STOP BREAKIN DOWN

STOP BREAKIN DOWN

stories

John McManus

Picador USA
New York

For my mother and father

Two of the stories originally appeared in the following publications: "Stop Breakin Down," *Ploughshares*; "Reaffirmation," *The Oxford American*.

Picador® is a U.S. registered trademark and is used by St. Martin's Press under license from Pan Books Limited.

Design by Maureen Troy

Library of Congress Cataloging-in-Publication Data

McManus, John.
   Stop breakin down / John McManus—1st ed.
     p.   cm.
   ISBN 0-312-26278-7
     1. United States—Social life and customs—20th century—
Fiction.   I. Title.

PS3563.C3862 S76 2000
813'.6—dc21   00-027723

First Edition: June 2000

10 9 8 7 6 5 4 3 2 1

Awareness is what happens when you malfunction.

—Stelarc

Contents

Megargel

Once there came a storm. She spoke to her grandchildren in a voice that was near a whisper. Luke watched his cousins: Every one of their eyes was wide. How can she whisper and still be so loud? they were wondering. Her whispers rang in their ears like shouts. Once there came a storm that was greater than any storm we had ever seen. There was so much thunder you couldn't tell where one thunder ended and the next one started. The dogs were howling out on the back porch. One of the dogs was named Thunder—the retriever was named Tipper and the setter was named Thunder—and it was Thunder who was scared of the storms. Once there came a storm and it was so windy that the rocking chairs blew off the front porch. One of them blew up into the oak tree. I looked up into the tree at the chair and watched the entire trunk sway back and forth, and I knew that if it fell on the house, we'd be crushed.

The boys watched her, and their eyes were open wide. She held her arms downward by her sides and rested her hands upon the cushion of the couch. She never gestured.

Your grandfather was only twenty-two years old then, she said. I held Eliza in my arms and cried, but your grandfather was never scared. When lightning struck, his red cheeks shone in the light from the window. He stared out at the swirling storm and narrowed his eyes. It was the most intense stare I've ever seen. He could have been powering the storm with his eyes, she said, her face quivering as she grew nervous. He was very strong. He was fierce and strong, she said, and I looked to him for comfort.

Grandpa's eyes were burning, and Luke looked into them and shivered. Do you think I'm your friend, you fool? they seemed to be saying. Do you think I give a fuck about you?

There was a creek in their backyard. Birds everywhere; they chirped in every direction, from the grass and from the trees and from the sky. Scents on the back porch: the early-morning dew, the coffee, the iced tea—Luke sat and inhaled them. Their house was a sanctuary, and it was good to be out of the suburbs. He looked in through the french doors and saw the morning sun rays reflecting off the country pink wallpaper. His grandfather had put up the wallpaper and the molding himself, and he had carved the hutch, and his grandmother had crocheted the dishcloths. There were so many birds; birds upon the railing; birds seemed to have been summoned from every swamp from Bay St. Louis to Pascagoula.

Luke was sitting cross-legged upon the floor. His knees and elbows protruded in four sharp points. Grandpa's face was red, and Luke's eyes met the stare. If Grandpa died right now, Luke thought, his head could fall forward and crack my skull in two.

Trey was eleven. Nathan was thirteen. Phillip was twelve.

One day that week they moved all the furniture around in Grandma's living room. They put the red couch where the piano had been, and they used the piano to block the door. They turned the tables upside down. They took down all the pictures. Luke watched them giggle; they always giggled a lot.

Grandma's gonna get mad, he told them.

Shove it, they said.

Maybe we should put it all back where it goes now.

Hey, Luke, Nathan said, do you sit down on the toilet when you piss? They all laughed.

No.

They laughed more. He didn't understand why they laughed when he said no. What is the right thing to say, then? What could he say so that they wouldn't laugh?

When Grandma came back home from church and saw it,
she yelled at all of them. He felt his cheeks turning red. I didn't
do any of it, he said.

She started crying.

Why are you crying? he said. Trey and Nathan held back
laughter. They looked at each other and started laughing, and
Phillip was laughing too.

You think it's funny that your grandma's crying? she said to
them. They tried to stop laughing. They were biting their lower
lips with their teeth. It makes you happy to see me upset?

Luke stood in the corner quietly and tried to tune out the
voices; he didn't want to start crying. Daddy always told him
he was sensitive. Maybe he could tell them he was just sensitive,
and they'd stop making fun of him; he could tell them that he
couldn't help crying—it was because he was sensitive. But it
wasn't only that he didn't want them to laugh.

He knew they would ask him why he was crying.

He knew he would just sit there and listen to them and cry
harder. How the hell am *I* supposed to know why I'm crying?
he wanted to say to them. *Hell* is a bad word. They would chant
at him: Luke said a bad word, Luke said a bad word.

Grandma and Grandpa had him for three weeks every summer.
Daddy said it would help his allergies to be so far south away
from the pollen. You're sickly, he had always said. He spoke
the word *sickly* like he was bragging. I'm so proud of you for
being so sickly.

Grandma served iced tea on the back porch. She bought them
Matchbox cars. Phillip and Trey and Nathan and Luke. Everybody gets a Matchbox car. His cousins picked out black Ca-
maros. Oh look, Trey said, there ain't no more black ones.
Looks like you'll have to get a pink one.

Luke's got a pink car. Luke's got a girlie car.

His cousins all lived in Gulfport. The houses were only ten
or fifteen miles away. How do you get to the beach from here?
they asked him.

You get on forty-nine and you—

Shut up. How the hell would you know? You're not from Gulfport.

He lived in Montgomery. It was a three-hour drive. Leave at four, arrive at seven. Leave at noon, arrive at three.

It was little things that always bothered him. He always had to take the last step on his right foot when he was walking. It had to be the right number of steps to the bathroom from the bedroom when he woke up in the middle of the night, and he had to end on the right foot.

He remembered that when he was three or four, he had been scared whenever his parents had gone anywhere after dark. He sat at the picture window in the living room and looked out at the road; he imagined them in their car darting toward the river as the green fields turned to black, the stars weighing down heavily, the summer heat stifling his breath as he heard the drone of the cars, the red lights flickering; it scared him. The fireflies, he thought, they're blinking in patterns, bright lunatic eyes, they're out there on the road driving, they're speeding through the night.

I'm gonna be a doctor, he had said to Mama. I'm gonna have an office on the twelfth floor and I'll have a big fish tank with big blue fish. He waved his arms swish swash through the air.

You can have as many big blue fish as you want, she had said. You're gonna be the best doctor there ever was; you're so smart you'll be the best anything you want.

He had asked her to tell him about the words. Tell me what I'd do with the words in the books, he said. She had told him the story: She told about how he pointed at each word and asked about it, so eager; what's that word, Mama, and what's that other word and what's the one after it.

You can never quit reading to him, she had said at the hospital. Luke sat in the hallway and watched the carts go by and listened to his parents talking through the door. He heard lots of noises. She was laughing but then he listened closer and she was sobbing. Read him twenty books a night, she said, always do it, don't you ever stop. Tell him what the words are.

. . .

You don't even realize what it is they're making fun of, Grandpa sneered. You don't even try to be like them.

Luke was startled.

You sit around the damn house and let them shove you around. You sit on the porch and watch your grandma make baskets. Like you're a little doll. Like you're her little fag doll. She thinks you're gonna be a preacher. Oh, he'd be perfect, she said. It's the devotion that I can see in his eyes; it's just like Eliza was. He swooned in her voice, hatefully, and he sneered with every word. Luke could hear her voice in his mockery.

He continued to speak. Look at your hair, he said. Look at your eyes. The symmetry of your face. You don't even see what I'm talking about.

Luke looked up at his grandfather's bright red head. He could see blue veins shining upon his cheeks, which were as rough as sandpaper. Luke thought he could see blond hairs still mixed in with the white ones. There was some yellowness stained on his mustache—that was nicotine—but Luke thought he saw yellow on his head.

I can see the person that I was, he said to Luke. It's genetic remanifestation. I'm jealous of you; you're going to get to do it all over again. Get out of Biloxi. Go somewhere else. Get out.

Luke wished Grandma would get home from the fruit and vegetable market.

You know I'm not the person your grandmother tells you I am, he said. Actually I don't know what she tells you. Whatever she tells you is wrong. I barely even lived with her until a year or so before you were born. I was in New York, Mexico City, São Paulo, Buenos Aires. When I was in the merchant marines they called me Megargel. That was the best they could say my name down there.

Luke listened to the sound of the name, and the syllables, and looked at the red cheeks. *Megargel* was an ugly word, he thought.

Grandpa rubbed his fingers against his cheeks. His eyes were shining. Luke could see the focal madness in his pupils. They're trying to get you to be a chickenshit, Grandpa said. You've let them make you a chickenshit.

Luke tried to keep his eyes from turning red.

Say, Grandpa said.

Huh?

Say.

Leave me alone.

I bet you're too chickenshit to even cuss, he said.

Luke stared back at him.

Say *fuck,* he said.

What?

Say *fuck.*

Luke was quiet.

Say it, you little shit. Say it, you little piece of shit. Say *fuck.*

Fuck.

That was pathetic. Say it louder. Say *ffuuuccck.* Say it like you mean it.

Fuck.

That's pathetic. She's making you into a little girl. She's doing you just like she did Eliza.

I wanna go home, Luke said when Grandpa had left later that evening.

What on earth would make you wanna go home? Grandma asked him.

He didn't answer.

I asked you a question.

I dunno.

Have you been fighting with your cousins?

No.

What is it then?

Nothing.

What is it, Luke?

He slumped down on the couch, trying to sink into the couch cushions. It's Grandpa, he mumbled.

What?

Luke was silent.

What?

Never mind, he said. I don't know.

You know your grandfather speaks out loud in his sleep, she said, her mouth curling down in uncertainty as if she feared punishment in return for what she had said. He talks like he's writing his will. He talks about his will, dictating it like I was his lawyer. You know he never tells me about it. I'm sure he has a will, but he never told me about it. He has money in the bank but he never tells me how much. Sometimes he talks in other languages; talks about people he never told me about. He sits there, upright in bed; he has one eye open looking straight into my mouth. He did it last night. I stared into his eye but it never met mine. He went on and on about his will. To you, he said, I leave nothing. To you I leave the skin that flakes off of my face.

Luke stared at her as she spoke.

Can you hear him when he does it? she asked him. He sounds so loud at night when the house is quiet.

Luke listened to her and imagined the images she had described. Late at night, when he was in bed, Luke could hear them snoring. The wind blew in through the windows on the south side of the house and out through the windows on the north side. All the lights were out. Trey and Nathan were asleep. Phillip was probably lying awake, but Phillip never talked to anyone but Nathan. Luke coughed a lot, and he was hot at night. The ceiling fans rotated slowly, and he watched the blades as they spun; he watched the shadows spinning in the darkness.

It seemed like everything in the house was fifty years old.

He smelled the cedar chest and the cheerywood trunk; the smells came alive in the darkness. He saw pine trees out the window. It's dark it's black bleck blick block bluck and the wolves will snare me when I'm unconscious. Half asleep, he lay whispering to himself not to be scared of the dark, and he heard the snoring through the walls, and he could feel his grandfather's thoughts seeping into his brain. He lay awake at four in the morning and the house was cold, and he listened to his grandfather's snores through the wall. The thermostat was always at sixty. He pictured Grandpa through the walls, buried beneath the three tattered blankets that he covered himself with every night, the blankets he had owned since childhood; he lay on the bed at four in the morning and imagined the red somnambulent body upright, standing with an agonizing lack of agility, inching toward the wall. He saw the withered body straightening its back, engaging its neck, the head rising slowly toward the hollow drywall, looming like a mechanized crane.

Slowly he fell into a dream. Lookit his face it's burning. Wrinkles that all are connected; black chasms; the wrinkles divide the red. One eye open and one eye shut, his forehead afire; he's speaking through its wrinkles. The downward end of his mouth slides open, a grunt forms in his throat; he emits its sound and speaks. The words slobber out of his mouth in uniform globs.

Luke tossed and turned in sleep. It was all made of words he had heard before, in the sermons, in books, on television, ordered for the darkness. Wrath implement spine. Mama, it's so scary when the words run together.

It was a waterbed that he and Phillip were sleeping on. There were waves when he jolted awake. There was one more voice from the dream: *Death is not the end.* He sat on the bed and sweated and stared out at the moon, saying, Please god, don't let him come through the walls.

He was alone in the room when he woke up. The sun shone into his eyes. He walked into the kitchen. Grandpa was at the table munching on corn flakes. His mouth was open as he ate, and he slurped the milk, and Luke watched the yellow teeth munch down on the garbled lumps of soggy grain.

Where is everybody? he asked.

Your grandma took the rest of them out to the toy store.

Why didn't she take me too?

You were asleep.

Why didn't she wake me up?

She's mad at you.

Luke felt his pulse jump.

She said you were saying bad things about me.

What? he said quickly.

She said you were shittalking me behind my back.

Luke felt his face turning red. He felt the blood pricking at his face like needles.

You'd better do something to make it up to her.

Luke looked into his grandfather's eyes; he was confused. What if she's really mad at me? he thought. I don't trust you but what if she's really mad at me.

I'm hungry, he said.

So?

Can I have breakfast?

No.

What do you mean no?

Why don't you just sit there and think about what I told you.

I'm hungry.

You just sit there and think about what I told you.

They came home at dinnertime. Luke was sitting on the couch watching television. Grandpa looked over at him. You just hush, he said; you just speak when you're spoken to.

They came in: Grandma Trey Nathan Phillip Charlotte. Charlotte was Luke's aunt, the mother of Trey and Nathan. He wanted to tell Grandma he was sorry, but he didn't want to talk in front of everybody. They were all carrying groceries in their hands, and they set them down on the counter. Luke wondered where the bags from the toy store were.

Why didn't you get anything at the toy store? he asked.

What made you think we were at the toy store? said Charlotte, and she laughed out loud and waved her hand in the air. I do declare.

Where were you then?

We told you yesterday, stupid, said Trey. We had to go to the doctor and the dentist.

Trey, don't call your cousin stupid.

It took the whole damn day.

Trey, don't cuss.

Grandma, Luke said, trying to get her attention. She didn't hear him.

You know I think you were right about the wicker, Charlotte, she said.

Of course I was right, Mother. You can't go wrong with wicker. She put her finger to her lips and glanced around the peach-colored kitchen. You know how much I love wicker.

Grandma and Charlotte cooked dinner together. Luke, said Charlotte, go out into the backyard and pick me three green tomatoes. He walked outside, obeying her, his head down. He didn't understand why they hadn't gone to the toy store. He walked out to the small square garden and picked the tomatoes; he moved his hand through the stagnant water in the birdbath and turned to go inside.

Luke, Charlotte said, these are ripe tomatoes.

So?

I said I wanted green tomatoes. Now what are we going to do with these ripe tomatoes? I guess they're just gonna sit there and rot.

I'm sorry, he said.

These are some of the best tomatoes.

I'm sorry.

Don't worry about it, said Grandma. We'll eat the tomatoes. It'll be okay. He went back outside to pick green ones. It cheered him to hear her say that it would be okay.

They moved around the kitchen in a flurry for nearly an hour, talking about cooking and about the garden and about the school where Charlotte worked. She was a teacher's aide. They hovered above the counter, chopping vegetables, speaking about things that did not concern him.

Trey and Nathan had to put the extra leaf in the table so that everyone could sit down for dinner. There were seven of them. In a circle they passed around dishes of fried chicken, mashed potatoes, gravy, cranberry sauce, green bean casserole, fried corn, stuffing, and fried green tomatoes. The sky grew dark outside; a storm was moving in. Charlotte said grace. Luke was always uncomfortable during grace because his father never said it at home before meals. He bent his head and glanced up at everyone; he watched their shut eyelids waver as he listened to the words. We thank you Lord for this meal that you put on the table for us and we thank you that we can feed our children well and that they can all be together again this summer; we thank you for giving us all so many reasons to be happy. Amen. They looked up and started eating.

Luke, put your napkin in your lap, said Charlotte.

Yes ma'am.

That's a lot of mashed potatoes you put on your plate, young man. You better eat them all, 'cause don't think you can just throw them in the trash.

Yes ma'am.

Grandpa sat across the table from him; he didn't seem to be eating. Luke watched him as he sat still, his fork balanced in his left hand above his plate, pointing out toward the door along the arrow that his eyes made, toward the door and toward Luke. Is he looking at me or is he looking through me? Luke wondered.

Do you like these fried green tomatoes? Charlotte asked him.

Yes ma'am.

Grandpa's eyes got narrower every time he answered her. Luke wondered whether he was trying to convey some sort of message. He could hear the sneering voice from the day before. Don't listen to her. Don't do what she says, you little pussy.

You know, she said, you should start playing a sport. Trey plays baseball and soccer. You're starting to get fat. Trey and Nathan giggled when they heard what she had said.

Grandma set her fork down. Why are you picking on him, Charlotte?

I just think he should be more active.

The boy is just fine the way he is, she said. Her hand quivered as she spoke. There's nothing at all wrong with him.

You're pampering him, Mother. She chewed on her chicken breast as she spoke. It's not enough for him to be smart. It's not enough for him to sit inside and talk to you all day.

Charlotte, she said, raising her voice, I don't want to hear you say another word about it. It made Luke happy to hear the passion with which she defended him. He ate his mashed potatoes and thought that everything was going to be all right.

Oh, for goodness' sake, Mother, Charlotte said. You treat him just like you treated Eliza, and look where it got Eliza to be treated that way.

She reached out and leaned across Nathan's plate and slapped Charlotte across the cheek. Grandpa stood up, throwing his chair backward against the floor: boom. Don't you ever hit my daughter. My daughter is safe in my house as long as I'm in it. Charlotte was wiping her nose; her mouth was hanging open, and she looked as if she hadn't dared to breathe since she was struck. Say you're sorry, Grandpa said. She was silent. He barked his order louder: Say you're sorry, woman, or I'll give you a damn fine reason to be.

She hid her face in her hand. I'm sorry, she murmured.

What?

I'm sorry.

I can't hear you.

I'm sorry.

Grandpa sat down. Damn right you're sorry. He looked around the table and rolled his eyes; he belched loudly and coughed and gulped his glass of tea, glancing around at every face in the circle, and he focused, locking eyes, upon Luke, who shivered. You see, there are winners and there are losers.

After dessert they were on the back porch. The air was humid. They sat on the porch and drank iced tea and breathed heavily in the moisture and watched the pink crepe myrtle flowers sway back and forth in the storm.

Roscoe was in the army, Grandma said. He went off to the army when I was a little girl and I couldn't remember what he looked like. I just remembered how he used to whistle. I thought about him walking up the driveway whistling. He'd whistle "Turkey in the Straw," over and over, and it was so clear and loud you could hear it a mile away. Well, one day Mama was all excited, she was picking flowers; I asked her what's going on and she said Roscoe's coming home. He was coming home on the train. I could hear the whistling in my head all over again.

We went to the train to meet him that night. It was due in at six. Six o'clock came and there wasn't a train and then seven came and went and eight o'clock and it was dark and we were all scared. You could hear the wind howling. I tugged on Mama's dress. When's it gonna come? I said, and she hushed me. The wind was blowing everybody's hair out of place.

It must have been midnight when the train people drove up. They came in a new Ford car. Everybody was going oh look at the car. They got out and everybody was quiet. The wind blew one of the men's hats off, and he bent down to get it.

You know what happened. I know I told you a million times. It was a train wreck. It derailed on the bridge. It went down into the water. I listened to him say that and I just watched his lips move and I watched Mama. She cried a lot. She must've cried for days after that. I don't think she was ever really the same. We went home and she locked herself up in her room upstairs and we could hear her bawling all night. But sometime late late after everybody else was asleep, real late, I heard a new sound. I'd been listening to Mama cry for hours, so I got all excited; it was something new. It was a melody. I was listening to Roscoe whistle down the driveway, and I heard each note, and it got louder as he got closer. The wind whistled along with him. That was 1931. He whistled down the driveway every night in June.

She stopped and smiled wistfully up at the ceiling; she let her eyes glaze over. I know it was him, she said. I know it was Roscoe.

Grandpa walked into the room. He walked over to her chair and stood above her. What are you talking about? he grumbled. His voice was deep and scratchy and loud. You never had a brother named Roscoe. She stared at him; she looked hurt.

You were an orphan. They got you out of the mountains up in Georgia. You never would tell anybody what happened to your family.

Her mouth was hanging open. Raymond, she said, the children are here.

Fuck the children.

She stood up and gasped.

Your family probably put you out on the street cause you lied to them so much. If you could call it a street. I'd say it was probably more like a little dirt trail through the woods.

Raymond, I'm gonna smack your face.

Give it your best shot. Just remember what happened the last time.

Luke shut his eyes tight. It was important for everybody to be nice to each other. He shut his eyes and swayed back and forth and whispered shut up, shut up, shut up. He could feel his cheeks getting red and puffy as his eyes swelled up. Grandma looked at him. Her voice was cracking. Come give Grandma a hug, she said.

Luke looked at her across the room. Her back was bent, and her fingers curled up in gnarled shapes. Come give Grandma a hug. They were all staring at him. Grandma and Grandpa and Phillip and Trey and Nathan. He could feel their stares drilling into his head. Grandpa was staring at him. He was grinning and drinking a beer. Go hug her, his eyes seemed to be saying. It was like a dare. He grinned and narrowed his eyes. Dimples formed on his face; they quickly became camouflaged by all the wrinkles.

Come give Grandma a hug.

Luke watched them all stare at him. He couldn't move.

There never was any Roscoe, Grandpa said. If I hear that goddamn whistler story one more time I'm gonna break something.

Grandma never cried—there was never any liquid—but she just hung her head and let it bob up and down, and she made squeaking noises. She bobbed and squeaked, and her face crinkled up and contorted, like a damp piece of plastic wrap. He listened to it in the penultimate silence. Tiny globes of spit slid out of her mouth as her eyes glazed over. He saw something escaping from her eyes.

Luke shuddered.

It had always looked like Trey and Phillip and Nathan were paying attention to her stories, wide-eyed, listening when she told them. He realized that their eyes had not been wide; they had been empty. Tell the fucking story and leave me alone, they had been saying to themselves.

He couldn't help crying. They all turned to look at him. Why are you crying? Trey said.

Why do you think?

If I knew why you were crying, I wouldn't have asked you. Nathan laughed.

Luke didn't respond.

Why are you crying, Luke? This doesn't have anything to do with you.

What?

Why do you give a shit?

Watch your mouth, Charlotte said.

Why do you give a shit what happens? You don't live here. You think you can come down here for two weeks and start living our lives.

Grandma's eyes were blank. She sat as still as if she had been paralyzed by a stroke, and she rubbed the sleeve of her shirt against her palm.

Grandpa drove him home.

But Daddy's coming down to get me, Luke had said before they left. Don't you want to see Daddy? He's coming down from Montgomery.

Everyone stared at him. All the people on the porch. The bluebirds were chirping out in the yard.

He packed his bags when Grandpa told him to pack them. He carried it out to the Buick in the driveway and laid it gently down upon the seat. How long a drive is it gonna be? he asked, but he knew how long it would be.

Three hours.

They sped along I-10. Luke looked out at the pine trees swoosh by the window. On the trees he saw crows and buzzards. They turned north and sped along I-65. It's a beautiful day, said the radio man. Luke looked out and saw big fluffy clouds; he saw that the sky was a darker blue than the usual blue. He thought about school: The year would start in three weeks. He made a list to himself of what he needed to buy: paper pencils folders ruler protractor and compass. He tried to see how long he could repeat one word at a time in his head, over and over and over. He shrugged out at the flat fields of cotton.

You hate me, don't you kid? said his grandfather.

Luke folded his hands in his lap and tightened his lips.

I've been thinking about what I told you the other day, his grandfather said. Luke looked at him. I've been thinking about the shape you'll be in when you realize.

Realize what? he asked stubbornly.

Realize what a little shit you were to have been scared of everything.

They drove over the Mobile River. Luke shut his eyes. Grandpa was laughing. Luke spoke the name above the cackle: Megargel. Drive off the bridge, Megargel, he said to himself.

Ten years from now, Grandpa said. He was still laughing as he spoke, wiping his eyes and smiling wickedly forward. It'll be ten years or so and you'll realize it and I'll be dead by then. Everything is different now, you'll say. He talked in Luke's voice, mocking the words that Luke would speak, mocking Luke's high-pitched boy's voice:

I realize that I should have listened to him way back then. I could have lived the chaos. I could have fucked myself up real good.

Die Like a Lobster

by'eck, it's gorgeous petal said the woman on the wall when I awoke. Speaking through slanted eyes as no light streamed in. As the day broke. As I turned side to side to side with half-opened eyes and pangs of chill and thirst, dizzy for an eternal moment. She's sipping a pint of Boddington's. Tilted and heady, creamy thick; her lips are puckered and her shoulderbones are gently crouching, cursive and angled.

Brrrrrrrrrrrrrtherainagain. Good God.

The woman winks her eyes. This is a beer coaster and cardboard like the many others around it, hexagonal heptagonal octagonal, yellow, flat. An unopened Hamm's beside me, strategically placed last night; I'll have it huddled beneath the covers brrrr. It's raining in Puddletown. Here comes the rain. Have you ever seen the rain.

Getting Pabstized already, Reuben said from the other room. This was the day he bit the bullet. The dimples showed up on his face even when he was frowning. He had brown eyes that wavered widely, blotchy skin. Pale as fuck.

It's Hamm's, I said.

No, he said, shaking his head. You, ya bastard. Off the wagon's what I'm getting at. Don't care what the damn brand is.

What wagon?

You know what wagon.

Ain't no fuckin wagon about it. You know.

He watched me smoke a cigarette, mouth half-cocked in a smile that powered his insidious stare as he scanned his eyes along the dark-walled cell. Do you want to know about the room? Black walls, black light, black witch-cat growling in sleep; smoke wafting over the dim halogen like a latent fire brooding. The souvenirs hung in patterns on the walls in English and several European tongues. De kroon op 250 jaar traditie; reinstate the draught; by'eck, it's gorgeous petal. It was Reuben's collection. When he was younger he went all over the world and saw more continents than I've seen states and he owned the coasters to prove it. They filled three walls. This was the back room behind the bar where I pretty much lived at that point.

He rested his left hand on the Captain America helmet on the cocktail table. His body bent into the papasan chair next to the photo of himself; he sat beside himself; staring up at himself, at many forms of space. On the yellow couch I puffed as the rain fell and I drank until I had to start working. Straight at me his image stared into my mind, cunningly silent as the slow glare burst upon me, sinking sharply into the buzzing of my skin. I was thinking about the things Frank had been yelling at me to do. Take inventory, clean the gutters, fill out your tax forms you've been here six months. I couldn't deal with it. Reuben fell forward onto me and knocked the beer right out of my hand. There was a beer in his hand too. They clanked together, aluminum versus aluminum, a metalcrumpling toast as pissyellow Hamm's splashed out onto the table and the floor.

Cheers, I said. I wasn't really awake yet. I said cheers, I said. I figured the old slob was just passing out again.

Looks like you'll be going on the wagon yourself for a few hours, I said.

Here's to the wagon, I said.

Portland is a young city they like to say. No young kids, senior citizens, homeless people. They're not old but they look like they're old. Pale and wraithlike so that chills run down your spine. Claybeaded hemp anklets. You think they're hunkered hungry dead but they just want to appear that way. Half the city looks like Matt Dillon and the other half looks like Ethan Hawke. Clovesmoking high-cheekboned boys who stand on

street corners nudging each other pointing to blondes in black
lipstick, the faces who loom for them in the grayness like mes-
siahs winking at them day in day out, high school waitresses
who stick their tongues out at me and all passersby and boy are
they hip to the scene. Smoking on the corner outside coffeeshop
number seventy-three thousand scowling on the brink of strobe-
struck gothness. Postpunk and look at all the spikes. Down on
eleventh toward Californageddon as Reuben calls it. They're
talking about the Modest Mouse show or the Dandy Warhols
show and their skin is pale. They're like Frank's crowd only
fifteen years younger. Below the punk they're pretty. Two random specimens:
    I'm so goth, I'm dead, she says in her huffy little voice.
    Purple hair twirling in little black-nailed hands. And the
oneupping response: Well, I'm so goth, I'm a cathedral.

The maggots were dead at the time of the autopsy but my what
a spirited bunch of vermin. The skull let us remember is one of
the thicker parts of the body. Especially in the case of Reuben.
I always told him he was thickheaded and he always knew it.
Like when he saw someone he didn't like the looks of wandering
into the bar to see what the music was all about. He stopped
right in the middle of a measure: down went his electric violin
onto the brick floor of the three-inch-high stage, silent, tapping
his foot, skipping every seventh beat and staring at Frank the
Fairy behind the bar until Frank expelled the intruder. He drank
nine pints of Exterminator every night. He drew the numeral 7
into the creamy head atop the glass and let it set for three
minutes as the tiny bubbles sank into the blackness.
    Are you *real?* was the first thing I asked him when I met him,
and he choked on his drink.
    That was some time ago.
    He had warts all over his face, and scars like a dozen dimples.
He was Frank's lover. He said he'd met twelve people in his life
worth knowing and he kept a list and he said when he'd met
twenty-five he'd go back to the Saskatchewan taigas, being careful not to meet anyone else during the course of his journey

home. So it was only one out of every five hundred million people or so who got to know him.

Kind of like a lottery, kind of.

So if you had wandered down Everett Street late on a Tuesday evening without an umbrella, racing for your car or for the place you thought you left it as you dodged between the gobbling raindrops, dripping trees, and wet purple neon as it bled into every glob of water, you might have glanced sideways at an empty brown storefront standing dustily vacant and two levels of apartments above it and not even noticed the dry space beneath a tattered gray awning, the unmarked staircase to a thick black door below street level and on each stair a letter of the bar's name in red bloodpaint. The dripping *M* beckoning all eyes down the hatch into the murky Morass. Where croaked the notes of Reuben the Rat boiling rawly out the airduct. You might have gotten back into the car to go back home to Rivergrove for the night and for twenty-five rain-drenched minutes hummed to yourself as you hydroplaned along the flat surface of the road and finally there was a chance for the water to grab you, send you careening right off the edge of an overpass, and there you went, exploding onto the Baldock Freeway, dead and it didn't even matter much to you anymore. Maybe your car landed on someone else's car and killed him too and neither one of you ever got the chance to see what happened to Reuben's hair after the bug spray.

Drenched every night for months on end. It looked like mousse but it didn't quite smell the same.

I was the one who told him about the maggots. Freaked him the fuck out by God I never saw anyone scared so shitless before. I wasn't trying to scare him. It was just a story. He got all huffypuffy and silent and opened his eyes wide and hyperventilated. He can't breathe well enough to handle shock.

(My dad went to school with this chick in the fifties who put her hair up in a bun all squeezed up tight don't ask me why and after three months when she hadn't taken the bun out, maggots crawled down into its crevices to breed: And lo, when a million squirming pupae awoke finally into maggotness they burrowed into her scalp and ate a hole in her brain.)

Heehehe.

Of course she died, I told Reuben, you think she didn't? I grinned and he squinched his eyes up in all horror. When maggots eat a hole in your brain, I said, it just happens somehow that you die you know.

Frank thinks I encouraged Reuben to go out and buy the Raid, but I didn't have shit to do with it. How the fuck am I supposed to know people are like that out here.

I came to Portland to fight the grunge, Reuben told me. This was some time ago.

Why didn't you go to Seattle?

Too late, he said.

He played every night and he lived with Frank in the room next to mine behind the bar and he called it heavy metal drunk calypso funk blues some nights or this blues or that blues or some other kind of blues on other nights. Two kids came down into the bar on Halloween wearing black leather and he stopped the music and said, Do you like the New Bad Things? They stopped in their tracks.

Yeah, one of them said, they're pretty cool.

Get out then. I don't want you here.

Huh?

Get out. I don't want any maggots in my brain.

It was a thirty-nine-hour drive when I came out here. When the oil light came on in Lincoln, Nebraska, I put another couple quarts into the tank and then I had to stop every couple hundred miles and add more. I picked up some old hitchhiker near Iowa City. He checked the oil for me. Yuppers, he said, it's empty but she ain't necessarily leakin.

Why's that? I said.

You done drove a long way. Maybe she just done run clean out.

Oil doesn't just disappear.

You never know, he said.

I would have made better time if it weren't for the oil and if it weren't for the little U-Haul trailer on the back holding a bed some chairs a shitload of clothes and a three-foot bong. I stopped in Idaho and called the guys at the house back home. I might be a little late this month getting you that rent check, I said.

How late?

Hard to say.

Where are you?

The office.

I don't know why I came to Portland. People come here you know. It's pretty close to Humboldt County so they figure there's good weed. I pour drinks at the bar, at Morass. You apply at a bar when you get to Portland. It's what you do.

They hired me for seven bucks an hour because there's no separate waiter's wage in Oregon. They give their applicants a test of manual dexterity. Frank yelled back for Frank Junior and Frank Junior brought five nitrous balloons out from the office. Inhale them all, he said. This was before Frank Junior moved up to Vancouver to cop crack.

I had to do the nitrous then make one each of twenty different mixers and serve them up on the bar without spilling them. I did it quite well. Reuben stumbled out of the back room in an encrusted velvet smoking jacket, rubbing the smoke out of his eyes violently. The tentacles of his hair crept searchingly up through the air as they waved in time with his steps. They were brown and black and sandy blond and gray and green and brown and purple and gray. They crept up through the air like jungle trees searching upward for the light. I've been here two months so this was two months before he died. That's how long it took was two months.

Howdy, he said, brushing hair out of his eyes. If you're the new barkeep pour me a damn drink, otherwise turn around and get the fuck out. Ain't visitin hours yet. I got him a beer and he sat down on a barstool to drink it. Back to my brooding, he said.

I looked at his ridiculous figure. Are you real?

I spose. I dunno what's real under all this hair though.

Later that day I tried to make conversation with him. He sat in the corner staring up at spiderwebs. Once in a while he strummed a few notes on his guitar. Why are you a musician? I said.

Eat shit.

What made you come here?

Suck balls.

I've never seen any dreads like that. They were brown with blotches of black and red, and they stank.

He dared me every day for the first couple of days to call in a bomb threat to the middle school down the road and eventually I did it. We drove past afterward and saw all the little punks standing outside in the rain getting drenched. Whatever man, the little fuckers were grateful to get out of class and wasn't I the considerate one to risk my good standing with the law to do it for them. They'll arrest you for that you know. I think the worst thing about getting arrested, I said to Reuben, would be not having any alcohol or maybe not having any weed but no not that so much as the alcohol.

No, he said, the worst thing was not having any KY. I stared over at him. His hair flopped around like rodent tails.

Huh?

That's what I said.

What the hell were you in prison for?

He shrugged and laughed. Well, you see it was like, it was either him or me, he said. You know how that is.

I nodded. You have to be agreeable. Who else was there to talk to? Was I supposed to talk to the vampire kids on the street corners?

It was in October when he bought the Raid. Close to the start of monsoon season. Are you sure that was a true story? he asked me.

Yeah. She died.

The spray hissed out of the bottle and coated his hair and it shone. The dreads bounced and then they stood still. Raid smells nasty. You can tell it's toxic.

I can't believe you're doing that, I said.

I don't want maggots in my brain.

Why don't you just take the dreads out?

He glared at me.

You're insane, I said.

He glowered down at me. He stood six feet seven and the

boots added a good two inches. You know it's bad to tell insane people that they're insane. He didn't answer. I've never been so horrified by a single look before.

The Raid smells nasty, I said to him. You can tell it's toxic from how it smells. You're gonna hurt yourself.

Vodka's the same though, Reuben said. How it smells.

Well, I don't put vodka in my hair, I said.

Well, I don't either.

Why don't you just take the dreads out?

Fuck off, he said.

His mother had braided them the month before she died and that's why he wouldn't take them out of his head but it was still pretty dumb if you ask me.

When he quit talking he stooped over to pick up his trumpet; he blew a few notes. That was what he did whenever he ended any conversation when he had his trumpet handy. He held his empty pint glass against the opening. People looked at him. He farted every few minutes for the rest of the evening.

It was the same at the bar every night. The same damn people in their same damn seats. I asked why they didn't get a marquee. Frank said that's not the way he operates. But think about the money, I said.

Think about your balls shoved up your ass, he said.

The sun rises earlier here. At sunrise before you go to bed, when you do the little hand-in-your-forehead snooze halfway through the last beer to remember that you are a body, you look out and see the sun coming up and it feels pretty good. You can't really see it though because the room is below street level.

All these people come here and no one is actually from here but they're from Denver Boise Chicago Pittsburgh and Cleveland and they get here in the summer when it's the land of milk and honey. That's what Frank calls Portland. I got here in the fall. All these people come out here and they work in bars and I'm waiting to meet them soon.

They kept saying they were going to go out to the desert. Reuben said he knew where the shrooms grow. He said you could pick barrels full of them. We were going to go east on I-84 on the steep part past the Dalles dam. I was going to sit in the back. I was going to tell myself I wasn't going to let myself feel awkward around them. I was going to try not to look while they fondled each other. When Frank was driving down the mountain Reuben was going to give him a blow job and I was going to look out the window and try not to see a damn thing.

There was this room under the bar where the floor was just dirt. It usually substituted for the desert for them I guess. Frank was an agoraphobe. I think he's left maybe twice since he hired me except for the time I'm talking about now and it's getting worse. It takes a leap of faith for him to step out the door. I do the grunt work like paying bills and buying things. It's not like he really needs me there at the bar for anything.

I don't know why they wanted me to go with them at all but Reuben insisted on it. Frank drove and I sat in the back. Frank scowled for three hours.

Why don't you ever get any letters or phone calls or nothing? he said.

Are you talking to me?

He just stared back into my eyes in the mirror.

How do you know I don't?

Cause you live in my fucking bar.

I shrugged. I don't know, I said. My scene's out here now. I don't keep up with those people.

Your scene is the two of us and whatever girls at the bar you get a chance to hit on.

I don't guess I'm following you.

Your scene is a pile of shit.

I just laughed and nodded because that's all you can do. It was true that I didn't keep up with the people back home. It was probably a relief to them when I left: I worried them; I didn't make the same connections. They had trouble under-standing what motivates me to do certain things.

It was several hours in the car. I was glad they were scared to go outside. Frank's eyes darted around as if predators loomed above him. I just nodded and laughed. That's what you do you know. That's how you get through it, you just act like you don't care or something and eventually it all turns around. Eventually Frank forgets about whatever he's been ragging you about. Reuben started telling jokes eventually. A blonde gets pulled over for speeding and asks the officer what she can do to get out of it. The guy pulls out his dick. She says, oh, no, not another Breathalyzer test.

His hair shook like a cyclone had taken hold of it.

A guy walks into a bar; you'd think he would have ducked. A giraffe walks into a bar and he says, the highballs are on me. A mule walks into a bar and the bartender says to him, why the long face?

We sat there and ate steaks and drank beer. There was a fire. The wind blew around us and it was light and then the sun set and then it was getting dark, cold. That was what they intended was the dark and the cold.

I thought the desert was supposed to be hot, I said.

Hell, Reuben said. Desert don't mean it's gonna be hot. Antarctica's got deserts, for Christ's sake.

The wind bit me till I felt like I was dead. Lying there numb with a sock in my mouth and a bullet in my brain. Sand's pulsing vicegerent lying spasmodic on the floor of the desert. Dead on the days that made me. All the coyote skulls in pretty ceremonial headpatterns and all the nightstars lapping on the shores of the nude eastern scablands.

It was a circle of skulls. Maybe they were too big to be coyote skulls. Maybe it was just some other kind of dog, like chihuahuas.

They just sat and stared at each other. I don't know if they knew all those skulls would be there or if maybe they had put them there themselves sometime in the recent past. The wind roared and skulldust pulsed up through the red bubbles of blood stewing eminently in our temples, up into the air to float against the mountains standing in the distance amidst the clouds like flying rib cages. The skulls' eyes were so big you could fit seven eyes in each eyehole. Through each eyehole seven eyes could peer out at the flaming rib cages of the horizon.

Why'd we bring him out here? Frank said.

Reuben looked at him as if he were trying to convey some subvocal threat.

Why'd you have to go and ruin it?

Shut up, Frank.

Why'd you bring him?

You know.

No, I don't know.

Shhh, Reuben said. You know.

He told some more jokes. I don't remember them. Frank laughed at most of the jokes. I was cold.

Hey, I said, I've got one.

Shut up, Frank said.

No, I've got one, I said. How does a fag take off a condom? Frank narrowed his eyes. This better be good, he said.

He farts, I said. They both were silent. You get it? I said. He farts.

Frank threw a handful of dirt at me. We shouldn't have left at all, he said. I think he might have been trying to throw it into my eyes but none of it went in my eyes.

We had to leave, Reuben said.

But what I'm saying is that we shouldn't have left.

That was when Reuben got his big drum thing out of the car and set it down in the middle of that circle of skulls. He started beating on it. His hair waved in the wind like big lobster claws flailing in the breeze. That's what it looked like really, was lobsters. There's really nothing else to compare it to.

He reached down into his hair and pulled something out. You have to understand how big his hair was. There could have been a grand piano in its depths. He reached his hand down in there and pulled out something colored gray or alabaster, coated with dregs of dried-up Raid. He laid it down with the other skulls and that's when I realized it was a skull itself, just like the others. He beat on the drum and cried out.

Aka aka aka aka akka. Like a pelican getting stabbed with a damn butcher's knife. Like dying boiling creatures of the sea.

He chose another skull and put it into his hair. He beat on the drum like mad. I saw where the bulge was from the skull but you never would have noticed otherwise.

Are you two like some kind of cult? I said.

Isn't two people a little small for a cult? he replied. Twelve more drumbeats followed. He moved the drum out of the circle. He jumped up and down on the old skull that had been in his hair, crushing it until it was stamped out of existence.

I don't know what the point was of all that. He said they had to do it and I guess you do what you have to do. I slept in the car on the way back. I was tired because I'm an insomniac and I'd gone three days without sleeping. Not even liquor can help when I get sleepless.

When I woke up we were back in Portland barreling down Lincoln. Heading west, they said. They were arguing in the front seat as I nodded in and out of consciousness. Loudly they yelled about how to get to the southeast quarter again, whether the numbers were going up or down.

But we can't have crossed the river.

We have to have crossed it.

It's not something you just don't notice.

But the numbers are going up.

A gasp. They woke me and I mumbled myself awake. Suddenly on a hilltop, facing a stop sign and open air in front of us, headlights pointed toward a misty paltrylighted valley. We gazed downward at the black Willamette.

We shouldn't be here, he said. This is Thirty-third and Lincoln and we should be passing the Kennedy School right now. What the fuck man, what the fuck. Gazing out past the metal barrier, he scanned the blackness. Birdshit fell on the windshield. He surveyed the panorama in shock and horror. He seemed so disturbed, so blankly dumbstruck, that fear gnawed briefly at my stomach, the chemicals swirling in the panic of their moment, fighting outward toward the late black dampness.

The street signs don't say NE or NW; they just say N.

But the numbers are going up.

That's the river down there.

It could be the Columbia.

It's not the Columbia.

It could be some other river, he said.

What the fuck. There is no other river.

They sat there like they were scared to death. Like it was the most frightening thing in the world; like they hadn't lived in the city for years and years. I think that's what scared me the most about them: how they didn't have any sense of place, of direction. If they can't tell north from south then who knows what the fuck they were ever thinking at all. I'm pretty easygoing for the most part but Jesus fucking Christ on a cross I mean really. I told them how to get home. They didn't understand how there were two sets of numbers. We went in the bar and I passed out and Reuben drank all night till finally he just plumb died. Not from the drinking though.

By that week his hair had lost most of its original pallor.

It kind of reminds me of a story he told me a few weeks ago. This was quite some time back and Reuben was in a hot tub with a few friends, drinking, et cetera, drinking quite a bit that is. They sat there in the hot tub for a few hours and it bubbled and they got drunk and there they were and then boom, one of the guys just up and died right then and there. Conked out and they didn't know what the hell had happened. They thought he might have gotten alcohol poisoning because they'd been taking shots of Aftershock. Turns out it was the hot tub because you can't sit in there for that long and especially if you've been drinking. It burns up your insides.

It's like if you cook lobsters. If you dump them into a boiling pot then they shriek and burn. But if you put them in water at room temperature and heat it slowly then they never feel it folks say. It's a nice little hot bath till your eyes slide shut.

That reminds me of the way Reuben died. Gradual so that you couldn't tell it was happening. It was just like the lobsters except no heat and nobody will ever know if Reuben felt any pain or not. He used to jab himself with razors to show how he didn't flinch at pain. So he never would have screamed.

Actually no one will ever know anything at all about anything because Frank buried Reuben under the bar. Reuben wasn't really living there in the real sense to begin with. He was a Canadian and went across the border long ago and never told anyone. No one is going to notice.

Frank thinks I made it all up about the chick with the maggots in her head. As if it was some kind of plot to poison Reuben. In which case I was the one who fucked everything up for everybody. In which case it was some sort of manslaughter on my part. I wonder how it even happened. I guess maybe the Raid got in his ears. There was white stuff coming out of his mouth a few hours after he died. That's what made us notice he was dead. I guess there's a good chance the Raid could have gotten in his ears. I don't know if his hearing got worse toward the end, because I tried not to talk to him. It's kind of funny. He did it wrong. You're supposed to get at the maggots before they're in your brain. It doesn't work to spray the Raid in through your ears.

What Frank seems to want me to perceive in him lately is rage but actually it is some sort of pathos. He loathes every unit of my being but it's essentially a weak loathing.

He said something to me about the Peruvian Mafia. As if it were a threat. His father is from Peru or some such shit.

What the hell are you talking about? I said, laughing out loud. What kind of crack are you smoking?

Be careful, he said. I may have no choice.

Of course, I said, it's Peruvian crack, delivered straight from the don.

Be careful.

If they have trouble finding me then maybe they could work in cahoots with the Saskatchewanian Mafia.

Shut up.

Because together, they'd be a formidable force.

Shut up.

I'd be a goner for sure.

I mean it.

Maybe they'll spray Raid on my head.

I don't know what's going to happen now but I hope it's not like this everyplace else. You probably think I'm kind of stupid but I just let myself focus in on one thing, you know one particular situation. Like not anything else no nothing for the time being. There are these spheres that barely overlap and I guess I'm crossing over now. You can't really say until it happens. I mean Portland is weird sometimes like with the deposit you have to make on beer bottles. Reuben explained it to me a bunch of times but I don't really get it. It's the little things like that you know. Not much point to the city as an entity at all.

It all seems very tangential, all of everything, except that it's not tangential to any particular thing. Nothing else is going on. I work at the bar. The other day we started carrying Magic Hat on draught. McMenamins' is opening another bar near us. This is what's going on.

I'm going to kill you pretty soon, Frank said as he threw darts at the board. He hit a triple twenty and then a seventeen. But I don't want you to quit working here.

I never said I was going to quit, I said.

I want you to stay where you are. Every day I'll work up a little more courage toward it. He played with his nuts through his boxer shorts. You know I joined the marines so I could kill somebody, he said, but there wasn't a war. He threw a double nineteen. They were going to promote me to sergeant and send me down to Parris Island to train recruits. I said fuck it. Fuck them all, I said.

You know it's not like I sprayed the damn Raid on his head myself.

Yeah, he growled, and a frog wouldn't beat its ass if it had wings neither.

The only way he'll kill me is if he kills himself and that's only ten percent likely. He can't leave himself with no errand boy. He hyperventilates when he gets anywhere close to the door.

Last night Frank talked to a few musicians who were looking for gigs to play. There was one electric guitarist with sandy brown dreads.

How long have you had those dreads in? Frank asked him.

Month maybe.

Well, just watch out for the maggots.

I beg your pardon?

That's what happened to Reuben. The guy you'd be replacing.

I beg your pardon, sir?

Maggots got him, Frank said, laughing. Got him right in his brain. And now there's one after me. Frank gestured at me behind the bar. I always thought it was just because of Reuben's hair, he said. But look at me; I don't have any hair.

The guitarist raised his eyebrows in nervous confusion.

You should play here, Frank said. We'd love to have you.

He averted his eyes.

It doesn't work just to spray your hair, Frank said. You've got to get at the source. He gestured to me again. One of these days, he said, peckerwood over there's gonna wake up in the middle of the night and I'll be spraying Raid down his throat. I'll stand on his chest and he won't be able to move. I can legpress six hundred pounds. He'll be one dead dead dead little maggot.

Well, I'd better be going now, said the guitarist.

Frank laughed. So that's how it goes, he barked.

They hurried for the door.

I walk the streets every day. I have a good pair of Gore-Tex boots now. If I keep it up I'll be hip to the scene. The bland junkie music and a haircut like Matt Dillon in *Drugstore Cowboy* and a good raincoat. A ring in my chin. You eat a tofu turkey on Thanksgiving and it's called a tofurkey. You walk down the streets and listen to the little punk children. I'm so goth I'm a cathedral. You let it echo in your mind. A cathedral. A cathedral. I didn't make that one up that is it's not original but I guess I could have thought of it I guess I was punk once. A dot in all the larvae. They don't speak to me now. Mewling out the veiny red kidwhimpers into the days and nights. Or are veins the blue ones.

The Magothy Fires

Listen to the wind blow listen. Ooooraroorarooo. Storms will rage all over Devon. Weatherman's report on ITV got it right for once. At the Bull's Head the telly was on while the run was being planned. Hope it don't blow out the fire.

No wind'll blow out that fire.

I dreamed the wind blew the fire into my face and scorched it off and left ashblack bits of soot—they weighed nothing— they were carried away on the wind. It didn't happen. Could have done. Didn't, no, nothing. When I ran into this soggy mossmuck field the wind bore fleshless air. Facelessness in distant western glow.

Pink in the sky. Whisper this. Pink in the sky is lit up all bright tight white in the whitewashed image of the light.

This is what I am smelling:

The wind coming up out of the heath. The peaty mix of fog and gorse and grass. The wind coming up out of the hoary heath shooting up whoowhooosh blowing all the dead scents down into the town, blowing the dead shrews' skin into the chimneys, the rotting blackcurrant mush atoss along the ground by Bickleigh Lane, dissolving beneath the gray cloak of constant clouds. Ales and bitters and stouts. The cold wind out of the heath, blowing east from the moorlands, whistling through the hedges. I remember the wind on Tintagel Head, forty miles an hour blowing in from the ocean, trumpeting itself in jagged currents as it blew the birds backward; they fell out of their elevation, down beneath the cliff edge. I looked out over the cliff at the gulls and the rocks and at the two hundred steps carved into the stone. I smelled the salt air from the sea; there is salt air everywhere but it was very strong there. Down by the station at night the moisture of the river, frigid, and the soft moisture of the water. Magpies.

Where is it you go at night, Jake said to me. He always looked like he was scowling. All his questions were phrased as statements, as if the answers were painfully obvious, ridiculous, unanswerable.

Just around, I said.

It's just a farm, he said. You've seen it all before. It's just a bunch of fucking fields and sheep.

I shrugged.

What the hell do you see, he said.

I don't know, I answered. The woods, and the river, and magpies.

Mum always talked about the magpies. The sounds they made at night. She was scared of their squawks at night in the fields in the grass. She wouldn't walk down the drive alone. In the middle of the night, surrounded by darkness, birds gulls goons quacking and moaning and a phantom sunrise hovering above the downs, she wouldn't move; as she stood stubbornly still upon the gravel she said, Let them eat me; at least they'll have to get up off the ground and come to my feet.

Numbskulls.

What I am smelling is the coal from the town. Up on the Yeomans Hills above Nympton Pyne. The steaming scent of fire, the trees, and the smoke as it rises and changes and flows. What I am smelling is the silence. The unbearable undertow of the wind, salty and slightly bitter, soaring above the hedgerows and the fields at night complicit in the stillness, the silent outer language of electric air.

The barrel race is on the fifth of November. Every year. November fifth, Guy Fawkes Day. People come to Magothy from all over the westcountry to see it—from Cornwall, from Dorset, from Bristol. They crowd into the streets. Only four hundred live in the town and the streets are narrow; people pack in surging through the cold night. Mashing themselves in the cold of the night into the bulging brain of bodies, drinking, glancing sidelong at the ambulances waiting at the edge of town and feeling fleeting pangs of fear. Maybe we'll get burned. Maybe some bloke's face will burn up in front of me. Standing around coldly in the cold air, hands in the folds of their coats, standing and waiting for the fires to surge and ignite all the ugly faces that will bleed in fire, surging red yellow gold.

Each pub has a barrel-rolling team. That makes ten teams. You wear fireproof gloves. The barrel is full of flaming tar. You have to see how long you can keep the barrel up in the air. It works like a relay. Four people on the team. You pass it to the next bloke when you get too hot and the barrel gets too heavy. You hold it high up above you and in your hands you rotate it; the flames shoot out into the crowd as you run down the streets. The people compact into themselves. You shout and the people duck down and run back and climb over each other and the flames shoot out at them and you laugh at the manic growls of fear and panic. There haven't been more than a few deaths. The barrel is burning up and you have to keep moving through the crowd. The barrel must stay up. You have to keep the barrel in the air.

Well well well, Reg said on Halloween. That fat shit Lewis is still in the hospital and your old man hasn't showed up. Looks like it's your turn to have some fun this year, kid. Reg runs the Bull's Head. The team is his choice.

He'll be back, Nigel said.

He won't be back, I said.

He'll be back, Nigel said, and he gulped down his pint and belched. We were in the pub watching Leicester play Arsenal. I had three quid bet on Leicester. Nigel slammed his glass down. Hey you old fart. Pour us another round of Stag.

If you're on the team, Derek said, Reg has to give you free drinks here for the rest of the year.

Bollocks to that, Reg said.

Give him free drinks for a week and you'll be out of business, Nigel said.

Bollocks to that.

Hanging around a bunch of old men all the time just to prove you can outdrink us. You slimy git.

I thought Mum wouldn't want me to do it. It's too unsafe. You'll get burnt. It's too dangerous for you to do. I waited till the fourth to tell her about it. They want me to take Uncle Lewis's place, I told her. They want to keep it in the family. Lewis has scars from where he has been burnt by the fire. One on his right cheek and two on his neck and scars all over his arms. I guess you don't want me to do it, I said to her. She shrugged. I guess you think it's too dangerous, I said.

Jake walked into the room from outside. She smiled at him. I got you some more Marmite, she said. He lay down on the couch and ignored her.

Did you not hear what I just said to you? I said.

I heard.

Do you care?

You do what you want to do, she said. That's the way you want it that's the way you'll have it.

Whatever.

I got you some more Marmite, Jake. Did you hear me?

He doesn't like Marmite, Mum. Your fucking loverboy was the one who ate it all last time. Sixteen years and you can't even figure out he hates that nasty shit as much as I do.

Ben, don't you dare curse in front of me. Jake, honey, you like Marmite, don't you, love?

He stared at her.

Don't you, love?

For the love of God, he said, leave me out of this.

But I bought it for you.

Just leave me the hell out of it, he screamed. Leave me alone.

I had been standing in place and staring at her the whole time. I yelled at her. You're going to argue about fucking Marmite but you don't care that I want to do the barrel rolling? Is that the way it is?

I care.

You don't care.

Don't change the subject, she said. She waved her hand. This jar cost me two pounds twenty and if your brother doesn't want it then he's damn well going to tell me himself so that I can take it back to Sainsbury and exchange it.

I left the room.

She fought with him. I listened through the door. The walls are thin and the wood is hollow. She yelled about the Marmite, and he didn't answer. You never smile anymore when you're around me, she said to him. He didn't answer. You used to be such a sweet and happy little thing, she said. I pictured to myself their movements as they spoke. She's putting her hand on his chin and tilting it upward, looking into his eyes. He's jerking himself away.

What are you talking about? he said.

You used to seem so much happier than you are now.

A few moments of silence: He's looking at her, I thought; his glare is belittling and derisive. The wood creaked.

I've never been happier in my entire life than I am now, he said.

You used to look so happy when you were a tot. Ben was never happy then but you were happy. Such a bubbly little boy. When you were six years old you were always so happy.

I wanted to kill myself when I was six years old, he told her.

She raised her voice and yelled at him. You don't know what the hell you're talking about, she said.

I don't think I want to kill myself anymore, he said. Maybe that means I'm happier now.

I listened to them from the toilet. The screaming and the sighing and the breathing. I waited for them to leave the room so I could come out. I stood in front of the mirror waiting for them, examining my face and looking for blackheads, squeezing them until each black splintered speck oozed out at the front of a small pink stream of pus and blood.

. . .

Our property is on a hill called Cairn Knoll. The house is called Cairnknoll House. The floors are uneven inside. It's large and white and secluded; you can't see it from the road. Jake used to say the only thing he liked about our house was that he could take a slash out the back door without anyone around to complain about it. But he would have done it even if there was a whole city street full of people to complain.

He called it the charnel house.

You're saying it wrong, Mum would say to him. She didn't get it.

I found a cassette tape in Mum's desk drawer with a label that had been crossed out with black ink. When I took it into my room and put it in my Walkman to try to find out what it was, I heard Jake's voice. I heard Mum's voice. There was a third person too, an old man with a Midlands accent. I listened to them talk and realized he was the psychiatrist in Bristol Mum had taken Jake to visit last year. Jake had refused to talk to her for a week afterward. She bribed him out of his silence with a hundred pounds.

I listened to the tape. Jake's pronounced, sullen breathing, intentionally labored as he sucked the air in and forced it out, was as loud as the words.

Is this your script on these papers?

No.

Does this refer to your girlfriend? Melissa is her name?

No.

Who wrote these?

No.

What are some of the things you'd like to talk to us about?

No.

Jake used to make up rhymes. He stared out the window of his bedroom at the sheep and the river, sitting motionless for hours on end, writing and thinking. He shook the pen sometimes, jabbing it into the paper. That was to express victory, I think, not anger. I could see it in his eyes when the connection was made. He wrote fast, in a scrawling hand, and he rolled his eyes up as if he had overdosed on a drug. What are you writing about? I said.

Dead people.

He spoke in a deep voice. It wasn't naturally deep, but he always tried to make it sound like it was. He spoke in a low vicious monotone that sounded like radio static, lorry engines, lowing cattle. He read aloud.

She stood upon a jagged rock. The waxing moon above. She howled and moaned into the wind and whispered to her love. *You coward now you've done it. You wretched little fool. The feral smile upon your face, the smile that is your tool.*

That's good, I said.

He spat out the window.

Dead people on the copses of the hills. He smelled all the lives the people used to live, the medieval people. He smelled the Black Death. He said he smelled their bones. The deadness knotted up in millennial trees, ancient rock walls, stone stairs that have become part of the earth. The grass is thick with the mulch of dead sheep. Such a vivid green. He said it is exhilarating. The fields, the hedgerows, the darkness. I listened to him speak in his dark raspy voice; I saw myself in the darkness and I saw him pirouetting in the air above Dartmoor. Magpies dotted the graves. Fog drooped through the blazing greenness of the pastures, the looming curvatures of the earth, the sheep that grazed the loamy ground. I floated in the air above the thinly carved peninsula. I smelled the draught ales from the pubs. Every finger of the wind was an arrow pointing me downward shivering into the dark smoky wooden towns of the night.

The week before the barrel run Mum brought the constable back to our house after work. We're having dinner together, she said to Jake and me; you two can walk down into town for a curry or something. Jake's hands were in his pockets as he stood and glared at her. He looked at the constable.

Well, if it isn't old Gaylord Cornworthy, he said.

Gerald Conningsbury, the policeman said.

Don't worry about it, Jake said. It's not like I'm trying to keep a written list of everyone who sleeps with Mum.

So Mum told him to get out and stay out.

I wouldn't need to write it down, he said. I can remember it well enough.

I've slept in the barn before; it's cold out there at night; it makes me feel like my bones are cold.

I read a book once where all the people got sick with something called the white death. It was a science fiction book; it was on a fantasy planet in a dark age. They got sick and called it the white death, and it spread from village to village, quickly, and men and women lay in bed with fever. Their bones ached. Outside the vultures howled while their bones creaked and shifted beneath their skin. The sun went down. In the germy darkness their glowing bones split holes in the skins of their arms and legs and stomachs, and the distorted limbs stuck out into the infected world like alabaster, shiny white.

At night I hear the frogs in the river. They croak on and on; the clouds streak across the sky. It feels to me as if my bones are cold.

I hear Mum's rhyming voice in my sleep. She used to sing the ballads back before Jake was born and when he was still a baby. "Long Black Veil," "Mary Hamilton," "Matty Carpenter." She rocked and softly sang the soothing folk hymns. I don't remember the tunes. I dream new words for them, and the wind provides a rhythm.

Sleeping.

Sometimes in the middle of the night I wake up and think to write down the words, but I just lie in bed with the blankets over me, and I fall back asleep before I work up the energy to go find a pen.

Lots of kids were jealous because I was going to be a barrel roller. It's a coveted position. They have a brochure that they give to tourists. It talks about how they cure the barrels. How they coat the inner surface with coal tar which is available from only one source in all of England. How there's a deep sense of tradition. How the origins of the race date back to pagan rites. The tourists read the brochure and go to the big bonfire; they

buy doughnuts for their kids. Some of them drive home at ten
o'clock because they're scared of all the drunk drivers who will
be out on the roads later but quite a few of them stay. They
want to think they might get burned.

It's a coveted position to be a barrel roller. There are fights.
You can get your face burnt off. A lot of kids were jealous. Jake
wasn't jealous.

I got to be a barrel roller because Lewis was still in the hospital at Exeter. Lewis had carried the Vic's barrel every year
since seventy-one. He got an ulcer in September. Mum said no
wonder he was in the hospital. You put yourself in that bed,
she said. All you ever ate your whole life was digestives and
coffee, white coffee and digestives; serves you right. Beer and
digestives and coffee.

That's all you feed Ben and Jake, Lewis said. I'm not the only
one.

Shut up, Jake said. Mum smacked him across the cheek.

I got to be a barrel roller because Reg had a thing for me.
That's what Jake said at least; he was probably right. Reg tus-
sled my hair sometimes. You look just like your father did when
he was a lad, he said. The same blond hair and the same rosy
cheeks. He said that to me just about every time I went in the
pub. You're quite a character, he said while I was playing pool
with Jake; he grinned through his eyes as the fat of his cheeks
dangled down over the hollow wrinkles of his chin.

You mean you wanna fuck him, Jake said.

He opened his mouth and shut it and opened it and shut it.
Now look here, he said. He didn't really know how to approach
the issue. Now look, he said to me, all I said was you look just
like your father did when he was a kid.

Did you wanna fuck our father too? Jake said. You had a
thing for him when he was a kid?

He didn't say anything. There wasn't much he could have
said. I was embarrassed for him, but there wasn't anything I
could do about it.

I got to be a barrel roller because I damn well wanted to be
a barrel roller. The team went to Teignmouth on a pubcrawl

on Halloween to talk about it. The old men and all their old friends. They took me around from inn to inn and bought me drinks and said well wouldn't you know it you little squirt, every single time, you can drink us all under the table, every one of us.

At nine o'clock the crowd was getting big. From the second-story window above the pub I looked out across the hatted heads. It was easy to tell who was a local and who was a tourist. All the people who had never been to Magothy on Guy Fawkes Day before were looking around worriedly, tiptoeing over the top of the crowd. Do you see flames yet are the fires burning? How are they possibly going to make it between people on these narrow streets? I looked out at them and laughed at all the wandering eyes. The bearer of the fire. The keeper of the flame the king goddammit, your father and your mother and your god.

Roger from fourth form used to try to slide-tackle me into the schoolyard wall when we played football. His team usually lost the games because he was always so busy trying to knock me down. It usually worked but it took half the year before it worked the way he wanted:

Ha ha you hit your head on a brick wall.

He pointed at the blood. Lick the wall, he said. Lick your blood.

I had to get five stitches.

I remember his face; over the years it ages along with me in my mind. I said to myself, I'll be looking for him tonight.

He was one of the people I was looking to burn.

Jake showed up finally. We went out into the crowd to buy bangers. He was pissed off about something, and he was already drunk. We waited in line at the stand and I watched him fuming. His face was red. We were out in the middle of the crowd, smothering, pulling in the cold air in excitement and desperation, surrounded by a thousand slobbering heads. I could see the glow of the fire shining above the bodies somewhere in front of us. No danger yet; no one is shoving. No one has been stricken by seizures. I listened to him and tried to balance; I tried not to stagger back and forth against the people I was shoved up against. There were kids crawling around the crowd, skirting between the legs of people everywhere on the road, slithering through the chamber of the street like serpents.

I need to get out of here, he said.

One more year of A-levels, right?

Fuck A-levels.

You have to finish your A-levels.

I just feel sorry for you, he said. Going to Uni down here. Living at home. You're such a stupid shit.

Shut up, Jake.

You could have gone anywhere. You could have gone to Aberdeen. You could have gone to Strathclyde.

It's cold up there.

It's cold down here too, you cunt.

Not as cold as up there.

You could have gone to Norfolk, he said. You could have gone anywhere but here. He lit a cigarette. You're here for three more years now. You'll be driving the A377 every day for three more years.

I shrugged. Look, I said, are you mad because I'm the one getting to do the barrel run tonight?

He scoffed. The barrel run, he said. The fucking barrel run. I don't give a shit about your barrel run, he said, coughing up a laugh. I don't give a shit about anything that happens in Magothy. In the fucking westcountry at all.

Whatever.

He swigged the last bit of vodka from his bottle and tossed it down on the ground. Getting drunk faster than me. The fucking barrel run, he muttered. When the hell does it start? Go run your damn barrel. Burn your fucking face off.

It's dumb to throw the bottle down when we're standing in a crowd like this, I said. You're just going to step on it.

Shut the fuck up, he said.

What's your problem? I said, and he smiled. There was another fifth of Smirnoff in his coat pocket. He got it out.

Glugluglug.

On knees rubbed raw from cold dark soil he kneels upon the lane. Howling blistered winds will blow. Drizzled draughts of rain. *Tell me why I'm seething. Tell me what to do.* Howling blistered winds will blow. In death you'll feel it too.

At nine forty-five we were drinking and watching the Ship's team. It was getting colder. Jake's cheeks were bright red from the cold. Watered-down piss, he said. We should have hit Kings Cross.

It's not that bad, I said. He rolled his eyes at me.

What's the difference between Churchill and Hitler, he said.

I don't know.

They're both English, he said, except for Hitler. He twitched his nose and sniffled and emitted a groping laugh. As the bonfire burned bright down on the football field half a mile down the street to our left, he and five thousand drunks shivered in the brisk air of the night. Singing to the songs that were being piped out onto the street. Shouting and drinking. There were warning signs posted on the walls. Prevent mishaps, be vigilant. I drank the beer and looked at the crowd. Vigilance. Everywhere is a vigil and everyone is my age.

What's the difference between sand and afterbirth, he said to me. I looked at my watch.

I need to get moving soon, I said.

You can't gargle sand.

Where'd you hear that?

I made it up, he said.

No you didn't. I've heard it before.

That doesn't mean I wasn't the one who made it up.

It was time for me to head back to the Bull's Arms. Squeeze through the crowd. I asked Jake where I should meet him afterward.

I'll find you.

You'll be on Queen Street when we do the run?

I'll be in your face. Burn me you bastard. Throw it in my face.

We were the eighth team to go. Everyone in the crowd was trashed. The air smelled like beer. Carling most of it was. I could see the reflection from where the fire was burning on High Street. That would be the Duke of York. Next the Turk's Head. Then us. So many people. Every other day of the year the town stood empty. Quiet shhh the silence. Desolate and one solitary blemish upon the countryside. Upon the open road it howls. The wind. Cutting into our coats. I can't get through the crowd. Piss on it get all these buggerin leadweight bodies out of my way. I could hear the distant siren of an ambulance. I heard an Irishman talking. Whoal coontrie smells funny, he said. The coal, the ale, the fairms. I don't know but it's soomthan. Can't quite put a finger on it. Ripe with the divil. Smells like we're ali goin to die.

That's true, his wife said, we're all going to die.

Not what I mean.

I made my way through to the pub. Thought you'd turned traitor on us, Derek said. Thought we saw you with one of the other teams. Whatever. They gave me the gloves. I looked around. A spot on the road was cleared for us to start. Fifteen minutes. The people closest to us were the bravest. We're going to run this fire straight smash into your slobbery shirts. Feel the heat of the heat. All beauty must die. Come closer.

Your hands are still going to burn through the gloves, Nigel said.

Yeah.

How do you feel? he said.

I don't know. Cold. Drunk.

Where's your little punk-assed boozer of a kid brother?

I don't know. He was staring out to the street, the dark plaid pockets of warmth and drink: into the arterial conglomeration of souls. Where is Jake now. Boozer. Laughed in the face of the officer. Silent about the whole affair. Fourteen. What are you doing you fool? Ask no questions. Ask no ask him yes what is this you foolish prick. What do you think you're doing? What are you trying to do? You wanted to kill yourself when you were six. I don't even remember those years. I would have been eight. You never talked to me. You don't talk to me.

Red eyes. You can feel the witches. Snotnosed slumchildren from the city kicking empty bottles down the road, fistfights breaking out between men with beersoaked greasy hands, the fires raging. The big bonfire down at the football field was still blazing and its smoke stained every breath of dirty townair.

Get ready now it's time.

We went to the barrel. I was starting. I don't know why they wanted me to be the one to start. Hope you been lifting weights, kid. It weighed six stone. Handcrafted by Bristol beerbrewers they say. Cured wood and wrought metal. Burn.

What's the record so far?

Twelve minutes twenty. Down at the Dartmouth Inn.

Over my cold dead arse will those shitchewers win.

We'll win.

Those old sheepshagging bastards.

One minute, the official said. We stood staring at the barrel. The smell was strong. Black noseturning tar. Enough to burn every inch of the wood. I'm freezing my bollocks off, Derek said.

Here in a minute you'll be wishing to God you could just say you're freezing your bollocks off.

Too late to back out now, kid.

Remember what Lewis would say?

Lordy lordy that Lewis.

Thirty seconds, the official said.

Your uncle Lewis, kid, at the beginning right before we started Lewis always said hey you old farts, if it gets too hot for you, just reach down and unzip my pants and point my cock up in the air and I'll piss the fire right out, if you get too hot.

The crowd was staring at us. Which way are they gonna run. Which way will the flames maneuver the crowd. They stared at me; they thought they could see it in my eyes. Which way will we have to contort. The official blew the whistle, and Reg lit the match and tossed it into the barrel. Bbrrkkclklooooowsh the flames shot out bam into the sky, shot their stink into the air.

Go!

I ran it forward. The bodies jumped back, and a path formed; people fell back upon each other, fell backward like dominoes into the crowd, knocking each other back all the way back to the walls. When there was no more space to be cleared I turned around and ran the other way. I went back and forth and back and forth and the corridor grew longer, snaked farther into the horde. I turned a corner. It was getting heavy. When my arms were aching too much to bear, I passed it off to Nigel.

Two minutes.

Heat. Hands burning. Sweat. Soak. See the steaming water. Eyesoaked sight of red watery fire. The barrel was starting to come apart. Hold'er together, lads. We followed him to help him if he started to drop it. The fumbling lurching bodies. The fear in their eyes as they fall duck and jump. Hahahah run away where are you going to run? See how quickly. Fire into your face. The heat the din. You want the flames to lick you dry.

Burn up up up, burn up.

Every eye gaping on us.

Nigel passed the barrel off to Reg. I looked around for Jake and didn't see him. So many faces. Old Marjery Black. Keith the porter. Mad Bill Buzzard. Jake you fool you'll miss it. The wind bit savagely gravely through the legs of my trousers. Burn me you bastard. What does that mean. Throw it in my face. Six years old and wanted to die. Why do you try to make everyone hate you. Let me in. No one at Uni cares. Ow the flames. Run run run.

Four minutes. He passed it to Derek, who lasted less than a minute. He passed it back to me.

Pay attention, Ben; it'll to fall to pieces if you're not careful.

Hell, Ben's doin better than any of us.

A clear corridor had formed for me to run through. Kids shot out of the crowd and when the flames came close they ducked back in. Don't think we've quite scorched any bloke's face off yet, Reg said. I carried the barrel back and forth. My arms were hurting. My hands felt numb beneath the gloves. The cinders burned my nose. One old man stared at us; he seemed to be always in front of me, following along, staring into my eyes.

Scars on his face. A bottle of scotch in his hand. Glen Ord. He drank from it and muscled his lips back and forth, curling them out toward the fire, quietly cackling. He looked like Lewis. The warts on his face. The dry air. Carry the fire north south east and west. Spread out through the dry air. Burn grass burn trees burn sharpbeaked birds. The wrinkled wizened women. All God's creatures must die. Fire was spurting out in front of me and it was eleven o'clock. In the bed Lewis lay dying at the stroke of eleven. The old man looked into my eyes and through him I could hear the moans ten miles west, howling across the hills in sputtered croaks.

The wrinkled old man looked straight into the fire and didn't squint his eyes or shelter them with his hand like all the stupid slags around him. Slimy gits and their slimy git kids. All the plaidcoated slags with their plastic cups of lager. He looked into the fire and seemed to hiss through his crooked teeth:

When the flames roar, when I see the wind, I wish I was crazy again.

Two Germans chanted a marching song. Tourist kids. Punk metal chains. Ein Hut ein Stock ein Damenunterrock. Walking behind me. Following in the wake of the fire in the tail of folding flames. Und vorwärts rückwärts seitwärts stopp und HOCH das Bein.

Eight minutes.

No one saw Jake coming as he approached. He smashed his fifth of Smirnoff onto the pavement. I had the barrel again. We weren't lasting as long. None of us could hold it up for very long anymore. Thirty seconds, twenty seconds. Thirty kilos is thirty kilos. You don't think about much else but your arms. Nine minutes total now. I held the barrel.

Und eins und zwei und drei.

Here he comes.

He jumped onto my shoulders, grabbing the barrel. The weight shifted and I lost balance; he floundered on my back reaching for the barrel. What the hell are you doing? The flames roared. He wrestled the barrel from me and flung it forward, raging splintering it on the road.

The redness of the west above the land in red attire. The redness of the cinders as he jumped into the fire.

Und vier und funf und sechs und sie—eee—BEN.

He stood in the flames. He looked into my eyes and his eyes looked to me like he was about to cry but he started to laugh. You don't get it, he said, do you? You don't understand me. You don't even understand why I'm doing this.

I'm sorry.

You're not on my side. Part of his hair caught fire. The hairs burned like pine needles.

Pull him out goddammit pull him out.

Men from the crowd took him by the arms and pulled him out of the fire and with a coat extinguished the flames from his hair. He struggled and kicked his legs and scrunched his face tight.

You're not on my side, he said. You don't even understand why I'm doing this.

Someone get the cop up here.

He kicked at the men who held him. Get the cop up here. I wanna see Gaylord Cornworthy. Front and center.

The crowd was clearing out to go to the next pub. It was on the other side of town, down toward the river. What was our time? Reg asked the official. Not that it matters anyhow.

Disqualified.

What?

Got to.

But Pete, come on now.

No way around it.

Reg cast his eyes down to the road. Reckon the Vic will win.

Derek looked at me. We would have won if it weren't for your brother.

Why didn't you tell us he'd try to pull a stunt like that?

Why didn't you do something to stop him? What the hell

goes on out there at your place anyway? Whole bloody family of neurotics. Entire bloody family. Don't know what you're doing spending your time with us anyway. Back when I was your age I wouldn't have been hanging around the like of us. What's the use in going to Uni if you're not going to live in the halls. What's the use in it.

Leave him alone, Derek.

Bloody cryin shame. Whole bloody family. Just stood there and watched him wreak his havoc. Who's older than who here anyway? Who's wearing the bloody trousers?

I'm sorry.

Whole bloody family.

He spent the night in jail. Drunken disorderliness. Possession of alcohol by a minor. Assault. I guess they were just fucking with him with all those charges but they kept him in overnight.

We lost.

I walked home a mile and a half up the hill. Tired. I almost passed out in the town. When I got to the barn I went inside and sat down on the straw. Don't want to walk anymore. Passed out in the barn. Cold crispedged air blading the shadows. What I am smelling is the coal from the town. Up on the Yeomans Hills above the distant rooftops.

A wee dram ae whiskey: Shoot that motherfucker down.

The wind coming up out of the heath whooowoosh and the dark squawking crow swooping medievally asoar toward the wintry sea, raw black redbeaked as it flies, a wodge of coal in its mouth and one shining eye in the sky. No wind'll blow out the fire. Ooooraroorarooo. Listen to the oooraroo yelping cold black and helpless and at night stomachgrowling dogs roam the hills a hundred years behind us.

It's all you need to think about.

She saw his cold and reddened chest; she stroked his bony cheek. She frowned upon the bloody ooze that trickled toward the creek. *It's crowded in the prison. It's crowded on the earth. I'll breathe again upon this moor you crowded with your birth.*

As I slept I felt an acute sense of dread and panic creep over me.

The sun went down around them, the darkness and the dews.
The hoarsely uttered donkey's bray that echoed from the mews.
I want to wake up now.

The heath is ripe with rotting things, with maggots and their
guts. With boars and with the oily pus that's flowing from their
cuts.

The Future Is Orange

Duane was drinking with Conrad on Saturday night at the bar on West Broadway. There was no sign outside the bar to tell them what its name was, and Duane didn't feel like asking. He sat with a bottle of Miller clasped in his right hand and a cigarette in the other and stared out the window at the desolate downtown street where no one ever passed by. This was Maryville. No one came into the bar while they were there and no one who was already at the bar ever left. Duane had asked what was on draught; the woman behind the bar said, without looking away from her conversation with the men on the barstools, We ain't got no draughts. He looked up at the large sign above the bar that read "Miller on draught here," shrugged, and asked for a Heineken. We ain't got no imports, she told him. He chose Miller because it was the only beer the bar served that wasn't a light beer.

Wendy got you down? Conrad said with a smug smile as he twirled his thick black hair with his fingers. Ain't she.

No, not really.

If they weren't no problem then you wouldn't be out drinkin with me.

Hell.

Hell my ass. You ain't drunk with me in months.

Duane shrugged.

So answer the damn question. Wendy got you down. Ain't she.

No.

Yeah she has, Conrad said. Look me in the eye and tell me she ain't.

We're fine.

Look at me, Duane. Look me in the eye and tell me that.

Duane looked into his friend's eyes. Everything's fine, he said slowly and calmly, with no hint of anxiety.

Well.

If that weren't the case then I'd tell you so.

Well, Conrad said, drawing out the word for as long as possible. Well.

Duane had no intention of talking about anything with Conrad or with anyone else. He wasn't going to tell him about the fight, and he certainly wasn't going to tell him about the banjo. He was upset and he wasn't going to tell Conrad why and he didn't want to think about it.

I feel like gettin plastered tonight, Conrad said. I mean I always feel like gettin plastered but tonight I wanna get fuckin *smashed.*

Okay by me.

You need to get smashed too, what with your fight with Wendy. Maybe then you'll tell me about it.

Duane raised his eyebrows.

Oh come on, Conrad said. I mean it serves you right for even takin a second look at her ass in the first place but I can tell you had a fight.

Duane shrugged.

They drank two Millers apiece at the bar with no name and then walked down the street to the Frog and drank two Budweisers. They took shots of Captain Morgan's out of the flask Conrad kept in his coat. Duane felt the warmth of the alcohol as it rose into his head and reddened the nacreous whites of his eyes.

She wants you to quit drinkin, don't she?

I already told you we're not talking about this anymore.

She thinks I'm a bad influence on you.

Well, she doesn't like you, Duane said. I'll give you that.

She thinks I'm a bad person. That I'm out of control. Duane stared down into the narrow opening of the beer bottle, and his refusal to look at Conrad as he spoke gave Conrad more confidence in his argument. She talks about your future, he said. She says how can you have a future together with her if you're out drinkin with your buddies all the time. Ain't that right?

Duane shrugged.

Well at least you ain't denyin it no more. Another four beers and you'll be cussin her right along here with me.

There ain't nothin for me to cuss her about, Duane said.

So it's your fault then.

He shrugged.

Wendy had been trying to persuade Duane lately that they should move south into Monroe County. She stayed in the house most of the time and never drove into the city anymore and cursed every time a car drove by on the road in front. There were subdivisions creeping out toward their house. West Maryville was growing. There was a new Food Lion and a new Home Depot. The highway was being four-laned. Wendy bought all her groceries at the little store in Greenback because she refused to go into town. When she wanted fast food, she drove all the way down to Vonore and ate at the Hardee's at Citico Road.

I don't know why you waste all that gas goin down there, Duane said to her.

I ain't goin into Maryville by myself.

What are you talkin about?

Don't even feel safe there no more. Gangs and all.

Duane stared at her. What the hell are you talking about?

That's what the preacher says.

Well that's absurd.

The kids at the county schools gotta carry see-through backpacks now so the teachers can see if they're carryin guns.

That's just the school board being paranoid, Wendy.

She just shook her head slightly and didn't answer; he could tell that his disbelief did nothing but convince her more firmly of her opinion. Property's real cheap down in Tellico Plains, she said.

What the hell would we wanna live there for?

It's right up there close to the national forest. We could go hiking more often.

Honey, all it is down there is a bunch of Klansmen and moonshiners.

It wouldn't really be any farther for you to drive to TRW from there.

His temper flared for a brief moment and then subsided. Honey, he said slowly, I ain't gonna move to Monroe County. I've lived in Blount County all my life and I don't want to live nowhere else.

She picked up her comb and began brushing back her hair, frowning, almost sulking. He examined her face, watched her yellow hair as it fell back against her black shirt. She had a scratch on her face from when she'd been hiking a few days before and had scraped a thorn; if she hadn't gotten the scratch, she wouldn't have told him about the trip at all. During the weeks when he worked third shift at TRW, he slept all morning and afternoon, and she took the car and drove around the back roads and the mountains, across to Robbinsville on the new road, stopping at the scenic vistas to stare out into the hazy blue and purple layers and thirst for their emptiness. She went on the hiking trails up around Bald River Falls. She drove the gravel road up to Turkey Pen Resort. Duane found out about her trips only through the discrepancies he noticed in the odometer's reading, and if that hadn't prompted him to ask, he thought, she never would have told him. Do you wanna be a deer or something? he said to her one time. She didn't answer. She never went with him to his relatives' houses anymore. When they came over, she stayed in her room. He made excuses for her. She's not feeling well, she couldn't sleep yesterday. He watched her late at night as she slept, wondering why all the freckles had disappeared from her face.

You know you could just talk to the moon every day, he

thought. A tent and a stove and a toothbrush. You could throw stones at the passing hikers from your perch on the laurel-shaded rocks as smoke rings rise into the treetops. You could watch the sunsets. You'd still smell the fumes from the Cherohala Skyway. You'd see the raccoons grow fatter slowly as the seasons change, their stripes expanding, the paws that nibble treebark and the eyes that shine in starlight. Would it be enough do you think? In the crickety night would your right foot as you sleep fumble for the accelerator, stretching down a narrow glass highway in darkness in winter, in the oncoming lane a headlit onslaught, beeping through your dreams?

She spoke in her sleep, no full words, no whispers: murmurs only. He watched her in the pale filtered light of the moonlit room.

How's that banjo comin along? Conrad asked him. The bar was filling up, and Duane wanted to leave.

Same as usual.

Conrad laughed. Can you play "Duellin Banjos" yet? he asked. Duane ignored him. Everyone asked him that. Can you play Foggy Mountain Breakdown yet?

I can't play shit yet, Duane said, raising his voice.

Conrad whistled. Whoa there, buddy. Sounds like I hit a sensitive subject. He waited for a reaction.

Let's get out of here pretty soon.

You been spendin all your time with the banjo and not enough with her? Or maybe she's been playin it too and she's twice as good at it and you realize how pathetic it makes you look in comparison?

Finish your beer.

Hold your fuckin horses.

I'm ready to go.

Or maybe she's wishin she never give it to you in the first place. You and me both know how she is about money. How much did that thing cost her anyways? Are you listening to me?

Duane stared at him.

How much did it cost?

I don't know, Duane said.

Can't have been less than five hundred dollars.

It was used.

I know it was used.

Wendy had given him the banjo as a Christmas present. He had wanted one for years, since before he had met her, but he never would have spent the money on it himself. She gave him a teach-yourself book by Pete Seeger and another one by Peter Wernick and a case and a set of picks and a capo and an extra set of strings and an entire book of tablature. She watched his eyes light up with childlike enthusiasm as he took the instrument into his hands and strummed it. He didn't know where she'd gotten the money. He couldn't believe she'd driven into town on her own to buy it at all.

Turn that one book to page 27, she said. He opened it; it was the tablature to the "Ballad of Jed Clampett."

Well how about that, he said.

That's what I want you to learn to play first.

Duane spent almost the entirety of his weeklong holiday from work practicing the banjo. He had taken guitar lessons when he was in high school, so learning to fret the strings properly was relatively easy for him. He learned how to play the major scale in G and C; he learned hammering-on, sliding. He learned to strum the melodies of several songs in the how-to book: "Old Joe Clark," "Bile Them Cabbage Down."

After New Year's he started practicing with the picks, because bluegrass banjo was what he wanted to learn. His fingers felt awkward and clumsy, and he kept looking at the pictures in the book to see if he was wearing the picks backward. They made his fingers sore. He read that bluegrass masters played eight to ten notes per second, but he had trouble playing one roll of eight notes in eight seconds.

He played the six practice rolls from the book over and over, for hours, until he was afraid the thumbpick was cutting off his circulation. He worked up to a level of frustration he hadn't felt since he had broken up with his former girlfriend, six months before he met Wendy. He felt redness flood his cheeks, his ears, and he stared down at the banjo and tried to keep himself from bashing it as hard as he could against the wall. When this happened, if Wendy was in the house he would whisper curses to himself, and when she was gone he would scream them until his throat hurt. He counted in time with his breathing to calm himself down. He didn't want Wendy to see his temper get out of control. His shoulders grew so tense by the time he was done practicing that he had to drink two or three shots of whiskey just to feel normal again.

When he wasn't playing the banjo, he found himself moving his thumb, index finger, and middle finger in the patterns of the rolls. At night he had trouble falling asleep because all he could envision was banjo tablature as he tried again and again to play it, never progressing beyond the first three or four measures before he made an error, causing a brutal, clangy sound to flood his ears.

At work Nathan Jones asked him why his eyes were so red all the time. It's that fuckin banjo, he said. I hate that fuckin banjo.

Then why don't you quit playin it?

I can't.

Sell it.

I can't do that.

He started playing it more and more every day. He stopped getting any better at it. He tried to learn a few of the other songs in the same chapter, and he got up to the same level with them; never any better. He couldn't sleep.

I sure am glad you like that banjo so much, Wendy said to him. He forced a smile. I was real afraid before I gave it to you that you wouldn't even like it. I don't know what I would have done if you didn't like it so much. It would have been awful.

Well, thanks again, he said.

Well, you're welcome, she said, and she kissed him on the cheek. I'm just glad it makes you so happy.

One day when Wendy was out driving around somewhere, he opened up her checkbook to find out how much it had cost. He scanned back through the entries until he found Tommy

Covington's Music written down. Six hundred dollars. Goddammit, he said to himself. Goddammit goddammit goddammit.

He practiced the "Ballad of Jed Clampett" over and over again, trying to get it right. He improved at first and then it seemed after a while like he was getting worse again. His fingers weren't fast enough to fret the A-minor chord on the third measure, and he never got his fingers close enough to the frets on the D chord, and when he got to "then one day he was lookin for some food" he couldn't do the rolls at all. He played it again and again and never came anywhere close to making it through the song without errors. He looked down at the banjo with disgust, wanting to rip the strings out with his bare hand, when Wendy walked in from the store. He started the song again and messed up on the fourth measure and stopped.

Hi, honey, Wendy said.

Hi, he muttered.

When are you gonna learn to play the "Ballad of Jed Clampett?" she said cheerfully. You've been playin that thing for three or four weeks but it don't sound like you're playin anything at all. Just a bunch of notes that all sound the same.

He felt an overwhelming urge to snap at her, to quit bottling his temper at all and scream that the "Ballad of Jed Clampett" was the ONLY goddamn song he'd been playing for the WHOLE FUCKING WEEK and maybe you just shouldn't have given me this piece of shit if you don't like the way it sounds when I play it and maybe I'm just not any good at it huh how does it feel to be married to a guy who's too stupid to learn how to play this goddamn thing does that make you feel any better? but he just breathed slowly, deliberately in and deliberately out, and smiled at her. I'm workin on it, he said.

How come it sounds all tinny? Is it out of tune?

No, honey, it's not out of tune. That's just because I'm not very good at it yet. These things take time, you know.

Duane and Conrad left the Frog and drove to the Cellar Bar. Duane felt himself getting drunk. He knew he needed to ask

Conrad whether he could sleep over at his house that night, but he didn't want to talk about Wendy anymore; he looked over at his friend, standing at the bar ordering drinks, and he tried to force the scowl off his face. He wasn't having a good time. With thick gritting teeth he faced the table behind closed eyes as Conrad brought the drinks and sat down, and he pictured himself whiteskinned and shiteyed, an amorphous blob, cheeks encysted with greasy lipotamous lardblots, bubble-headed, speechless.

I tell you what, Conrad said. You know what would solve all your problems?

What?

Hell, it'd solve everybody's problems.

What?

If piss were flammable.

Duane laughed.

Then everything would just be perfect, Conrad said. Just get yourself a Zippo, light her up, hold it right there under the stream and let physics do the rest. Wendy bitchin at you again? Just point a finger down at the bulge in your pants and she'll shy away and shut right up.

Conrad shook and fidgeted in his laughter.

I tell you what, wouldn't be no more fights between me and my dad neither. I'd just unzip my fly and I'd burn his whole goddamn place down while he stood there and watched. I'd walk over to him and you know those last couple drops of piss well I'd just light them up and they'd fall down to his feet like little balls of flame and catch fire. I tell you what.

Duane was frowning again, and Conrad wondered why he wasn't cheering up.

All the niggers that play basketball over on Hall Road and stare at you when you drive by. You could just piss out your window. And all the wiggers that go cruisin up in town.

Them and their fuckin ten-foot-diameter subwoofers too, Duane said. Put a whole new meaning in pissin somebody off.

Conrad drank quickly. He had bought two pitchers, and he drank one of them in little more than two minutes. He told

Duane about his dog dying. He told Duane about the Lady Vols game he'd watched on television the night before. He talked about how he hated everyone he saw around him in the bar.

I tell you what, Conrad said, it just might work if you was to drink gasoline.

What would work? Duane asked. He wasn't paying much attention to what Conrad was saying.

Flaming piss.

Christ, you're still on that?

Conrad laughed.

Well why don't you go drink some gasoline then and tell me what happens. Get that high-octane shit. You might as well. Texaco's just down the road.

Conrad slapped his knee. Goddamn, he said.

What?

You know how grain alcohol has a warning on it not to strike a match near it.

Yeah.

Are you thinkin what I'm thinkin?

No I ain't and I hope to God you ain't neither.

Let's drive across the county line and hit the liquor store.

That's the most ridiculous thing I ever heard.

Well, it's a good excuse to go buy somethin to drink, anyways.

You're drunk already.

Ain't no crime in that.

They left the bar and drove over to Highway 33 and headed for Vestal. Duane fumbled for a cassette tape between the seats; when his hand found his three banjo picks, he lifted them out of the ashtray and threw them out the window onto the road.

What was those? Conrad asked.

Nothin.

What was they?

Just trash.

No it wasn't.

Just never mind.

They sped down the highway. Duane was screeching the tires

on every curve, and just past the bridge over Stock Creek he went around a turn so fast that Conrad flew halfway out of his seat and hit his head on the steering wheel.

Be careful there, Duane said.

You better be careful yourself, you little shit.

At the liquor store Conrad went straight to the grain alcohol. Looky there, he said to Duane. One hundred ninety-five proof. Flammable. Keep away from flames. Beautiful.

You are one crazy bastard.

I'll be crazier after we drink some of this shit.

I ain't touchin it.

Hell.

I ain't.

I got ten bucks says you drink more of it than me.

You ain't supposed to drink this shit straight. You mix it with jungle juice.

Well, we ain't got no jungle juice.

You'd probably die if you drank that shit straight.

Well, you gotta go somehow.

They bought the grain alcohol and a fifth of Seagram's and headed back toward Blount County. Conrad took swigs out of the bottle as they drove. Lawdy law, he yelled. You want some?

Well, I guess I'll taste it. He took a shot out of the bottle. Goddamn, he said, contorting his face, that there is the nastiest shit I ever drunk in my life. Conrad laughed. I suppose you probably like the way it tastes, Duane said, don't you?

I've had better. He laughed. But I've had worse too.

There ain't anything worse than that shit.

Conrad laughed and drank more. You better call out the fire brigade, he said, cause I'm gonna be pissin myself up a storm.

Duane drove to Sandy Springs Park. The weather was unseasonably warm, nearly sixty degrees, and they sat on the hill above the softball field and drank. The water fountain was turned off for the winter. I never thought I'd use gin as a chaser, Duane said.

What's that sound? Conrad said.

The squirrels I guess.

No the other sound.

I don't know. They both laughed.

Duane was losing track of time. He couldn't tell if they'd been at the park for thirty minutes or two hours. They had made a significant dent in both bottles. His head was spinning, and he felt like he would have motion sickness if he chose to move ever again. We better slow down, Duane said, and then he couldn't remember what he was going to say afterward.

Why's that?

I don't remember. They both laughed more. Duane momentarily forgot where he was. The green of the grass and trees was black in the darkness in front of him and bright jade green when he saw it in his mind. The dark and the stars and the rustling in the trees above him were rampant and overpowering as he staggered through it all and even though he sat motionless upon the dewy grass of the park he felt as if he were careening through a virgin forest in the wilderness of the tallest eastern mountains on no trail or path and he stumbled past chestnuts as tall as redwoods, hemlocks as large as sequoias; in the midst of a brave hooting cradle of owls' cries he proceeded unflinchingly ahead toward the threshold of the cloaked leafy dais upon which he strode, arrow-eyed, beasts and winged things of the night calling him tensely forward.

Hey.

What?

You see that?

What?

He grinned and shut his eyes and tried to decide whether he wanted to open his mouth to answer and what he would say and what he had been talking about in the first place. The sky was a circle above him. He was cold but it didn't really matter. Eyes closed in drunken satisfaction and his chest gently rising, falling, gently as he breathed; he shook his head to decline the request for explanation. It was getting colder. The grass was wet. It was all clear.

He heard cascading liquid; he saw flames.

He noticed several things as he faded into dream. How the

dew was wetting his socks through holes in his shoes. The distant lightning. How the sky was pink from the glow of Maryville. They call it that old mountain dew and them that refuse it are few. That was in the songbook. Twenty pages ahead in the intermediate tablature section. He had spilled beer on that page; he had stared at it and laughed. He had taken the compact disc included with the book and thrown it off his deck like a Frisbee and shot at it as if it were a skeet. The temperature was dropping. The car took several minutes to heat up and he noticed how Conrad hadn't spoken in the longest time and how it was disappointing to think it was two in the morning and they were going to pass out soon. How his headache was a cross between dizziness and nausea. How the white lines vibrated like banjo strings as he drove. He knew as it was happening that he didn't know what was going on. He stared in confusion at the darkness. In black the trees were big black waving leafblobs and when his eyes were open they waved at him in the wind. Time was passing, he thought. A lot of minutes but not a whole hour but maybe. He was smiling and there were things going on outside. Little bugs and gnats flying around going glunk against the windows and they're all flying sideways. He heaved the bottle across Conrad out the passenger window because it needed to be out of the car definitely but he hadn't realized as he launched it that the window was closed. The bottle was one-third full. He didn't want to throw it out his own window and have it hit a car or something else that he couldn't predict. There was humming. The moon was rising or setting or just hovering there above the treeline. There was water. He heard birds, or planes maybe. The road didn't look familiar. There were curves.

He was overcome by vertigo and disorientation as he pulled out of a dream. He was playing a song on the banjo: "Worried Man Blues." It was the one on the page opposite the "Ballad of Jed Clampett" in his songbook. He was playing it quickly, in darkness, accompanied by an invisible fiddler, no bodies to be seen but the music was alive and awake and he wasn't making any mistakes. He sang, and somewhere a chorus sang with him:

It takes a worried man tooooo siiiiiing a worried song,
I'm worried now, but I won't be worried long.

He went through the song again and again, never missing a note. He listened to the applause and was happy: They're stringing me along and speaking to me, the little disembodied babblers, they like me, they know me, I'm drifting through their domains; they're granting me admittance to their thousand glowing underworlds.

When he opened his eyes he was overcome by disorientation and vertigo as he saw pink. Everything was pink. It shouldn't be pink.

He was cold. His shoes were gone.

It was a rectangular room with a concrete floor. His belt was gone.

As he rubbed his eyes and tried to figure out where he was, his head throbbed. His memory of the evening was murky and unclear and almost nonexistent. He remembered being on Highway 321 headed for Friendsville, out on the straight empty stretch by Uncle Dave's Market. Where was Conrad? As he scraped his teeth with his tongue, he realized their surface was thick and scummy with the residue of vomit, but he didn't remember vomiting. They had been at the bar and the liquor store and the park and everything was hazy and disjointed; all he could recall were single images: passing the mall, running the traffic light out by the industrial park. He looked down at his hands: They were scratched and splintered, with jagged lines of dried blood running in all directions, like razor marks.

Fuck you all, screamed a man in the corner who looked like he was dead.

Duane looked around and surveyed the room: Everything was pink. Every wall. There were ten or eleven men in the room. There was a metal door. He was still only half-conscious, and he had trouble keeping his eyes open. He couldn't tell if he was speaking out loud or mumbling or making no sound at all. No one was looking at him; no one seemed to notice his presence. As he reached the moment in his awakening when he became aware that he was not dreaming, that he existed in space and what he saw was where he was, he jolted into alertness. Where am I what the hell is going on. What the fuck is this place. His wristwatch was gone, and he didn't know if it was morning or afternoon or still late at night. His heart pounded with fear.

Drinkin just ain't it anymore, the man with the food caked in his beard was saying. Seem like ever damn time I get drunk the law come and throw me in the pink room. I seen the pink room, sugar pie, I know the dagblame pink room like it was the back a my hand. I'm sick to my bones a the pink room. He stood up and wobbled slowly forward with a blurred, crippled rhythm, all the way to the wall. They ain't no more pink room for me baby, he yelled toward the door, and his laugh whistled through a missing tooth as he fingered the hard places in his beard. They's great things a-comin, he announced. Ain't no more drinkin, that ain't the future.

What's the future, Mack? someone yelled.

Buds, he said. Buds is the future.

Naw, the black man said. County's got them copters now.

Don't make no difference.

You best be careful.

Ever time I take one goddamn drink I wind up in the damn pink room. Don't make no inch a difference. Ever damn time I put the bottle to my lips.

Well, that's the way.

Ain't nothin ever happens though when I get high.

You know what I want? said the black man.

What?

A drink of water. Makes me thirsty to hear you talk. I want a goddamn drink of water so bad right now I'd give you my left nut for it.

Well, you can want in one hand and shit in the other, Mack said. He picked a visible wad of earwax out of his right ear with his finger. I'm sick to my bones a this pink room, he said. He fingered the curled ends of his beard, leaving bits of wax stuck on the ends of his hair. Them buds don't get me sent to no pink room.

Pink room won't be the same without you, Mack.

They's great things a-comin, Mack said. Duane leaned back against the pink cinder blocks and groaned as he listened to them. Just you keep a eye out.

He passed out again.

In the dream he was having when he reawakened, he was playing the banjo again. The song was the "Ballad of Jed Clampett," and he was getting it right. It was going even better than "Worried Man Blues" in the previous dream. He was picking the strings so fast he could barely discern each individual note, but they were all there, sounding clearly, and he was accenting the melody notes and doing everything right and he didn't screw up the last D chord like he usually did and when he finished he started in on the second verse and played it as perfectly as the first. Wendy was in the room watching. Everything was coming naturally. He wasn't thinking about what he was doing; he wasn't even looking down at the strings as he plucked them. He burned with satisfaction. He probably wouldn't have woken up from the dream at all, he thought later, if its plot hadn't twisted around so that Wendy said, in what seemed to him to be a non sequitur, Why don't you ever make Conrad wear his seat belt when he's riding with you? The way you drive, I just know somethin's going to happen one of these days.

He awoke as she spoke. For two seconds the dream continued as he struggled to open his eyes, as if they were glued shut; he forced his way out of the dream. He jumped sweating into consciousness, and Mack, who had been looking in his direction, laughed.

Kid, he said, you a mess. You are one hell of a mess.

Where's Conrad? Duane said.

Who the hell is Conrad? He that one old guy the cops was bringin in every Friday night there for near two months?

Duane stared forward, sweat rolling down his nose and dripping onto his shirt.

Say, Mack said. He the one got sent to prison? Say.

In a panic Duane tried to remember what had happened. The bar. The liquor store. The park. The highway. Why were they going down 321? Conrad's ex-wife lived down 321. He'd wanted to go piss on her house maybe. He'd gotten so drunk and stoned he was hallucinating and he actually believed he could piss fire and had they ever gotten there? He couldn't remember. They had been looking for a lighter. There wasn't a lighter in the glove box. There weren't any matches.

You gotta help me, Duane said, but as he said it he realized that he was only mumbling. No intelligible words were actually coming out. He wanted to get up and bang on the door and demand to be let out but his head hurt and his body felt like his bones had liquefied and he had a strange foreboding sense that something had happened. As he thought back on the events of the day, searching for some clue about what had led him here, the evening retreated further and further into the opaque membrane of his memory, and he found himself unable to remember clearly what had happened at the Cellar Bar, at the Frog, even at the bar with no name.

Why were they out drinking at all? He never drank with Conrad lately. He didn't even like Conrad very much anymore. What was going on, he wondered in desperation. Suddenly one memory came clear to him, blindingly clear, and he remembered why he had even left his house at all that evening.

He had woken Wendy up with all the noise he was making. She had been taking a nap after her Garden Club meeting, and so he had decided to practice the banjo out on the deck behind the house. It was only about sixty degrees outside, and the cold weather probably made his hands stiff; he might have made more progress as he practiced had it not been so chilly, had the wind not been blowing quite so hard. He made tick marks on the deck railing with his Swiss Army knife for every time he started the song and made a mistake somewhere in the middle of it, and he began again every time there was a mistake. Stubbornly he forced himself to stop in his tracks whenever he picked the wrong string, fretted the chord incorrectly. He started the song three hundred times before he went back inside. He carved sixty sets of ticks into the wood. It seemed to him that each time through the song it sounded worse than the previous time. On the last fifty tries he never even made it past the first six measures.

It was the electric blender that had probably woken Wendy up. It was on; it was blending. Everything was loud but it was probably the blender, he thought later, that brought her out of the bedroom. He had hit one of its buttons along with every-thing else on the countertop as he destroyed the kitchen, appli-ance by appliance. For eleven seconds the blender pureed empty air that whirred within its lidded space. Duane knocked it off the counter with his weapon; early in its spiral it pulled its cord out of the countertop socket with its own weight. He swung the banjo. He hit the toaster, the knife set, the spice rack, the hang-ing fruit basket. The toaster made a hollow tinny sound, and the spice rack gave a solid wham. He held the banjo like a baseball bat, left hand down close to the peghead and right hand just above the fifth string peg. Wendy was watching him in the open doorway, he realized afterward, as he bashed the wall, the counter, the cabinets, the yellow linoleum floor. Dents and then cracks appeared in the oak as Duane made his way into the living room. Take that you piece of shit, he yelled as he smashed the banjo's head into the brick wall of the fireplace and swung back and smashed it again and again. The armrest and tailpiece broke off.

Wendy probably heard the bridge, he thought, as it crunched and pierced the head. Duane picked up his pocketknife and sliced the head open; laying the instrument on the floor, he stood up on the tension hoop, one foot on either side, and he knelt down and positioned the knife beneath the strings and at a right angle to them. They didn't all snap at once. When the last one finally whipped up toward his face he fell backward, catching himself on the armrest of the love seat. He reached down for the banjo, swooping it up in his left hand, and he banged it against the mantelshelf as picture frames fell off onto the floor. Fuck, fuck, he was muttering, out of breath and raspy-throated. He swung harder and harder. In one final blow he burst open the polished, shining wood disk of the resonator against the sharp corner of the shelf. Fuck you you piece of shit, he said.

Drool swung back and forth as it hung from his mouth. Grabbing the banjo by the gaping crack in the wood, Duane bounded for the sliding door. He threw open the glass, ran out onto the deck, and flung the battered instrument through the air. Without style or grace it spun twice and sank. As it fell, two pegs came loose; the three objects descended together toward the rocks at the bottom of the hill and struck at almost the same time. The pegs disappeared but the banjo tumbled across a long sequence of boulders; the sound of its cascading fall, he thought afterward, was surely dissonant and ugly in Wendy's ears. Duane stood listening, still and silent, until the faintest prick of noise had faded into silence.

He saw Wendy through the glass when he finally turned around. She had slumped down onto the floor from where she had been leaning against the doorframe. Duane's eyes opened wide and his pulse quickened and he realized what he had done, stepping gradually forward ohshit and her body in shadow from the setting sun against the glass, silhouetted so he couldn't see but weeping and every muscle now rocking in the fullbodied action and oh shit she's crying, she saved up six hundred dollars to get me this banjo. Acorns exploded like bottlerockets against the rusty tin roof of their cabin.

Do you want to recede into the brownness of the woods? Soil rich in scent rotting in front of your nose and the pine needles alive beneath your back. Companions infinite in webbed retreat around you. Worried now but won't be worried long.

The door opened. Two deputies shoved a half-conscious kid into the drunk tank; he stumbled forward onto his black bruises and passed out on the floor. There was blood on his ear and on his jeans. This one thinks he's Muhammad Ali, one of the deputies said, so keep an eye out.

The two officers boomed with laughter. Cause when he done slept this shit off, said the second deputy, the kid'll be hell on wheels. The door closed.

Wait, Duane tried to yell, but it came out as barely a whisper.

The room was wholly silent for almost a minute, and then Mack started singing: Once two strangers climbed ol Rocky

Top. How's it go after that? Lookin for their still. Ain't come down. How's it go.

I was gonna learn that song on the banjo, Duane said. He didn't want to talk to anyone and he hadn't had any intention of saying anything at all but something made him speak out in the low raspy voice which was all he could manage.

You play the banjo? Mack slapped his knee. Kid like you?

I'm learning.

Get out, Mack said. Duane shrugged his shoulders. What kind you got?

Gold Star.

Mack shook his head and whistled. My papaw, he began, why Lord have mercy. You know what my papaw had back in his pickin days?

Duane shook his head.

Nineteen thirty-seven Mastertone, Mack said. When Duane showed no response Mack started talking again. He'd play that song about Liza Jane. The one I always liked so good.

Duane stared at the wall and tried not to think about his headache. Just shut up, he was repeating to himself. Everybody's papaw had a banjo and if you believed old drooling fools in county jails they were all Mastertones from the Depression and the papaws were all clawhammer virtuosos and they all knew Bill Monroe and played with him once or twice, had a few beers with him, taught him a thing or two. Mack started singing:

*She went by the newmade road, and I went through the
  lane
Stuck my finger in the crack of the fence and out jumped
  Liza Jane.*

He shook his head and whistled. Wasn't nobody could sing it like papaw. He shook his head again. Wish I could remember the words to that ol Rocky Top.

The man in the corner with the spider tattoo stood up and stumbled toward the toilet. His pants were already unzipped and falling down; his beer gut hung out from beneath his shirt and seemed to droop halfway down his legs. He moved forward as if his mutant knees pointed in directions perpendicular to each other: one step left and one step forward and two steps left he shuffled, eyes clenched shut. Spit dangled out of his mouth in tangled strands that hung behind him as he walked; they fell against his shirt. He reached down and fiddled with the fly of his boxer shorts.

You can do it, Mack yelled. I'm with you, baby.

The stream of piss that rainbowed toward the wall fell a foot wide and some inches short of the dingy brown toilet and splashed and steamed in a puddle on the floor. Duane stared up at the man, who coughed as if he suffered from black lung and had black hair emerging from his ears. The pisspuddle grew larger and then smaller as small streams began flowing toward the drain. One of the men who had passed out on the concrete floor lay on the slope between the drain and the puddle; Duane watched as a head of carrotred hair absorbed liquid from the twin streams that ran beneath it and came out from beneath the man's downturned ear on the other side of his face. If piss were flammable, he thought. We could do some cleaning up and I see eleven logs to start the fire. Twelve if you count me too and you might as well. He stared with disgust at the pastel walls and imagined a glowing glottal cave of screaming flames and it raged and defiled with black skinsoot the four emprisoning pink slabs and as it burned it sparkled, shone. If piss were flammable. Get yourself a lighter and slam some beers and the world waits.

That's how come drinkin ain't the future, Mack said as the fat man tried to zip his jeans up. Cause we'd be pissin away the future ever time we went to the fuckin bathroom.

Duane tried to remember the evening; he saw himself at the no-name bar thinking about the banjo and he saw himself in the matte-pink drunk tank and everything in between was a blur. There was Conrad and there was the grain alcohol and what was it that had happened, the bad thing that had happened because there had been something bad, he was sure, just across the dusky event horizon and what a supernatural dreamlike air his mind had taken on suddenly where memories lasted five minutes and then ducked out of existence. Frowning and scared and the night's indelible absence hovered in his eyes clear, unjumbled. It's a nightmare, he thought, pinching himself several times and hard. Why can I not why can I not remember. All the cells in his body shot forth like panicked lemmings. Who are these drooling thugs? Where is Conrad? Where the hell am I? he said, his voice hardly a murmur. He concentrated on the words, the act of speaking them, the motion of his lips; he tried again. Where am I? His voice was that of a scared child.

You in the pink room, pretty boy, said Mack, and you here cause you been drinkin.

Duane was suddenly cold, and he huddled and shivered in the corner, rubbing his arms with his shirtsleeves.

This drinkin shit it ain't the future though, kid, and I got a mind to suggest you be gettin away from it. I orta know; I was in the pink room when you was in diapers.

How long are they gonna keep me here? Duane asked in a timid voice that bordered on a whisper.

Mack laughed. Oh, I'd say they gonna let you out pretty soon. Six months, say.

What?

Mack roared in high-pitched laughter.

Duane shut his eyes and leaned his head back against the cinder blocks as mucus dripped down his throat. He listened to the men repeat endlessly the same conversation. Bars clanged in a cell down the hall. His stomach growled with hunger and his eyeballs were alive with pain that shot backward into the splitting center of his head, and he kept an eye on the puddle to make sure none of it would defy gravity and flow upslope toward his outstretched legs. He tried to ignore his own full bladder; he focused only on his throbbing head. Maybe the pink helps headaches go away, he thought. Maybe that's why they painted it pink. The men in the cell snored and farted and coughed and belched and cried. Duane stared at the pink wall out one open eye, silent, wondering if the door would ever open again.

June 1989

The bathroom was only five feet by six feet and in the corner behind the toilet the floor and wall were rotting. Two six-inch-square floor tiles had sunken away entirely; in their place crept brown dirt smelling of mildew that barely covered an exposed floorboard. Sometimes mushrooms grew out of the dirt and Matthew flushed them down the commode.

To the left of the hole was the shower. The thin tiles on the wall by the tub had fallen off; at the level of the faucets was one broken tile coated in grime like the grime on the floor. The green-black sludge snaked upward into the shower and weaved and wound between every tile connecting the entire grid of dirt to the murky pit behind the toilet. Sometimes the stain patterns on the drywall above the shower tiles reminded Matthew of his mother's varicose veins. The wall was tan and brown and yellow and it looked like it might soon crumble away into a gaping window to the kitchen, just as the floor would probably soon collapse and leave a dark hole down into the crawl space. The fan on the ceiling had been broken for several years. The smell in the bathroom made Matthew think of his cousin's freshwater fish tank that never got cleaned, in which swordtails and tetras and a guppy with a tumor on its tail swam eternally in a monstrous mass of algae.

Go put towels over the hole in the floor, Matthew's mother said to him when they were expecting company, although they hardly ever had company. Matthew was embarrassed at the filth of the bathroom, and he made sure the shower curtain stayed closed. Once he tried to scrape the caulk clean with his finger-nails.

Don't get that gunk on your fingers, his mother snapped at him. They sell shit at the store for that. It's called Tilex.

Do we have any? he asked.

No.

Why don't we get some?

Because we don't have any money, Matthew. That's going to be the answer for whatever you ask us to buy you this month, so I wish to hell you'd quit asking me.

The condition of the bathroom embarrassed him but it was okay because they never had any company come over to visit. The people across the street were always having parties. Matthew looked out the window and watched their driveway fill up with cars. He moped into the kitchen. Why don't we ever have anyone over to the house? he asked his mother. Don't you and Dad have any friends? She stared at the television without answering. Don't you hear me? he said.

What? she snapped in irritation.

Do you and Dad not have any friends or something?

Her eyes narrowed. What kind of a damn question is that?

Matthew looked down at the floor. He wasn't trying to make her mad or hurt her feelings, and he was sorry he had spoken. I just wanted to know why no one ever comes over, he said.

You don't have any friends either, she said, so you can just shut the fuck up. She munched on a bowl of Ruffles. The chips were cold because she kept them in the refrigerator. I don't see you having company over every day either, she said.

But when I want to have Brandon over, you always say no.

She stared at the television.

His parents don't understand why we never play at our house instead of down there, he said.

She answered him without averting her eyes from the screen. I don't want a bunch of screaming goddamn kids running around the house, she said. I'm tired when I get home from work.

She watched *Wheel of Fortune* and *Dallas* and then the Home Shopping Network. When Matthew went into the bathroom she yelled at him to remember to wipe his ass.

Brandon lived a quarter of a mile down the road in a split foyer. It was white with black shutters and the yard was neatly mowed. There were pink azaleas lining the front porch and walk. There was a birdbath.

The neighborhood ended behind Brandon's house. The two boys climbed over the chain-link fence and ran down a path into the woods. The trail wound down the hill past hickory roots and twisted poplar saplings and in the summer they didn't need to go far before the trees grew thick and the houses disappeared behind them. When the trail reached deeper into the woods it split into three parts. The left fork went up to Eric's house and the right fork went over to Suicide Hill where they sledded down the packed dirt face of the slope on blue slabs of hard plastic. It was the middle fork that went straight down to the water.

The pond was about twenty-five feet across. It was underneath a TVA power cut. The farmer who owned the land grazed beef cattle in the fields, and the pond had been built for the cattle to drink out of. Brandon and Matthew played football and baseball and soccer and Frisbee in the broad expanse of mile-wide fields that snaked farther into the distance than they could see, and they sat by the pond afterward drinking Nehi. They couldn't see any houses or roads from the pond; the fields were empty. Sweating through the humid afternoons, they walked from Brandon's house down to Oasis Market to buy grape drinks and Topps baseball cards, and then they walked all the way back into the neighborhood and down to the pond before they looked to see what was in the packs.

The day the farmer came to chase them out of the field they were opening baseball cards and eating ice cream bars that were nearly melted. It was the third day of summer vacation. The temperature was ninety-five; Brandon had a thermometer on his watch. They lay in the sun with their shirts off and looked through the cards. Holy shit, Matthew said, I got a Dwight Gooden and a Darryl Strawberry in the same pack.

So what? I got a Jose Canseco.

Dwight Gooden's better than Jose Canseco.

I hate the Mets.

He's still a good pitcher.

I hate that nigger.

My mom said you're not supposed to say that word.

Nigger nigger nigger nigger.

You're just jealous cause mine are worth more in the price guide.

They wouldn't be worth a penny if I threw them all in the pond.

You wouldn't do that, Matthew said.

I would if you pissed me off enough.

I haven't done anything to piss you off.

Just about everything you say pisses me off.

The farmer drove up along the dry dirt tire ruts that led all the way over to Morganton Road. He drove a beat-up light blue Chevy pickup truck. His skin looked like burlap and his arms were nearly eight inches in diameter.

We should get out of here, Matthew said.

Don't be a coward.

Aren't you nervous?

Brandon shook his head. Matthew thought he was lying, but he wasn't sure.

The farmer drove up to the pond and got out of the truck. He was smoking a cigarette. Who the hell are you? he said.

Who's asking? said Brandon.

I own these fields.

TVA owns the fields.

I own the goddamn fields, kid.

Then why are there TVA power lines up above us?

Cause TVA pays me to get to have them there, he said, scowling into the sun. Now get the hell back on your side of the fence and don't come over here again. I don't want you climbing that fence and pissing in my pond and scaring my cows.

They sat still and stared up at him.

Well, get on with it, the farmer yelled. Get the hell out of here.

Who's making us?

Are you stupid or something? I'm making you. His rough cheeks held deep cavities that expanded when he spoke. Matthew thought they looked like ants might crawl out of them at any point in time.

Give us each one of your cigarettes, Brandon said, and then maybe we'll go.

The man stared at them with piercing eyes.

Or I'll tell you what, Brandon said, we'll trade you a pack of our baseball cards for your whole pack of cigarettes.

I ain't givin you a goddamn thing, kid.

We got a Dwight Gooden and a Darryl Strawberry in one pack.

You better get the hell off my property.

Matthew got his cards and stood up. Come on, Brandon, he said, let's go.

What if I don't want to?

Come on. Matthew shuffled his feet uncomfortably. Come on.

Brandon stood up. Well, I'll go, he said as he looked into the farmer's eyes, but only because I'm hot and I want to go back to my house to play video games.

They trudged through the Queen Anne's lace and ironweed to the fence at the treeline and they climbed over it. Don't yuns come back neither, the man yelled. If I see yuns crossin my fence again I'll call the cops. I'll have you sent to reform school. Brandon turned around and flipped him off.

Aw shit, Brandon, Matthew said. They ran up the trail.

Brandon's parents had bought him a Nintendo for his birthday that spring. He owned Super Mario Bros., Metroid, Simon's Quest, Double Dragon, and Rad Racer. He had a subscription to the *Nintendo Power Magazine*. When they got back to the house from the pond they got Cokes out of the refrigerator and ran to Brandon's room and turned the Nintendo on as they caught their breath. Let's do Metroid without the Justin Bailey code, Matthew said.

That takes too long.

We can save it at the end.

I don't want to.

They took turns playing Rad Racer and bet a slushy on who would get farther. Matthew liked the first level the best: the beach and the palm trees and the sunset. It was supposed to be someplace in California, like Malibu maybe. The sand and the sunset and the sportscars.

Have you ever been to the beach? he asked Brandon.

Of course I have. We've gone every year except last year.

Oh.

Haven't you?

We were gonna go once but the car broke down on the way.

What beach were you gonna go to?

Toqua.

Brandon laughed. Toqua? That ain't a beach. That's just a bunch of sand on Tellico Lake. He threw back his head laughing. You've never been to the beach?

No, Matthew said quietly.

That's pathetic.

Matthew stared at the orange and purple beach sunset on the animated screen and wrecked the car because he wasn't looking at the road. You dumbass, Brandon said. Matthew had to buy the slushies when the slushy man came at four. The sound of the truck as it played "Pop Goes the Weasel" faded into the distance as they sat in Brandon's neatly groomed yard sipping the syrupy blueberry drinks.

It sucks what happened at the pond, Matthew said.

Yeah.

You think he meant what he said about reform school?

They can't send you to reform school for trespassing.

Where the hell is reform school, anyway?

I don't know. Maybe down in Greenback or something.

You don't think he could really do anything?

Brandon laughed. There's only one way to find out, he said.

Matthew looked down at his shoes nervously. I don't know if we should go back down there, he said.

You scared?

No.

Yes you are.

No I'm not.

Well, let's go then.

Matthew ate dinner at Brandon's house. They played Monopoly after dinner, and they went back down to the pond about an hour before sunset. They sat on the bank facing the hill that climbed up to the higher field a hundred feet above the pond, and they skipped slate chips along the surface of the water.

How deep you think the water is in the middle? Matthew asked.

Probably about fifty feet.

I dare you to walk in and see how long it is before it's over your head.

Hell.

I dare you.

Why don't you?

I asked you first.

I asked you second.

They sipped out of their Coke cans. On the hill above them the wheaty brown grass waved in the breeze. The sun's shining reflection upon the surface of the water faded and vanished. I bet there's cows down in there, Matthew said.

Huh.

I bet when they die, the farmer doesn't want to have to cart off the bodies somewhere, so he just throws them on in.

Yeah.

I bet there's horses in there too.

Russell Goins says his cousin drove a Volkswagen Bug into the pond. Crashed it all the way down that hill.

Well, Chad Walker says there's two dead bodies in it. Kids that lived right here in our subdivision.

My half brother told me they put nuclear waste from Oak

Ridge down there, Brandon said, and if you touch the water then you die in seven years to the day.

That ain't true.

How do you know? My half brother works at Y-12 and he says it's true.

It just ain't.

Well, let's see you touch the water then.

Hell.

Let's see you walk in and test how long it takes till it's over your head, he said. They heard a gunshot, and Matthew was startled. What's the matter? Brandon said, you afraid it's that farmer?

No.

He's got a big shotgun and he's gonna come back and shoot us for crossing his fence.

Shut up.

He's gonna shoot us and drag our dead bodies to reform school.

Shut up, Matthew said. People hunt in those woods over there all the time.

Or maybe he'd just put us down in the pond with those other dead bodies. Brandon looked over at the fence. You know what we should do? he said.

What?

Tear that whole goddamn fence down. Then we wouldn't even have to duck under it or climb over it. Dumbass thinks it's his pond or something. We go here more than he does.

Yeah.

All that's holding the barbed wire on is little plastic things, Brandon said. You just gotta kick them up with your shoe.

Matthew looked over at the fence, squinting his eyes. Yeah, you're right.

We could get it all off. All along the woods and then where the fence stretches through the field along the bottom of the hill. We could stretch it all the way across the pond.

That guy could send us to reform school.

He wouldn't ever know it was us.

He saw us down here, stupid.

But he don't know who we are.

But he'd know we did it.

That's the whole point, Brandon said. We'd be saying, hey look, we're coming back down here and crossing your fence, and what the hell are you gonna do about it. He doesn't know who we are. He can't find us.

They sat silently, staring at the fence. Matthew could see in his mind how they could fence off the pond away from the fields by knocking the wire off about twenty or twenty-five posts. They could stretch it across the water and redraw the property boundary. That would get the guy back.

You know, that fence probably cost him a lot of money, Matthew said.

What the hell do you care?

I don't know.

They flipped through a *Penthouse* that Brandon had been carrying in his backpack as the mosquitoes buzzed around the muddy herd of cattle. Bugs skimmed across the murky water. They watched the sun set over the distant treeline in shining streaks of orange as cowpiss splashes sounded from behind them, and in the calming air of the dusk they relaxed silently as their sweat evaporated into the fading light.

When Matthew got home his mother was watching TV. It was nearly ten o'clock. He walked into the kitchen and poured himself a glass of milk and sat down at the table. I'm home, he said.

She glanced over at him and then turned back to the television.

He looked at her for a minute. There were bags under her eyes. She had dirty dishes stacked next to her on the table. Aren't you mad that I'm late? he said.

She rolled her eyes. What do you want me to do, whip you?

No.

Well, just don't expect me to fix you dinner this late.

I ate at Brandon's house.

That's nice.

The kitchen walls were plastered with dirty green-and-gold wallpaper filled with green apples and bears and gold grandfather clocks and fruit baskets. The few white patches bore brown-yellow stains from food and dust and nicotine. Matthew wanted to peel the paper off and repaint the room but his mother refused; it would be too much work, she said. The refrigerator and stove were olive green. The curtains were gold and covered with a thick layer of dust. The thrift-store table and chairs were metallic gray.

Holes the size of his shoes had been chipped out of the linoleum. The ceiling light loomed overhead like a yellowed rotting fungus. Spiderwebs stretched in yardlong strands across the corners. There was no dishwasher or second sink basin, and the walls had no outlet covers. The washer and dryer stood conspicuously in an alcove next to the door that led out to the garage because there was no separate laundry room, and dirty clothes cascaded out from the laundry machines in a cluttered heap. The tiny Zenith TV sat on a wheeled stand that could be rolled back and forth between the kitchen and the living room, and Matthew's mother munched on potato chips and watched *Family Feud*. Matthew sat at the table watching her, trying to think of something to say.

Mom, he said, why don't we have a back door?

She stared at him.

Mom, he said, don't you hear me?

She shrugged and glared at the television screen. Well, what the hell do you want me to say? she said.

He was confused by her response. I guess I want you to tell me why there's not a back door, he said.

Hush, she snapped, staring at the screen. They're about to say something important.

Mo-omm, answer me.

For God's sake, Matthew, will you hush? The blueprint didn't have one. They didn't build one. I don't know. What the hell do you want me to do, knock a big hole in the wall?

No, he said quietly.

If we're not good enough for you then you can just march down the road till you find a family with a back door and a great big deck.

Mom, don't say that.

Brandon's house has a back door. Maybe you should just move in with them.

Mom, don't.

His parents make more money than we do. If you lived with them you could have all the ice-cream bars you wanted.

Mom, I just wanted to know why we don't have a back door.

Hush your mouth, she said, they're about to say the next category.

Matthew went to his room.

He sat in his room in the stark light of his fluorescent bedside lamp and read *Treasure Island*. He didn't understand everything that was happening in the book but he kept scanning his eyes across the lines, scything through the pages. He stopped every few minutes to glance around the room. The paint was peeling off the walls. Every piece of furniture was a hand-me-down: the old sewing table that he used for a desk, the green chest with broken drawers, the bed that was really a couch without the cushions. The wide six-shelf white bookcase leaned left against the wall for support because otherwise it would collapse; he wasn't allowed to put any hardback books on the top shelves because they would be too much weight. Covering the window was a broken wicker shade that wouldn't open. A hundred nail-holes dotted the dirty walls. He counted them when he got tired of reading. He paid attention to the clock as time passed: eleven, eleven-fifteen, half past eleven.

When his father got home from work at a quarter to one Matthew was still lying awake in bed. The key turned and the door opened and closed; there were footsteps into the kitchen, footsteps on the hard tile floor, a muffled drone of voices. His door was shut and he couldn't make out the words, but it was a comforting sound. He liked it when his parents had conversations with each other. It was soothing when they relaxed and reminisced and talked. He closed his eyes and listened for fluctuations in the volume of their speech as his mind wandered sleepily.

The door to his room opened. Matthew kept his eyes closed as he felt his father's presence move stealthily into the room. He heard the quiet sound of breathing. He wanted to talk to his father, but he kept his eyes shut anyway because he was supposed to be asleep. He tried to open them enough to see out but still make them appear to be closed, and while he was doing it he heard his mother's voice.

Why aren't you listening to me? she said. Don't just walk out of the damn room when I'm talking to you.

I don't want to hear about it anymore.

You're on his side, aren't you?

I'm not on anybody's side.

You don't listen to what I say to you, she said. You're not home to see it. He thinks we're not good enough for him. He tries to hurt my feelings.

Whatever.

I'm used to the shit you say to me and I can handle that but I can't take hearing it from a snotnosed little kid.

Don't talk like that in front of him, he said.

He's asleep.

Well, then don't wake him up, he said. What the hell's wrong with you anyway? Don't start this while Matthew's trying to sleep.

If you care so much about waking him up, dumbass, then why the hell did you come in here when I was trying to talk to you?

He raised his voice. Because I wanted to see him. I go to work when he gets home from school and I get home after he goes to bed and I never even get to talk to my own goddamn son.

Then you should have found a better job.

Well, that's just brilliant, Wanda. That's just the most brilliant goddamn thing I've ever heard.

It's not my fault you work evening shift.

Well, it's not my fault we have fifteen thousand fucking dollars of credit card debt. Fifteen thousand dollars, Wanda. That's how much you earn in a whole goddamn year.

She put her fingers in her ears.

Fifteen thousand dollars, he said.

Shut up, I'm sick of you. I'm sick of you both.

You're sick of us both. That's just great, Wanda. You know, you act like you don't even like him. I know you don't like me but you're his mother for Christ's sake.

He mopes around all day and night like he's depressed. Always expecting something from me. Staring at me like he thinks we're denying him something.

We *are* denying him something. He goes without lunch at school so he can afford a pack of baseball cards because we don't have the fucking money to buy it for him otherwise. If you're depressed about the money then why the hell shouldn't he be depressed?

How the hell can a ten-year-old boy be depressed? What the hell does he want, a goddamn shrink?

Maybe he just wants you to be nicer to him. Agree to get him that new dog.

What?

Like I've been saying all along.

Right. A dog. That's just brilliant, Warren.

Well, maybe he wants one.

We're not getting another damn dog, Warren. If there's one thing we definitely can't afford it's a dog.

We could scrape up the money to have a dog if he really wanted one.

She rolled her eyes. Good God.

Well, you don't know until you ask him.

Ask him then.

He's asleep.

Matthew opened his eyes and sat up. I don't want another dog, he said.

His mother jumped back. Why the hell do you try to trick me like that? she said.

I wasn't trying to trick you, Mom.

Whatever.

I told you you'd wake him up, his father said.

I didn't wake him up. He was lying there awake all along.

Matt, his father said, there's kids all over the world that would do anything to get offered a dog.

I don't want another dog.

You'd have fun with a new dog.

I don't want any dog but Bear.

Hell, that old fuckin mutt.

Any other dog would just get run over like Bear did anyways.

His mother chortled. Goddamn, Warren, she said, he's right, that's the last thing I need around here is him blubbering about another dead dog.

Hell, woman, it's no different than all the blubbering you did back when that dumbass stepbrother of yours died in that fight.

Oh, fuck you, Warren.

See, everybody blubbers about something or other once in a while.

You were there, goddammit, you coward. Didn't raise one hand to do anything but run away.

I'm not going to listen to you go through this again.

You know what I was thinking when I was crying after he died? How it should have been you. I was crying cause it was him and not you.

Matthew got out of bed and locked himself in the bathroom. He covered his ears but through the walls he still heard the sound of breaking glass and his mother's shrieking.

Don't you cuss at me in front of my son, his father yelled.

Fuck you fuck you fuck you fuck you fuck you.

Matthew heard more glasses breaking. He found a washcloth on the bathroom floor and wet it in the faucet; with it he cleaned the mirror and the porcelain surface of the sink. He rinsed it out and began wiping spiderwebs off the wall underneath the basin. There were dead bugs and egg sacs. He scraped at dirt stains on the walls with his fingernails, and he heard the sound of stomping. The mildew smelled unusually strong that night in the bathroom, and he wondered if there would be more mushrooms growing out of the floor when he woke up in the morning.

When he woke up the next day it was already one in the afternoon. His father was still asleep and his mother was at work. He went into the kitchen and made himself a grilled-cheese sandwich, washing all his dishes afterward and drying them and putting them back neatly in the cabinet in the stacks he had made. The design of the plastic plates and bowls was gold and green; his mother had bought them all at Goodwill. Most of the glasses were actually plastic cups from Hardee's and McDonald's.

He put on shorts and a T-shirt and walked down the road. The woods were quiet. None of the birds or squirrels seemed to make any noise. No cars passed on the road behind him. He turned left on the trail when he got to the empty lot. When he saw glass bottles on the ground he stopped over to pick them up, and he busted them against tree trunks.

He stopped at the swinging spot. Beside the trail there was a box elder tree that was maybe five or six years old. Matthew liked to pull its trunk sideways and hang from it, swinging, and when he let go and dropped to the ground he liked to watch the tree bounce back into shape like a taut spring. The bark was rough and flaky against his hands. He swung back and forth and built momentum as the leaves shook off the treetop that was no longer any taller than he was.

When he got to the tree he stopped to swing on it for a minute. He jumped up and grabbed the thin trunk with his fist and pulled it sideways to hang from it, but his feet dragged on the ground when he bent it down. When he let go and the tree slowly lifted back into the air, he noticed for the first time the effect of his swinging on the trunk: It was bent like a hunchback. The tips of the branches pointed only diagonally upward, parallel to the slope of the hill in the distance. He tried again to pull it down, jumping higher to grab the trunk, but his feet dragged even more than the first time. He let the tree spring back upright, but it didn't work; its entire body wobbled uncertainly and finally came to rest in the misshapen curl of its fracture. Matthew gazed at the bent trunk and thought about how the tree would keep growing and the mutation would expand and the trunk would never be straight, always misshapen. He looked around and saw all the perfectly straight trunks of trees that were hundreds of years old. They had trunks that he couldn't reach his arms halfway around, and they were straight all the way up into the sky. He pulled at the bent trunk of the sapling but it stayed bent. The magnitude of what he had done seemed suddenly upsetting, and he ran the rest of the way down to the pond. Birds twittered as he raced forward, and the woods smelled dry and acorny, scoured by bark and decomposing heartwood.

When Matthew got to the pond he did not immediately notice Brandon standing on the hill with Ian, the third-grader who was three years younger than them, who lived in the house behind Brandon's and got suspended from school for cussing out his teacher. A rock sailed through the air and splashed into the water, and Matthew heard the chatter of laughter as he jumped back in surprise.

I didn't see you, he said to them, looking up and shielding his eyes from the sun.

No shit, Sherlock.

I went to your house but you weren't there.

That's cause I'm down here, Brandon said, and Ian laughed. They walked down the hill to the pond.

I thought you weren't allowed to come down here, Matthew said to Ian.

I go wherever the fuck I want to go.

Do you now, Matthew said.

Yeah, I do.

He gets to roam around more than you do, Brandon said, and he's only eight.

Yeah, Ian echoed.

His mom doesn't just scream all the time the way yours does.

Yeah.

And his mom doesn't look like Elvira either.

Matthew felt his face turning red. He didn't want Ian to be there. He was used to Brandon taking Ian's side when the three of them were together, and he wasn't in the mood to deal with it. He walked up to the fence between where he stood and where Brandon and Ian loomed above him on the face of the hill, and he kicked at the lower plastic bracket on the fencepost, snapping it off and sending it flying in an arc through the air. Stretching his leg back, he kicked upward and knocked off the middle one and then the top one, and the post was disconnected from all three wires. He looked at Brandon with eyes gleaming from the mischief of his act, and with a struggle he managed to pull the metal fencepost entirely out of the ground. Like a spear he threw it into the pond, impaling the calm film of plant matter, sending concentric circles bubbling outward.

Shit far, Brandon said, and Matthew's eyes burned with the glint of a vandal's satisfaction.

Are you just gonna sit there on your ass with your little buddy, Matthew said, or are you gonna work on this with me?

Hell, I didn't know you'd actually think to do it.

Well, I guess I'm just not the big pussy you seem to think I am.

I guess not.

Brandon got up and started kicking at the fence beneath the big walnut tree a few posts down from where Matthew was standing. Ian refused to help. Matthew moved methodically down the rank of posts. He threw some of them into the pond and left some implanted in the ground. Because he had started in a corner from which the fence angled out in a vee, the barbed wire fell loosely onto the ground, and it formed a tangled intestinal mess as more and more of it piled up. He thrust his leg upward in fake karate kicks as he aimed for the plastic connectors, and Ian yelled Hi-ya, hi-ya, like actors he had seen in karate movies.

You know what to do if you see someone coming, Brandon said to Ian, don't you?

Run like hell up that trail.

No, you stupid little shit, you tell us he's there.

Can you imagine the look on that farmer's face if he drives up and sees all this?

They all laughed.

When both arms of the fence had been knocked down well beyond the edges of the pond, Matthew began to tug at the wire cords with his hands. He picked up all three, being careful not to let his fingers touch a barb, and he pulled them toward the pond. Get over on the other side and do what I'm doing, he yelled to Brandon. He stopped to take his shirt off. Cattle lowed in the distance. The treetops rustled in the wind.

Why the hell do the two of you give a shit about this fence anyway? Ian yelled down from the hill.

Cause it gets in my fucking way, Matthew said.

Well, ain't you just cussin up a damn storm today.

It took them nearly fifteen minutes to get the wire across the pond. They had to stop and knock connectors off more of the fenceposts. Eventually Matthew realized that if he pulled hard enough from the opposite end of the pond, he had enough leverage to make them snap off without having to kick them. His arms started to grow sore.

Hey, he yelled to Brandon, what the hell is this pond called, anyway?

Fuck if I know.

We should give it a name.

How about Fuck Pond? Brandon said, laughing.

Yeah, Fuck Pond. It was fun to say it. Matthew repeated it to himself and suddenly remembered his mother screaming in his room last night. Fuckyoufuckyoufuckyou. Probably sticking her fingers in her ears while she did it so she wouldn't hear any response. He wondered what she would do if she ever found out about what they were doing with the fence. The hickory tree was dead, so she would have to get a switch from the oak tree.

As he pulled the cords of barbed wire across the pond he thought of the rotting bathroom. How it was ugly and it stank and he didn't want to go home. The bathroom at Brandon's house was clean. It had striped wallpaper and hand towels and little pink soaps shaped like scallop shells. It had a plush throw rug and a shower curtain with big ruffles. Brandon's parents smoked and his father had been laid off at the plant but they had a nice clean bathroom. As the fence skimmed the green surface of the water it was the slimy black strings of muck in the sink drain he thought of, and as he tugged the wires closer to the far shore of the pond he imagined them together to be a giant fingernail tearing the scabby sheet of algae that clung to the slimy water's ceiling like a festering cancer. Sweat beaded on his bare back as he gripped the slicing metal with the raw palm of his hand. He pulled as hard as he could. He forgot his place and time entirely as he tugged with a red face and sweating eyes, pulling the wires behind him as if he were a struggling beast of burden.

Matthew snapped out of his daydream to the sound of Brandon and Ian yelling. He looked over at his friend standing across the pond.

What's your problem? Brandon shouted. I've been screaming your name forever.

Sorry.

Let's go.

But we're not finished, Matthew said.

The hell we're not. We're gonna miss the slushy man.

Matthew walked around to the hillside and climbed a few feet up to survey the damage. They had pulled the wires farther than he had realized. He looked out toward the horizon and back down at the water. The pond had been refenced. It's on our side now, he thought to himself. I guess the farmer will be trespassing now if we ever see him walking around our pond. The fields laid out before him appeared neat and tidy with nothing out of place, and he didn't want to go back up into the cluttered shabbiness of the neighborhood. They had a pond of their own now. The barbed wire shone brightly in the light of the afternoon sun, and the fence lay with symmetry upon the ground beyond the water's edge.

Matthew, you slow sonofabitch, come on.

Hold your damn horses. I'm coming.

We're gonna miss the slushy man if you don't hurry the hell up; I can already hear the music.

Flies buzzed at them in pursuit as they moved into the woods, and Matthew's skin itched violently from dirt and sweat.

When he got home his father was sitting on the porch drinking a beer. There was trash scattered through the monkey grass from where dogs had torn open the garbage bags that had been left on the sidewalk.

Where have you been? his father said.

Down at Brandon's.

You see him about ten times as much as you see me these days.

No I don't.

Oh, his father said sarcastically, never mind. I guess I was wrong.

Dad, don't start that.

I guess we spend a lot of time together. I guess everything's just great.

Dad, he said, quit it. He stood on the porch and traced the line where the coat of paint stopped and the cream turned to green. His father had started painting the exterior of the house the previous summer but never finished. The old paint was foam green with brown shutters and the new paint was cream-colored with tan shutters. The cream color had been applied to the garage door and to nearly half of the front of the house, but everything to the left of the front door was green. On the sides and in the back the cream paint had been splattered onto the wood siding in erratic patterns. From the road, when Matthew went to get the mail, he looked up at the house and saw that it was shabby and half-painted. The grass was weedy and overgrown. The hickory tree was dead and the garage door had a big hole in it and the variegated wygiela bushes were all dead.

When the entire front gutter had fallen off, crashing against the wrought-iron porch railing before it fell down into the holly bushes, Matthew's father had said, Fuck yeah, now I don't have to paint it.

Dad, Matthew said, when are we really gonna finish painting the house?

What the hell do you care?

It's ugly. It looks bad.

Eeennnhh, it's ugly, his father repeated, mocking him.

People on the bus make fun of it.

School's out, his father said.

But they'll still make fun of it when I start back to school if it's not painted by then.

Well, why don't you just kick their ass?

Daaddd, he said. He heard the whine of frustration in his own voice. Come on, Dad.

Kick em in the nuts.

I'd get in trouble, Matthew said.

You'd get in trouble, his father grunted. Huh.

Dad, you didn't answer my question.

What the hell was your question?

When are we gonna finish painting the house?

I'm the one working a full-time job here. Why don't you paint it?

Dad, I can't paint the house.

Well, I can't either.

Other people have jobs too and they don't leave their houses half-painted for a whole year, Matthew said, and after he had said it he realized he sounded ungrateful, critical.

Well, if it bothers you so much, I guess you'd better get off your lazy ass and do it yourself.

Dad, I'm only ten.

Well, it's time you started earnin your keep.

Mom won't let me get on a ladder.

Well, we'll see about that, he said. As he spoke Matthew's mother arrived home from work, pulling up into the driveway in her old Mercury. She got out of the car and walked up the sidewalk to the porch.

Get out of my way so I can get inside, she said.

Matthew says you won't let him get on a ladder.

No.

Why the hell not?

Oh Lord, don't start this right now. I've had a long day at work.

You always have a long day at work.

Well, it usually is a long day.

Every day it's the same goddamn number of hours, Wanda. Eight to four every damn day. I don't see how one's longer than the other.

Matthew gazed out at the yard. There wasn't much grass because they had waited so long in the fall to rake the leaves. The brown grass that was there in scattered splotches was mostly dandelions and wild violets and weeds that looked like grass if you kept them mowed. The yard was green in the narrow patches above the septic tank and brown everywhere else. It had been three weeks since their grass had been mowed; Matthew couldn't do it himself because it made him break out in a rash. Next to the road was a large charred spot where they had burned the leaves that spring and the fire had gotten out of control. Dandelions were starting to pop up out of the gaping black scar. His father's old Buick sedan that hadn't run in three years was parked in the ditch beside the burned patch. The dead cherry tree on the other side of the driveway that had fallen over in February from the weight of the snow had not been moved, and its wood was starting to rot. The mailbox had been knocked over a few weeks before. Three of the four house numbers had fallen off the side of the house, and the fourth dangled upside down. Matthew's father gulped his beer.

Oh Jesus Christ, Warren, you know we can't afford for you to drink.

It's one beer, Wanda.

Well, we can't afford one beer.

We both work full-time jobs and you're telling me I can't afford to have one goddamn beer?

We owe Norwest eight hundred dollars by the end of the

month and a thousand to the transmission place and four hundred to the dentist and a hundred to the bank for those four overdrafts and five hundred to Sears and a hundred for your speeding ticket. We're a month behind on the mortgage. The insurance down payment's coming up this month.

Matthew's father stared into his beer.

We owe five hundred to your father and two hundred to Citibank and a hundred to the phone company or they'll disconnect our phone in a week. Her voice had been building up until she was almost yelling. She shook with nervous spasms. They stared at each other.

Can you afford to pay it all? Matthew said quietly.

They both turned to look at him. No, his mother screamed, of course we can't afford to pay it. We can't afford to pay half of it.

Well, what are you going to do? he said. His parents had been worried about money for as long as he could remember but nothing bad ever really seemed to happen. His mother yelled about not having enough money to pay the bills but she always ended up paying them. He looked up at her worriedly. He thought about the fence.

What are we going to do? she yelled. You want to know what we're going to do?

Don't take this out on him, his father said.

How the hell am I supposed to know what we're going to do? We'll rob a bank. We just won't pay it. We'll get arrested and you'll become a ward of the state. I don't know.

Everything's going to be fine, Matthew, his father said.

Everything is not going to be fine at all, his mother said.

We'll take out another loan or something.

No one is going to give us another loan, she yelled. Tears welled in her eyes. We can't even afford to buy any food, Warren. We're gonna be eating pinto beans and cornbread for every goddamn meal. We're not going to buy any beer. There aren't going to be any more baseball cards, Matthew. She sat down on the porchstep beside him, and his father tossed back the rest of his beer.

I hate pinto beans, Matthew said.

Then I guess you're gonna get pretty hungry.

Matthew felt his stomach growling, and he was sweating. Dogs barked in the distance. The three of them sat in silence, crowded onto the tiny porch.

The phone rang while Matthew was watching the Braves game that night. The Braves were his favorite team. They were losing seven to one, and they were in last place. This was the last game he would get to watch, because his mother hadn't paid the cable bill and their service would be disconnected the next day.

It was Ian on the phone.

What are you doing calling me? he said. Ian had never called him before.

You're in trouble, Ian said.

Matthew breathed into the phone.

You're in trouble, Ian said. I was just down at the pond and guess who I saw.

Fear disseminated through Matthew's bowels and stomach.

That farmer, Ian said.

No you didn't.

His name's Sam Williamson. He asked me if I knew who did it.

Matthew waited for Ian to say something more but there was only silence. So what did you tell him? he asked.

Ian laughed.

Stop it.

He laughed harder.

Matthew was panicking. Tell me what you told him, he said. Tell me, goddammit.

He gave me his phone number, Ian said. He said if I find out who did it I'm supposed to call him and tell him, and he'll have you sent to reform school.

I don't believe you.

The number's 983-3010. Why don't you call it if you think I'm lying?

Matthew breathed heavily into the phone. He shut his eyes. Shit shit shit shit shit, he thought to himself.

You scared?

No.

Well, you should be, cause if you don't give me a hundred dollars by tomorrow then I'm gonna call the number.

What are you talking about?

That's what it costs for me not to tell on you.

What?

Are you stupid or just deaf?

Matthew breathed into the phone.

Bring me a hundred dollars, Ian said, or I'll tell him it was you. I'll call him up and say it was Matthew Boring at 1212 Hilltop Road and I'll give them your phone number and your parents' names and where you go to school.

How'd you know my address?

It's in the phone book, dumbass.

Matthew stared at the dirty green refrigerator as his mind raced.

Bring it down to my house by tomorrow, Ian said.

You know I don't have a hundred dollars.

You better find the money somewhere then.

Why are you doing this?

Cause I want two hundred dollars.

You said a hundred.

Brandon's gotta pay it too. If one of you doesn't give me the money then I'll turn in both of you.

I thought Brandon was your friend.

Brandon's a dumbass, Ian said, laughing. Hey, what's the matter? You sound like you're about to cry.

Ian hung up. Matthew sat on the dirty living room floor leaning against the browned beerstained wall wondering what to do. In dread his heart pounded viciously and his mouth went dry. He pictured himself sitting with his parents in juvenile court; he saw himself being carted away to reform school, whatever that was. He thought about what his parents would think, what the people in his class at school would think. He always made As. He always turned in his homework.

Matthew, his mother shouted from her bedroom, put the clothes in the dryer. He sweated and felt distant from his own mind as he heard her voice in his ears. The ceiling above him was stained in a circle two feet in diameter from where the roof was leaking. Sometimes when it rained they had to put a bucket underneath the leak. Once it rained while they were gone to Elizabethton to see Matthew's grandparents, and the carpet reeked for two weeks from the water that rotted in it and beneath it.

Matthew, his mother shouted, did you hear me?

Yeah.

Are you gonna do it?

Yeah.

The laundry room had not been cleaned in years. There was kitty litter scattered around the floor from when their cat had still been alive. The dryer vent had come loose, and in the thick, humid air that poured out into the room a jungle of lint collected on the walls and window. The curtains were two tattered gray bath towels that his mother had fastened onto the rod with clips. Soda had been spilled into the toolbox on the floor, and the disorganized pile of screws and nails inside it had solidified into one immovable metal unit. Spiderwebs draped from the ceiling in curves and spirals. As Matthew moved the heavy wet clothes from the washer to the dryer his heart pounded through each passing second.

When he had finished with the laundry he called Brandon's number but there was no answer. He called it again and again and on the fifth ring of the third call Brandon's mother answered the phone.

Can I speak to Brandon, please? he asked.

Brandon's asleep, she said.

Oh.

All of us were asleep.

Oh, I'm sorry, ma'am.

Don't ever call here again this late, she said, and she hung up. Matthew put the receiver in place on the wall and paced back and forth down the hallway as his mother snored. He counted the times he reached the kitchen door and turned around. Two hundred. Two fifty.

He thought about walking down to the pond to see the damage they had done. There was a half-moon. He could find his way through the woods at night, he thought. It upset him now to picture the fence lying torn apart upon the ground, and he wondered why he had done it at all. It had been fun but it hadn't really been fun. He realized they would never be able to relax beside the pond again. They would always have to be on the lookout for the farmer. It would always have to be a covert action; they would always be on edge. He tried to suppress the hammering rhythm of his heartbeat.

He took his jar of coins into the bathroom to count them and locked the door behind him. There was no lock on his bedroom door and his mother never stayed asleep for very long at one time. He didn't want to arouse her suspicion by counting the money in front of her. There were no quarters because he had spent them all on slushies in the last two months. A medium-sized slushy was two quarters. He had some dimes and nickels and a lot of pennies. There was barely room for him to sit down on the floor between the toilet and the wall. He sat on top of the air-conditioning vent; the air conditioner had been broken for more than two weeks, and no air was coming out.

He had six dollars in dimes, three dollars in nickels, and seven dollars in pennies. It took nearly half an hour to count them all. It was sixteen dollars. He had a dollar bill that his grandfather had given him the previous weekend. That was seventeen dollars. There was some loose change on top of the dryer in the laundry room. He could sell some of his baseball cards at the card shop, but tomorrow was a Saturday and it would be closed. His parents didn't have any money. Their change jar was empty because they had wrapped coins just two days before. There was no money in his piggy bank on the bookshelf. There was no money in his mother's wallet on the table, and he felt guilty for having looked in it at all.

The wires in the bathroom light fixture protruded from their casing in dusty orange tangles; the mirror below the light had fallen off the front of the medicine cabinet, exposing to the room two scummy shelves and dusty jars of cluttered drugs upon them. The bathroom looked like it had been vandalized ten years before and left to rot unhindered. He flipped through a copy of *Southern Living* that his mother had left beside the toilet; he looked at all the sparkling sinks and cabinets in the pictures. He wanted to clean it up but it wasn't stuff you could just clean up, like the clutter in the living room and the dirty dishes. The tiles were crumbling. Smeared upon the wall opposite the toilet was a shitstain that had been there since they had moved into the house seven years earlier. The sink was coming loose from the wall. Caps covering screws on the base of the toilet were filled with streaked and hardened dirt. The throw rug was caked with bits of torn toilet paper. Inch-wide circles of dark green mold grew upon the surface of the tub. Behind the locked door Matthew sat on the floor staring down at his piles of brown pennies. The battery died on his digital watch. Through the wall he listened to his mother snore. He thought about what might happen if she found out about the fence; he wondered whether she would care. Jarflies buzzed above him on the roof. He rested his head against the wall and wished he still were young enough to sleep in her bed at night when his father was working, young enough to bury himself beneath the electric blanket, lying awake to the thick sound of her breathing.

The Body Painters

Last night Billy had a twenty-dollar bill in his hand when he locked the door. So you didn't need two hundred from me after all, now did you. Rubbing his nose he glanced intently upon the money, the tight rolling of the bill's edge to its face to build a cylinder. Hey wait guys, I said, peering around the corner. They were meditating, they said; no one can be in the room but us. Then why'd you take the mirror in there—you use a mirror when you meditate? Silence at every point upon the wood.

With them was Greer.

I sat on the couch in the room by myself and picked small wads of piss-yellow Styrofoam out of a hole in the upholstery. Fools: they think that I am new to their scene; they ignore me because they think I am ignorant. The TV was on with no volume. I fiddled with the foam and listened to the music, waiting for the chorus to sag, to echo in a loop aligned:

This monkey's gone to heaven.
This monkey's gone to heaven.
This monkey's gone to heaven.

If I drive home now, I wondered, will Greer wonder where I went; will they call my apartment spouting at me: shit Jim I didn't want you to leave Jim, I wish you hadn't gone? Fiends, lying upon the floor, obstinate in unreason, smiling they sing, rejoice without me. This is what I am thinking.

Come to the party, Billy said. You never get laid.

That's not true.

You should go out to clubs more often, or to bars or to Buzz.

I don't want to hear that anymore.

Why don't you go out to a club you never talk to anyone you haven't already known for the last five years you just sit around the apartment don't you wanna find some pussy?

I don't feel like it.

You're too cynical.

I just couldn't be bothered.

You've been drunk the past three weeks.

So.

When we go to a bar you call home every five minutes to check your voice mail.

No I don't.

I don't know who you think is going to call you.

You're coming to the party, Zeet said to me. He moved in last week when his landlord booted him. He sleeps on a cot on the living room floor, and his friends drink late into the night. He has a lot of CDs, so I don't mind him living here. They got his nickname from *zeitgeist*, he told me. Then you're pronouncing it wrong, I said. What do you mean, he said. He moves his finger beneath the newsprint when he reads the newspaper. Everyone likes him; he's chill, they say, he's chill. His hair stops up the shower drain. I don't think he knows what *zeitgeist* means. He and his girlfriend screw in Billy's room when Billy's at work, or at a bar, or wherever. I told them that they're too loud. Have some sympathy, Zeet said, you know how it is.

I know how it is but I don't guess I have any sympathy.

I sit and talk to people at the photo lab. In the darkroom they examine my work: Who are your influences? they ask. I talk to them; I tell them what they want.

I wear white T-shirts and tight jeans and eat one meal each day. In the mirror in the bathroom over the double vanity I glance sideways as I walk, examining my strides, eyeing the bones protruding from my back as they bulge out of my skin. In the mirror I watch my hand as it covers my crotch, my nipples poking through the cotton tee, my torso outlined in wrinkled fabric, and I take a drag off my cigarette and blow it toward the glass at my face, at my body, at a figure sculpted in glass. I see myself naked in winter, sliding on the icy streets. My mouth a living hole, a culture. I see myself screaming things out suddenly in crowds. As everyone turns to WATCH. In shock they place their hands over their MOUTHS. I shout and it gives me a BONER for them all to be STARING at me.

Sometimes when people talk to me I don't answer but I stare straight at them into their EYES, at the tics and dilations and the balls of spitshined white, and I say nothing. The eyes tell it in order of time. I should quit wasting so much time. I'll have plenty of time to be dead and I have plenty of time now to be SCREAMING.

I'm trying to figure it OUT. Why time has become such a raw quantity for me. I'm trying to understand why I don't even want to FUCK ANYMORE.

I remember some things my mother used to say to me. If you like a girl a lot, swallow a slug and she'll fall in love with you. Don't eat an apple without washing it. Don't write on your hands; the ink will sink down into your blood and kill you.

Victor, Zeet, and Billy got dressed for the party. I wore a T-shirt and blue jeans. Billy called Warren to make sure he was coming. They whisked themselves around the room, tightening their belts, fluttering like fragile insects.

Bring money.

What for?

The body painters.

They were slicking their hair back with gel, framing their faces with the structural weight of slime and goo. They examined themselves in the mirror. You got a rubber in your wallet? said Billy. I stared at him through the silence and shrugged.

I remember the staircase of their apartment building from when I was there two years ago. Rising from the stained brown linoleum I can smell the odors that I remember; I can sit upon the stairs and recall the smell, when I smelled it, what I was doing and who I was with, but it is not the people or the actions

I remember; it is an abstract quantity which can never be replicated in space or in the mind or in time or in all the little things that combined in those moments like a chemical reaction, the musk incense, the Goldschlager, the snow, and I get restless when I'm trying to remember something.

I smell all the empty THINGS in the staircase. It smells the same as it did two years ago. I'm not really the same PERSON now.

Two blocks off of Hillen near the blinking red radio antenna perched the mansion that is shutterless black, rising sirens screaming in stereo, rocks in the yard, a housesunken hole of brick and block; the dirt is falling down. We had an argument about whether or not the house is a mansion. The bricks grow thicker with the years. It is a brick city.

Warren brought Toast to the party with him. Toast is a chicken. One evening two years ago Warren phoned his cousin and said Hey, man, I'm horny, bring some chicks over. His cousin lives on a farm. He gathered up twelve chicks from the barn and threw them in the back of his pickup truck and drove them to Warren's apartment.

Warren said, Dude, that's so totally not what I meant.

The dog ate eleven of them. The survivor ran around the house and slid around on the kitchen floor and squeaked when it was hungry. That chicken's gonna be toast pretty damn soon, someone said. That's why they call him Toast. They tell the story over and over.

What a nice story.

If you lay it down on its side it will scoot around in a circle, never moving its head. It thinks it's a good party trick. I don't know why it was never eaten by the dog.

Toast ran around the room and shat on the carpet and squawked, and Billy bought ketamine from a couple of girls from Morgan State and puked for three hours into the kitchen sink, and they were both hubs of entertainment.

· · ·

What brings you back to town? said the guy who always wears the black hat.

Denver wasn't working out for me any longer, I said.

How come?

I don't know. The weather.

I moved all my photography equipment back here. A dumb stoner girl in Denver broke my tripod. She offered to buy me another one; I said okay, buy me another one, and her mouth hung open and she stared at me. Yeah, I said, it cost eight hundred dollars, you're damn right I'm gonna take you up on it if you offer to buy me another one. She was typical of the scene.

My point is not that it's different here. Warren dashed on a whim out to Boulder last year with Chank to buy five sheets of acid, drove twenty hours straight in the Corvette, seventeen hundred miles methed to the brim, got to Boulder and paid nine hundred bucks to God knows who, drove back east, got home, slept thirty hours straight and woke up only then to discover that he had bought nine hundred bucks' worth of blank white paper, blank as fuck.

Chank. Zeet. I don't know where they get these nicknames.

My point is not that they're dumb.

My point is that they drove through Denver without stopping. They didn't even realize that I was LIVING there. I don't hold it against them though; it's not something they really would have THOUGHT of.

The heat of indoor summer rose upward through the many-bodied tangle: Every joule of warmth pushed inward to play off another, each body an oven careening, colliding to the beat of the music's blaring in the strobe. Sweat pissed off of the heads and chests of bodies one drop at a time, a deluge viewed frame by frame. My eyes processed it in images of stillness, droplets of salty sweat transfixed in air. Fulguration.

In the crowd was Greer.

They didn't know that they were fulgurating but they were fulgurating; they were fulgent; they were fulgurant tangles of electrodessication, bleating like sheep. My beautiful bodies.

. . .

Have another martini, Greer was saying to the silver man.

Why?

I want to watch you drink it.

Her body paint was mostly green, forest green, with silver highlights, brown, black, some blue. It was a fifty-dollar paint job. A forest at night, a jungle, vines entangled, spiders crawling over slimy moss and peat. Her left nipple was the nose of a squirrel. Her right nipple was a point within the canopy of trees. Below her navel and above her waist was a horizontal diamond's shape: a murky black pond that shone in the full moonlight, and two boulders in the foreground, and water poured out of the pond in a triangular waterfall that led down into her crotch. I know those nipples. Red blanket radiator sirens rising through the ceiling. It was Greer. The silver man examined his palms and mumbled and walked away as I approached her: You are Greer; you're standing in front of me.

We smiled at each other and embraced.

I'd heard you were back, she said.

Yeah.

Get too cold out there for you?

Hm.

I admired the artwork. Twining vines were rising up her legs, bending at the knees, a pulsing camouflage. I saw bugs and beetles, crawdads, the crawling creatures perched upon their nimble legs; I saw leaves brown upon the branches, dying from wrinkled arboreal blights. Her hair was green. She wore green corrective lenses. As she stood before me, she appeared to me to be a giant hovering arachnid, creeping outward upon her web. I admired the artwork and sucked on my joint, drawing all breathable air into my lungs.

I thought you didn't like it here, she said.

I shrugged.

I thought you said the city suffocates the soul.

It grows on you.

What is there to say. She laughed. I'm glad you're back.

I was sweating. Excuse me for a minute, I said; I'm gonna go outside and sit on the porch. Maybe I'll see you later.

I stood on the porch and shivered. My jacket was somewhere beneath a pile of coats, and I couldn't find it. I stood on the porch and smoked and shivered and looked up at the pink glow of the city.

You know they're doing some crazy shit with physics these days. When the moon is not in the sky we cannot look at it—this was already known—but now they're saying that when we are not looking at the moon then the moon is not in the sky. There is a mathematical proof. Each of us has one quantum reality in which the moon is the moon while we fix it in space.

When I looked at her I shivered. As if my head and throat were shuddering at the thought of taking a double shot of tequila. Her face made me shudder.

Greer appeared to me to be a giant hovering ARACHNID. I stood on the porch and smoked a cigarette and looked up at the unadorned pink sky, at the hole where I should have been able to see the moon. I stood there and hoped she wouldn't want me to SLEEP with her.

You saw Greer? Victor asked me when I was back inside.

Yeah.

Some paint job, huh?

I shrugged.

I wouldn't mind hooking up with that shit later . . . you know come to think of it you've got the best chance of any guy in the room . . . you two used to be close . . . I'd forgotten about it. You two were together back then.

We weren't together.

Yeah you were; I saw you together all the time.

But we weren't together.

How come?

I never asked her.

You wanted to be?

Yeah.

But you never asked her.

No.

Lights were flashing in the next room. My shoulders were tense. The drumbeat in the music went on and on. I saw fire.

She's just walking around naked, I said.

But there's the paint.

She's basically just walking around naked.

So are a lot of people; it's what you do when you get your body painted.

She's let herself go downhill since I left, I said.

What do you mean?

You know what I mean.

No, I don't know what you mean.

In Denver I ignored all the girls. None of them was what I wanted; Greer was what I wanted. I bought a phone plan and called her every week. How's it going, I'd say.

Good.

What's going on there? I'd say.

I don't know. You know. The usual.

I drank a Miller Genuine Draft. I drank a Hempen Ale. I drank a Natty Boh. I could see her across the room, wine in hand, talking to the silver-painted man again. He was drinking another martini. Warren pointed her out to me. Who's that guy with your woman, Jim?

She's not my woman.

Things have changed, Jim. Better find out who that guy is.

She twirled a strand of her hair with her finger, stared past it toward my side of the room, toward the wall, toward me, shadowing herself beneath the light. Her face became an alien construct: two eyes a nose and a mouth connected only in the past. Her eyes lit up. She was green. Her breasts were green globs of gutted peat.

Two years ago I wanted you so badly.

Billy came over to me; a bunch of people were following him. Let me borrow some money, he said. He was shuffling his feet impatiently.

What for?

Goddammit why the hell do you need to know what for, he said, and then he lowered his voice. Sorry, Jimmy, I didn't mean that. Look I just need some money.

How much?

Two hundred.

You don't have any money at all?

Jesus God Jim I've got three hundred already now do you have the cash or not? I don't have a lot of time.

I didn't want to give it to him, but I shelled it out anyway; I didn't want him complaining behind my back that I was stingy. He ran off with it. I saw him talking to the others: Zeet, Victor, Warren. I felt the usual tension rising up. You just keep me around for the money. You brought me here to pair me off with Greer because you don't want me to live with you anymore. It's different now you know. You wish I would go back to Denver.

Stop it, I said softly to myself. I went into the kitchen to fix myself another drink.

I listened to an argument between two women to my left. One of them was crying. I felt the intensity of their argument. I never have arguments like that one. Maybe I haven't met the right people. Maybe I don't have the passion to argue like that. Maybe it's a question of luck.

Billy had a twenty-dollar bill in his hand when he locked the door. Five people followed him. That means you spent eighty dollars apiece. They slammed the door shut. With them was Greer. She glanced back at me before they disappeared into the confines of the bedroom.

Why didn't you ask me? You think I haven't changed in the two years since you knew me. You never asked me whether I'd gotten coked up before; do you think you can read it in my eyes or something?

I sat on the couch. Everyone else had either gone home or gone out to Valentino's. Incomprehensible voices were drifting through the wall; they coalesced into a uniform murmur. I tried to think about what would happen if she came out of the room. I picked the wads of foam out of the couch and tossed them toward the wall and listened to the stereo: It was set on random play, and ten albums switched back and forth in a night-long loop.

Hey darling what's in your eyes. I saw them flashes across the skies.

I saw her in a dark bedroom alone with me. The blinds had been drawn, and her body in the smoky air was translucent where she sat. Magnificent green eyes, green that gushed, oozed and splotched, the little green dots like infected bits of a spleen, the tumors blotting her soul. The paint. Flop floppity flop. To bleed on sutured throats. Her lap robe over her legs as the pulse was staged—there needs to be red paint—a personality in red, grounded, disgorging blood, the lard on her larynx. *Per-* . . . *per-* . . . *perceive me,* said her voice at last, and the beauty of her murmur as she tossed and turned, and I understood the demons in her face that had made me want her for so long, the crazed amazement in her eyes, feeling my wish as it arose in my mind: to drown in every decibel of those moans and murmurs.

The music was gone. I had fallen asleep. I heard the voices of the people who had gone to the diner, and I listened to them without opening my eyes.

He's out already. Looks like he can't drink worth a shit anymore.

Never could if you ask me.

Funny to have him around again; he hasn't changed a bit. Probably still chasing that bitch around like always.

Yeah. I wouldn't worry about her though. She knows what's up.

Everyone was looking at me; I could feel their stares pierce through the stretched skin of my skull (perceive me), and I could feel their silence. They were all looking at me TOGETHER. I had been asleep only a couple of hours but I had a hangover. I wanted to go back to sleep, but it would have been unacceptable for me to have passed out on their couch. I stood up and stumbled toward the bathroom and spoke to NO ONE, and my eyes narrowed in irritation and disgust.

Vlad the Nefarious

when i wake up i look in my coat pockets to see whats there. sometimes theres a lot of things there.

mostly lighters or ashtrays or a shot glass. last tuesday it was the 8ball and the qball is that how you spell it from a pool table. crash em together bam bam its like those balls you squeeze around in your hand except for bigger.

coz when i see the shit in the morning then i remember where i was the night before. i saw the balls and remembered how trent was like yeah yeah take it take it and dennis was like no no its a nice bar theyll have to pay for new balls and trent laughed at him.

ive got a 2ball already if i keep it up ill have an entire set its too bad i cant stick the whole fucking table in my coat pocket. up in my room i got pint glasses foosball balls, lots of crazy shit. the glass clanked in my coat when i walked. it was cold that night so i was wearing gloves & scarf & a hat & people bitch about the cold weather but if its cold ive got plenty of pockets.

why im writing this shit is i got kicked out of poly for packing a blade. i took it there coz a sophomore told me to do it, it was a dare, it was to show i aint a poser. but then the pigs did a fuckin locker check the rat bastards.

at the suspension center the counselor said keep a journal.

i said piss on that.

she said watch your mouth & i said watch your own or ill smack you upside of it.

i mean i always wanted to have a journal but i couldnt tell her that. i said fuck off i aint keepin a journal, she said its a requirement, i said pissonit.

so im doing it anyways i just aint lettin on to that old diesel-dyke bitch about it.

why its lowercase is coz thats what trent says you do if you write stuff down, if your good you do it lowercase. like he says if you write poems thats what they all do all the poets do he said.

i dont know.

kids made fun of me before for doing what all trent does but i fucked them up good when they said that i put concrete & gravel down in their skin. they were calling me a fag. well i aint no fag i just wish i looked like trent i just wish my face & eyes looked that way. but i cant tell kids that though, it dont come out right.

trents not dropping out of school though like im doing. thats all me.

you have to be 16 to drop out of school. thats fucked up isnt it. fuckers expelled me but i still cant drop out.

ill be 16 at the end of the month. have i said yet what im gonna do

my older brother works in boston, ill drop out get a job up there with him save up the money to buy 2 motorcycles 1 for me 1 for him. we'll go to mexico. its warm down there so ill have to quit pocketing shit.

wont you miss your parents, trent said.

well their nice people but their the only ones left that can make me cry, it looks faggy to cry

its cool being expelled i just wander around looking at stuff. kind of like that kid pecker in pecker except i dont take photos. thats what i did today was look at stuff all day just lots of all different stuff.

i spend a lot of time on the web too.

i took the bus coz there wasnt any other way to get downtown. i just walked around & looked at shit. i saw on eutaw st where fuckstick was sprayed on the brick in black, you know i never heard that word, im gonna start saying it.

i listened to people talk while i walked around. people say some fucked up things. i dont remember any of them now though.

everybody says how in baltimore they dont say baltimore like baltimore instead they say balmer but i never do hear people say it balmer. nobody says balmer. no one at my school says it that way or in my family.

maybe some dumbfucks down in the ghetto say it that way, who knows, i doubt it

im gong to bed now

today i got my spikes all done up for fever.

its like how i had them for the offspring show where there was a mosh pit & i jumped in & jab jabbed all those fuckers

like a sword in your fuckin chest man
we got some pills trent & me all we could get was mitsu-
bishis oh well its ok
they were $20, their little, their white
we're gonna candy flip
we'll be out in space

this time we wont quit looking till we find the shit & eat it. at the trance allah show we couldnt get hold of any acid we took robitussin instead. on a $7 botle you trip your balls off thats called robotripping. funny how it costs more than acid. i dont know what you call it when you do E and cough syrup together. it aint candy flipping thats for sure its a lot harsher than that.

its fuckin out there

all those kids like 1000s of them just fucked out of their heads and theres cops in there that cant do a thing & you walk in the bathroom & theres kids crammed into the stalls in 3s & 4s dealing pills. fuckin self destruct, man when i heard fever was back i called up everybody & told them. i called trent & said hey man, we're going to fever.

he said i know.

i said no man, we're *going* to fever.

my mind feels all blank & stupid like im cracked out or something, i cant think, ive been fucking around on the web all day but my eyes started to hurt so i quit. now i cant think straight. sometimes when i sit down to write in this damn thing i just stare at the page for an hour. like just now. i put some music on to help me write & all i can do is copy down the lyrics. the whole tapes just a bunch of long dubs but the guy talks a while like different words

drown boy drown in me
out loud
boy

if i still cant write after the music then i just do some html code. im working on hyperlinks to a bunch of porn sites and ive got links to some chat rooms.

my name on i.r.c. is vlad the nefarious.

its a word we learned in ms wests class which i liked how it sounds it sounds like what it meant bad. bad like evil death mean fuck bad, so thats what i use on i.r.c. when i use it. vlad comes from vlad the impaler which is the name of a trance deejay who spins some good trance.

i get on there and im vlad the nefarious and everybody on there likes it. theres this one channel called ragefuck and i get on there and they like me

their talking to me

they like me

their taking me into their lives, their talking to me, all the shit scrolling down the screen, the words & shit, the thoughts & sounds

· · ·

its money time man. we went back & got more pills & this time they were different ones cheaper better the kid said. we paid $500 for 60 do you know what kind of profit that is if we sell them

its a lot

that should get me started toward the motorcycle

trent thinks we can move it all at fever well i dont want to spend the whole time at fever worrying about that shit, i wanna dance, so i been making the rounds. i sold 5 just today

i even put an ad for it on the web page. heres what it looks like on the page. dennis said hey dumbfuck you can't put that on your web page, i said sure i can stupid there aint cops on the net

he said oh is that so.

well, nobody born before 1976 can use the web at all period, nobody before 1980 can use it good like us, thats what i told him

so heres what it looks like on the page

[drawing it in for you]

---

these are the pills im selling

their pink, their called "email" coz of the E on them—

is this what your looking for

---

before we drank yesterday we drove around in trents car. hes got a wicked camaro. hes had his license for a few months now its great. theres no other way to get around in this city.

have you ever been on the baltimore metro

i havent

its dumb it doesnt go anywhere. just the ghetto and the hospital. its a good thing trent got his license when he did or i would have just about killed somebody from impatience.

use to be we took the bus but it quit at 12 thats early. we took the bus all over the place, ive spent a shitload of time on the bus, ive puked on the bus ive done just about anything on it.

this one time on the school bus i remember. it was on glenmore it was on the way home it was a dare. it was back in the middle school like 8th grade. there was 10 of us there in the back seats. they all said theyd give me $2 thats $20 total & i was saving up for a playstation. i undid my zipper & i did it i beat off right there. it went all over the back of the seat in front of me, i got my money. all the stupid girls in the front of the bus never even noticed.

its probably still there on the seat

anyway now we can drive

down off eastern avenue theres bars where even kids our age can get served no question. i aint gonna rat them out & say their names but their there. theres this one around butchers hill thats run by an old fighter pilot that was in the air force, his names pete. we went in there asked whats on special

that nam shit, he said.

that what shit?

nam shit. as in from nam.

vietnam?

what the hell other nam is there?

i dont know.

i aint sold a single fuckin bottle of it all year, he said.

so it's bad?

hell.

it's not bad?

gooks was so pissed they lost the war that they pissed in a bunch of bottles and sent em over here to try to trick us into drinkin em.

so we got degroens instead. we each bought three at a time then we bought three more. pete said careful, it dont take much for kids your age to get wasted, i said yeah, thats the great thing about it.

pete had this parrot in a cage that cussed like a damn sailor. its name was callie, when it got done cussing in english it cussed in egyptian. before long i saw it wasnt even in a cage at all coz the cage didnt have a door. i said can i hold him, pete said eat your heart out kid.

we talked for a while and some shit happened etc etc & then i didnt remember anymore till i woke up this morning. my legs were all sore & shit. i looked in my coat pocket and there was a dead parrot. mouth hanging open.

twat. callie want some twat.

i threw it in the trash

fevers tonight but i cant find trent anywhere hes not home

this is 3 days later, i just threw my little league trophy against the wall & broke a picture frame

i aint gonna talk about fever im way too pissed off to talk about it

this is another 2 days

im too hungover to write anything

fuck

so much for the motorcycle

so much for having the money for any fucking thing at all

trent yelled at me about the bird. he remembers it all. he said we were pretty close to being fucked. he said you dumb shit that was my favorite bar, he said they chased us, he said you really got shit for brains dont you.

he said why dont you just sit on your ass & talk to your internet friends for a while

he said its not just the bird its everything your always doing

we didnt go to fever. i got stuck with all these pills. i havent sold anymore except a couple 3 days ago. i ate 2 myself but its no fun by yourself it sucked it was bad. trent said why dont you just go by your damn self you dumbass but it was him i wanted. the kids on the net said it was the best time at fever theyd seen. talbot said the jungle was vicious, he said dj wack spun for 3 hours & it was bitchin.

you wanna know what i did that night

i wrote fucking linux code
thats what i did
i can hear the music in my head. all the little beats. fuckin rrraaah. you just lose yourself for hours at a time dancing watching everybody else dance everybody theres so pretty. their all so thin, they all have bellybutton rings, their skins real clear. they look like the kids in the abercrombie & fitch ads the ones that are all so pretty. all the lights are going. everythings metal like your under the entire city. like that big room on aeon flux where shes bleeding & the bloods like wine & it fills the room & the rooms metal, the rooms metal around you outside & the rooms metal right there under your skin. all the eyes are so wide. big blue eyes big green eyes big brown eyes. their watching you it feels warm, their eyes. theyve all got glow sticks their in their shoes, their hands, their hair. this one kids got nipple rings with blinking red lights, hes got a glowing nunchuck, he waves it around its shining, your rolling & its just one big flow you feel it in every little piece of your body, where do they get all these beautiful people. their all tan, theyve got their shirts off theyve got lots of muscles, stringy blond hair, theyve got tattoos. the lights up above you are flashing like a bunch of spaceships, spinning around, the floors purple green black white and the shadows are dancing back and forth so fast, so long, so dark. everybodys rubbing on everybody coz everybodys rolling, their giving massages, waving lightsticks in your eyes, it goes back and forth like lightning.

the beats all you can hear. its drum & bass & the kids arms move like snakes. rada-rada-rada-ra puh-DOE puh-DOE puh-DOE so many times it builds up so good. their all sweating. their all thrashing their bodies around its so pretty. this is it, you dance next to people & your in it together, your all in the same cage in hell. they know it you know it too. dont stop dancing dont stop, oh theres the boy with the french hat, come over here dance next to me. the sound gets thicker like its the bottom of the ice, its like a thousand toads ribbiting. it all feels so good in your eyes like your watching a porno, like everybodys just there for you to watch them, theyve got their shirts off their all like look at me, look how pretty i am. the storms in everybodys eyes growling real fierce its scary, their eyes go black its blackness. it feels good to be hot, it feels good to be sweating. your giving yourself to everybody. the boy with the glowing claws on his fingernails waves them around in your face and the blue lightstick boy is behind him, their working around each other, its all so good. four hours fly by like its nothing but while your in it thats all there is. their sweats shining in the strobe light, the beat goes darga darga darga, it spins around forever.

thats what was going on while i wrote linux code.

kal84 said thats gonna be the last fever.

now that im kicked out of school i dont see anybody much.

trents met some new people their the new batch of transfer kids their all blond like him. they have spikes coz their skaters their like my spikes were except for their blond. trent got a board thats red & black.

i dont know how to skate

their good though

i went to dennys last night with them. trent & the skater kids. it was while i was just starting to get the flu, i could feel the fever setting in. trent didnt pay much attention to me so i felt kind of dumb sitting there. we were all smoking lucky strikes & this one kid with a triangle chin says hey, who gives a shit about cancer man, you dont get it til your over 50 anyway & who wants to live that long.

trent laughed & said fuckin A, fuckin A

thats what he did with everything they said.

i remember when he said fuckin A to everything i said too

i went home & got online i was in a real pissy mood, i was real sick by then, i felt like shit. i got on the channel, everybody said hey, they #ed me coz its set automatic, they said where you been all week.

here & there.

i sat there & watched them talk, they werent saying much, it all looked so stupid. just cussing & going on about the next show. most of the kids were from DC so they were talking about all their DC shit. the scenes better down there but i remember when it was better up here. talking about DJing & how stupid everybody was who doesn't understand DJing. well i just started in on all of them. i made sure i pissed each one off. i thought how the whole internet was just all the nerds & geeks out there all connected into one big thing, sitting in their houses slobbering on theirselves jerking off, all the people who dont have any other friends, all the losers in the world. how before the internet they all probably just sat there in their rooms thinking jesus, there must be other people out there just like me, if only i could meet them. their fucking pathetic.

so i told them so. i told them the internet did for the pathetic losers what the wheelchair did for the cripples.

whats wrong with vlad, they said.

krexx said hey, maybe someone else broke onto his account, maybe its not really him, he wouldnt say all that shit

like how their all worthless, how their wasting their lives. i said get out & make some real friends, thats what i did.

then i just stared at the screen & it quit scrolling for a minute coz they were all so surprised. not for long though.

my computers got an hourly chime when it was midnight it said

　　EEP EEP EEP EEP EEP EEP EEP EEP EEP EEP EEP EEP
& at 1 it said
　　EEP

when i got done i thought well shit, thats the end of that, it was weird. i looked for another channel but they were all dumb so i went to bed. i couldnt fall asleep though till 4 A.M. thats whats happening again tonight, its already 3, im wide awake.

this is a little while later
　　the skater kid was right
　　who wants 50 yrs of this shit
　　you know its only been two weeks past since i got kicked out of school but the time sure does seem slow while its happening.
　　i put on my headphones & listened to that berlin dj but it

didnt put me to sleep. it reminded me of what mom said about
techno. its just the same sound over & over, she said. its like a
broken record. i laughed at her but i guess shes right.

i couldnt sleep so i got back online. i got on ragefuck & it
was empty.

where did everybody go

it wasnt empty though. they went & blocked me from the
channel so it sent me to an empty room. they blocked me coz
of what i said before. i was gonna say sorry but now i cant.
well you know what, im not sorry, those assholes, i can stand
on my own.

id be happy if i could just fall asleep at night. if im not drunk
i cant go to sleep at all ever. its 530 A.M., the rains beating on
the window, im staring at shadows on the ceiling. my eyes hurt
when i move them around in my head. if im gonna be sick i
wish id at least get delirious with a high fever, all fucked up,
that would be kind of fun. when i was little like 8 years old i
had a fever of 105 & mom says i kept crying,

where is everybody?

where is everybody?

where did everybody go?

i remember being scared. there wasnt anybody there except her,
the room was empty, it was quiet. i dont remember the words
but she probably said hush up, kid, there never was anybody
here in the 1st place.

The Feed Zone

He knew the man on the Litespeed. It was the tall, the blond, the balding man, who was bald on top but with his helmet he was young, twenty-five or going on thirty at most, Cajun accent, sitting atop his bike like a lifeguard, fixing the horizon in place with beady lifeguard eyes looking at all the cars out there, all the little pebbles; his eyes were angry, halfway heartless, and as the group waited for the race to start Jay looked sidelong at the man's boyskinned hairless arms and the double silver crosses in his ears.

Can you believe the purse for this race? someone said.

How much is it?

Three hundred for first place.

Goddamn.

Course you're a cat five so it don't matter none anyway.

Yeah, shut up.

You think about your little trophy, I'll think about three hundred bucks.

The fifty riders huddled in their pack together in the heat. Jay was already sweating. Above the inlet of the lake rose humidified air currents ninety degrees and rising. The heat against his face was the opposite of a breeze. He reset his odometer and stretched his arms up and to the side and fastened his helmet and ate a PowerGel. He looked around at the faces around him, the cocky smirks. Before a race he was always nervous, apprehensive, and everyone else always looked so confident, so smug and set in their fates. His hair itched beneath the plastic of his helmet.

The official chirped her whistle and stepped in front of them.

Okay folks listen up, it sure is a fine day for yall to race bikes. These are some good roads we got for you to ride on. Now listen up because I ain't gonna say this but once. This sure is a fine course we got for yall today and I think yall are gonna like these roads. These roads yall are gonna be riding on are some of the finest smoothest roads in all of Tennessee, and there won't be one speck of gravel on em. Now I've been with the Tennessee Bicycle Racing Association for three and two-thirds years and traveled all over the state and I can tell you for sure right now these are the smoothest roads in all the whole state. These are some good roads we got for you.

I hate this bitch, muttered the rider in the pink jersey to his left, number 301.

The man's teammate nodded. She's at every race in this goddamn state, he said. Her and her center line shit.

Probably never got her fat ass on a bike in her whole life.

The woman's blond hair bobbed up and down as she spoke and she gestured with both arms and chewed on a wad of gum as her jaw drooped down in sloppy indifference. Her breasts shook beneath a white Dollywood T-shirt. She kicked patterns into the gravel at her feet as she spoke and the pack stared blankly back at her as her arms pointed and hovered in the air before them.

Now there's one rule I wanna make sure all of you know about and that's the center line rule. I think you all know about the center line rule.

Here it comes, said the pinkjerseyed man.

They had been assembled for nearly ten minutes, straddling their bikes and waiting to go. Jay was impatient. I see you cross that yellow line and you are DIS-qualified. You see that white pickup over there? I'll be right behind you in that white pickup and if you cross the yellow line you may as well just stop and sit your hind end down on the grass and take a rest cause you'll be DIS-qualified.

Just shut up shut up shut up shut up, he repeated to himself, and he was sweating profusely already, just start the race. The woman kept talking, and after another five minutes of agony the whistle finally blew and they moved forward.

Shit, someone yelled, dude wrecked already.

Jay looked down at the body on the ground to his left. Couldn't clip into his pedals maybe. Writhing on the ground. Jay didn't know what had happened, but he rode on and accelerated into the pack. They rode for two miles in silence. The leaders set a quick pace.

Hey, said a man in a red and yellow jersey, I thought you said you couldn't afford the money to race anymore.

Jay shrugged.

Where'd you come up with the entry fee?

I took it out of my mom's wallet, he said.

No, seriously.

Jay shrugged again and moved up into a gap ahead of him.

The pack shifted and flowed and from above it was a fluid mass of water rolling along the road up hills and down them and the riders swirled around within it as if blown by the wind. Jay stayed on the wheel of a man in a TVBC jersey and together they moved to the front, the back, the left, the front, everywhere in the group and at all points within it. He looked to his right and saw another man he knew from the summer before. They had trained on the same schedule and had ridden in century rides together.

Hey, Jay.

Hey.

Finally hit the senior circuit. You just turn eighteen?

December.

Damn, you must of lost thirty pounds.

Jay kept breathing steadily and watching the wheel in front of him, and his breath was his only response.

You been starving yourself?

It's one way to save money, Jay said.

Starving yourself is no way to lose weight, the man said.

It's actually a pretty damn effective way to lose weight.

The pack reached the first major climb. It was steep and at least a quarter mile long and when Jay saw it he struggled to move into the front of the group because he knew the hill would cause a split between the category three racers and the cat fours. He felt strong, and he didn't want to be caught with the slower riders. He rubbed his tongue against his lip's edge and got closer to the wheel ahead of him, staring and darting alert and he was a machine aware of all observable objects. His fingers draped against the sleek brake levers with sharp intent as they began to climb. Jay watched the muscles on legs ahead of him and saw who was going to stay in front, who was going to fall back, who was breathing the wrong way. The riders sliced left and right and darted sideways to vary the motion. Jay watched them and laughed. There were so many who didn't know how to breathe.

This is gonna split up the peloton, said a man to his left riding a Bianchi, struggling between gasps of air to force out barely uttered words.

The peloton, said Jay scornfully. You're racing in Tennessee for fuck's sake.

Huh?

You don't call it a fucking peloton when you're around here.

The man stared back at him. Jay smiled smugly toward him and shifted up and darted to the top of the hill. He was gritting his teeth but making sure he showed no outward sign of pain, and he reached the top at the same time as the other fastest climbers, and the stragglers behind them inched their way over the hill and latched onto their wind tunnel on the way down the other side.

When they were on flat road again Jay moved back to the rear of the pack. There were still twenty-five or thirty people riding together. It was eight miles into the race. When he saw the size of the group he inched his way toward the front again. There needs to be a wreck, he thought. Right behind me. Block everybody up for good. The road was bumpy, and he felt hard jolts as he crossed sinkholes and bumps on the pavement. He was drafting the man in the pink jersey. The man's tire wobbled; it was out of true, accentuating the man's lack of control. Every bump seemed to take him by surprise, and Jay watched him swerve and weave and bump against the rider to his left. Jay wanted to get behind a different bike but no one was shifting positions, and he was on the far right edge of the road. They rode over bump after bump.

Remember guys, someone yelled, these are the best roads in Tennessee.

Best roads in Tennessee my fuckin ass, said the pinkjerseyed man. I'd hate to see the worst ones.

Several people around him laughed. The man reached for his water bottle and in doing so swerved three inches to his right and crossed the white shoulder line. He tried to steer back to the left but his weight had shifted, and his wheel drifted to the pavement's edge. Jay saw that the dropoff to the dirt was at least two inches high, and the man floated right and right and he was off the side skidding along the road's jagged bank like a trolley against its track, and in the space of three seconds he crashed down against the road and Jay leaned sharply to the left to swerve around his flailing body. Someone yelled oh fuck and the man's helmet cracked and bones snapped and split and in the helmet's airhole the skewer bolt of Jay's front wheel snagged and caught and jerked him forward. He clung to his drops to keep from being launched into the air and his bicycle dragged the man's head forward three inches along the road, scraping his stubbly cheek against the gritty stiffness of the pavement. Jay thought he would surely crash too and he closed his eyes and braced himself for his journey through the air, his crash, but in a split second his wheel came loose and he opened his eyes and continued riding, turning the cranks in fury, aiming for the leaders. A gap had formed between him and the dozen riders ahead of him, and he sprinted to catch them and behind him the man screamed in pain and as he hurried forward he tasted raw blood against his lip where he had bit it.

The blond man was still in front of him.

He caught the pack and downshifted two cogs as he fell into

their slipstream. They were easy to catch and he knew they had not even noticed the crash because if they had noticed it they would have sped up and tried to break away. Gotta stay ahead now, he thought. He considered leading a breakaway himself, but he wanted to rest. He breathed heavily and reached behind him for a PowerGel from his jersey pocket and tore it open with his teeth and sucked the gooey sludge out of its wrap and tossed the package down onto the road. The pacecar was still back at the site of the wreck and no one would notice.

Fuckin litterbug, said a voice from behind him.

He looked back, startled. The man on the Klein had stayed on his wheel as he had bridged the gap. No one else had kept up.

You just about went down with that guy. The man rode up beside him to his left to join the double paceline. I mean goddamn, the man said, I don't know how you stayed upright with your wheel caught like that.

Jay shrugged.

What were you thinking when it happened?

I don't know.

Well it sure scared the shit out of me for one.

He shrugged again.

Weren't you scared? the man said.

Jay thought for a moment. I guess I was just thinking how I needed to speed up so they wouldn't get away, he said. How they might try to make a run for it. The sound of the man's splitting helmet echoed in his head.

In a torrent of air they rode into a forceful headwind that kept the front-runners each from pulling the group more than twenty seconds at a time until the blond man got in front and pulled for three minutes straight. He's still in front, he's still in front. That's what I was thinking about, Jay thought, about how I wish it was the blond guy that went down. Their tires scoured the road of dust and dirt and the spokes in their celerity were invisible. Jay felt a mosquito barrel into his nostril. The air smelled of sheepshit as they eagled forward speeding through their transit of the valley. They stayed at twenty-five and twenty-six miles an hour.

You know what I could do with three hundred bucks? some-one said.

Upgrade to nine-speed, that's what I'd do.

Hell, I got that shit more than a year ago. I'd get a second helium wheel is what I'd do.

Waste your fuckin money.

Shit.

Titanium Speedplays, the bearded man said, that's the way to go.

You weigh too damn much for Speedplays. You gotta be un-der one fifty of they'll snap in two.

I'm right at one fifty.

Shit.

Shit's ass.

Titanium training wheels, that's what you need.

The bearded man squirted Powerade at him in response.

Why don't you get yourself a titanium kickstand while you're at it.

In the monotony of the next ten miles words and sounds stuck in his head and repeated. The last song he had heard in the car was what he heard over and over in his mind when there was no sound: There is no pain, he sang to himself, you are receding; sweating he heaved out lumps of air as muscles ripped in his calves beneath him turning. The riders moved forward like a rumbling herd of swift gazelles, and sunrays fell fast upon them, and a hot wind swept cattletrodden dirt against the rough sweating hide of their cheeks. The pinstripe sunbeams that raced through an endless succession of pine trees conjured blinding white rainbows in the periphery of his plutonite eyeshades. Birds lit down on the steaming road behind his popping ears and squawked and pecked at rocks and birds rose in harried takeoff from the flat mirage of watery road ahead. The spooling revo-lutions of the riders' hundred tires bound them all in rubber friction to the road as their gleaming frames rattled like dying kingbirds, and they dashed across long black asphalt sinkholes and sinking heatsplit cracks that snaked into the ditches and his legcells shrieked in their endless dizzied circuit and his muscles were moving toward agony and on the boiling pavement his sweatdrops fizzled.

What the hell kind of a bike is that? the man in the Pilot jersey asked him.

What do you mean?

Vitus. What the hell kind of a bike is a Vitus?

That's the brand.

Where the hell do they make it?

France.

Does it sprint pretty good? asked the man in the blue jersey. I hear those sprint pretty good.

Maybe if you put a good sprinter on it, Jay said, and the men laughed.

Hell, that thing don't even have STI.

He didn't answer.

I ain't used downtubes since I don't know when.

Seven years, said another man.

I could never go back to that shit, the first man said. Hell, I wouldn't be caught dead at a race with downtube shifters.

How much did that thing cost you, kid?

Twelve hundred, he lied. He had bought it used in Chattanooga for four hundred and twenty-five dollars and a case of beer and he had spent three hundred upgrading the drivetrain. All the men around him were riding three-thousand-dollar bikes, Litespeed titaniums and Colnagos and Klein Quantum Pros. They'd spent their three hundred dollars on titanium skewers and water-bottle cages and all the expensive little things they would buy to make their bikes an eighth-ounce lighter.

How much does that thing weigh, kid?

Twenty pounds.

Twenty pounds, Jesus H. Christ, why don't you just put some bricks and stones in your jersey pockets while you're at it?

Jay glared back at him without responding.

How much does yours weigh? someone asked the man who had spoken.

Seventeen point two three, he said.

Mine's seventeen even.

Damn.

You could get lighter cable housings than that you know. Save point oh two ounces. Maybe even point oh three.

The blond man was still leading them. Jay knew he was the strongest rider in the group. He tried to will a crash in his mind, a spoke jamming in the man's wheel. He tried to picture whether the bike and the body would go forward, backward, up or to the side, whether it would flip with the ease of a baton, whether inertia would make the bike go forward but not quite so much as the rider. Jay ignored the putrid algae in roadside ponds and the edgy heartthump that stretched his tingling fingers outward as they rested on the faded yellow bartape, and he ignored the heat and the drenched itching of his hair, the horns of oncoming traffic, the jagged hills foreboding in the distance and the gelcoated grumbling of his stomach; high on the diesel fumes of trucks that raced the opposite way he ignored the crazed escape of groundhogs under barbed wire as they dashed headlong into tattered brown acres of okra and of horses and of corn. He tore the fibers of his muscles in gritted confidence and ignored all but the brittle hiss of his drivetrain as it went rawking and thromping up the steep scalene hillside as bugs danced in blinding air. His muscles scraped against the outer casing of his legs like redlined pistons as he propelled the radial spokes along in a solid circle whizzing and the chain jerked forward in broken oily spasms; his pain was coldly growing and against the bony saddle fabric his testicles scraped in aching numbness as they recessed into the folded muscle matrix of his crotch.

They formed a rotating double paceline. He stayed in the seventeen-tooth cog and relaxed and worked his way forward in the column as the front riders drifted back to refasten themselves onto the tail of the lines. The wind pressed against his cheekbones and he could feel it constant in his sinuses as empty air moved through them. Warring clouds were general upon the white skyline. The wheel he followed swerved suddenly to the right and flew behind him and he was in front, and he felt the spearhead of resistant wind against his head and torso and up-shifted to maintain the group's pace and breathed deeply to combat his cramping stomach. He counted the seconds, and they crept in excruciation toward their end, and after half a minute he fell back and hooked onto the rear.

He looked at the cattle in the field beside him, and they looked back at him and tossed their mouths in ovals.

Brake, someone yelled.

Everyone was stopping. Jay screeched to a halt and in doing so slid sideways and unclipped his left foot in time to right himself from landing on the road. The two riders in front had crashed. There were three down, four, tangled up in each other's bikes and bodies. They had been going thirty, maybe thirty-five; it was a slight downslope. Jay clipped back into his pedals but there was no path through the men down and riders were standing across the road blocking it, and Jay dismounted and thrust his bike onto his shoulder and he was in the high grass running, and they were all running, and in the ditch he ran past the crashed riders and their blood and the gravel embedded in their red road rashes as their bruises rose up purple-red against the surface of their skin and they cried out in pain and lesions formed beside furious wheels spinning and their trapped legs beat against spokes.

He rode to catch the men ahead of him and men behind him rode to catch his own wheel. There were seven of them. A new paceline formed. The blond man wasn't there; Jay looked up into the distance and saw a dot speeding around a curve. He had broken away. The blond man was going to win and the feed zone was still ahead of them and the man would steal any bottle he wanted. Jay saw red blue and yellow flashes of anger. They rode silently but swiftly. Jay wanted to keep the gap between them and the riders who had been blocked behind them, and he took the lead and scissored against the wind at twenty-six miles per hour for three minutes straight before he fell back and finally allowed himself the luxury of the slipstream, lurking behind the foreign muscles that now propelled him, exhausted and anaerobic.

There is no pain. You are receding.

The first time he had seen the blond man was two weeks ago, in a race near Johnson City. They had ridden eighty-seven miles that day; the feed zone was at mile seventy-two. It was just him and the other man; everyone else had fallen back long ago. Jay was exhausted and in agony and the only thing keeping him going was the bottle he knew would be waiting for him. He breathed a sigh of relief when they finally rounded a curve and saw the men and women standing beside the road, arms thrusting Gatorade and PowerBars out toward them. Phillip was done with his cat 5 race and there he was with the bottle, cold ice dripping from the side. Jay struggled ahead, riding his opponent's wheel.

The man's hand was out but there were lots of bottles and Jay never thought—

What the fuck, Phillip yelled.

The man snatched Jay's bottle out of Phillip's hand and boom he was gone, sprinting ahead to the base of Beehive Ridge.

Phillip chased after him on foot and stumbled and fell into the ditch and Jay thought he could see blood on his arm as he rode past. Catch him, Phillip yelled.

Jay skidded and righted himself and barreled forward along the road. He looked ahead and saw that the man wasn't going very fast anymore, was slowing down to enjoy the quenching of his thirst. In a burst of anger he found the energy to catch up. The burn of his muscles lacerated his bones and legs and skin and everything he could feel. He looked left at the man's scowling face. Droolbars connected his sweating lips and his teeth were strong and shining and Jay felt the wail of the wind sounding in his ear. The man laughed, his cackles spaced out by his struggling aerobic intake as they ascended the hillside two abreast and he was laughing violently, laughing through hollow scoops of snorted air, slicing up the slanted runway laughing and Jay stared up at him agape and drooling spit and sweat and struggling to keep pace.

Gimme my fuckin bottle, he said, grabbing for it.

The man giggled. Jay turned the cranks with brute force and halfway up the hill he felt a wave of numbness flowing through his legs. He was strung out from the heat and the exercise and exhaustion and you can't convey the suffering and Jay's horror at the man's laugh kept him laughing harder as he breathed in waves of energy through his grinning teeth.

Jay downshifted.

The man took the bottle from its cage and opened the pop-top with his teeth. He sucked down the ice-cold carbohydrates and turned to Jay and smiled and licked his lips. Jay's eyebrows drew together in rage. The man upshifted. His bike rocked back and forth from the force of his newfound vigor and with one last sip from the cold plastic container he turned it over and squeezed the purple liquid out onto the sloping asphalt and in ten seconds the bottle was empty and the man laughed and the puddle steamed upon the road.

You fuck, Jay yelled.

The man looked again to his left. Jay was a wheel's length behind and falling back. The man watched Jay's number flapping against his jersey. It was number sixty-three. One of the safety pins had come loose, and the square paper noisily blew around in the wind.

You little fucker, Jay said.

The man smiled. He tossed the empty bottle up into the air, and it spun around and landed on the road in front of Jay's tire. Jay swerved and lost his balance and regained it and zagged across the yellow line and back.

Center line violation, the man yelled. I'll have to turn you in for that one.

You bitch.

Remember what the nice woman said. If you cross the yellow line you better just sit your hind end down on the grass and jerk yourself off cause you'll be DIS-qualified. The man pulled away. He pedaled faster and Jay fell a bike's length behind him. Bye number sixty-three, he yelled over his shoulder.

I'm gonna kill you.

But number sixty-three, he called back. Number sixty-three, don't be mad at me.

That was a bad day. He had bonked that day. Didn't even finish. Today was better. He dreaded the hills but he did them all, got to them and found he had the strength to climb them. You dread them whether you feel good or not. They were fifty-five miles into the race. The hill stretched up as far as he could see. He dreaded it. At the back of a seven-man paceline he braced for a painful ascent and downshifted to increase his cadence while he still could. So steep. They began to rise. The snake of their staggered bodies slowed and stretched and regrouped slower and jerked forward with no fluidity or grace and they struggled to ignore the burning lactic flames. They were going eight miles an hour. They were going seven miles an hour. He followed behind them and thought only about staying against the wheel ahead of him, six inches back forever, restless and overheated and struggling. Could quit right now and I wouldn't have to climb it, could stop, lay my bike down beside the road and rest. His heart beat rough against the thick sweaty film of his jersey, and he watched his pulse climb on the monitor's display to one eighty and up again and his ears ached and spasms shook his legs.

What the hell?

Startled, he jerked to the left. He had rubbed the tire of the man in front of him. The riders were all slowing down. What the hell? He didn't understand how he could be going faster than them. He had thought he would have to struggle to keep up. They were all falling back. Jay kept his pace and rode up past the rider whose tire he had hit, past the rider in front of him, past number seventy-seven and number thirty-nine and number sixty. They were staring at him. They didn't know who he was; he hadn't raced with them before. He felt their eyes upon him as he passed them, and although his legs burned terribly he sliced into the revolutions as if they were gladiatory swordstrokes and he was passing them and suddenly faster, nine miles an hour, and his pulse broke two hundred. His heart raced, and it was exhilarating, and in the corner of his eye his competitors fell down the hill behind him. He climbed and watched sweat droplets salt his top tube and imagined himself hooked onto a towrope that tugged him mercilessly up the hill, don't think about it, look at the rope and the pulley is racing toward the hilltop, glinting metallic, always tugging.

Someone coughed behind him. They were scattered along the full length of the visible road. Fuck all of you, he thought, chuckling back at their distant struggle.

He rounded the hilltop and descended and swallowed the cold vast air. He shifted into the twelve. Pinetwigs crunched beneath him as he flew into the valley's hazy vista stretched elongated and on the edge of cliffs he leaned into curves that were wedges, curves that were snakes, curving into them and out again and he was alone falling, sinking into ever-thicker air, the altitudes all scurrying into space.

Don't be mad at me, fifty-three. Pole through the wheel maybe. How the arc would form. I wonder. Forward, or backward, or up and to the side, launching straight into space, or loop-de-loop in a vertical figure eight, or into a roadside oak, or down onto a cow. He rounded the sharp corner of the hillcrest and breathed deeply the cool rock-shaded air in gasps and spurts and shifted into his hardest gear as the downslope pulled him forward. The speedometer raced into the thirties and the forties and he pedaled until the cranks turned too fast to pedal and flies collided with his face and his eyes secreted a blinding film in the wind. He leaned into switchbacks until he thought he would surely fall over. As his ears popped he gripped tightly onto the drops and crouched down into a tuck position and the wind went over him and under him and stroked thin streaks of his hair through his helmet's airstrips. When he got to fifty-nine miles an hour he tucked himself down even further and was at sixty and a bleeding streak of color against the dying drought of brown in fields around him. He couldn't see anyone behind him anymore and the blond man was the only one in front of him and that could be dealt with; air swirled everywhere invisibly, cyclonically, so many pockets and swirls. The only sound was the hiss of racing air. Air was the only smell.

There was a sign for the feed zone. Five miles. There wasn't going to be any water bottle of his at the feed zone for blondie to steal this time because no one had come with him to the race, no one had come to hold it, to stand and wave and encourage him; he'd had to beg Phillip to come the last time and he'd finally bribed him, and his father was working extra shifts over the weekend, and his mother was still in the hospital, and there wasn't anyone else.

You better come home with some cash to show for yourself this time. After all your talk. Or you ain't takin the truck no more.

Only blondie in front now.

When he reached a flat stretch he practiced his victory sign. He held his arms up for five seconds, back straightened, and lowered them; he raised one arm in muscled strength and waved it and smiled; he held up both arms for a quick two seconds with clearly formed fists, eyes plaintive, looking forward at the road ahead.

Okay listen up yall are here to race and ain't it a fine day for yall to race. There's nobody else in sight they're all way back there somewhere you're coasting along Lantana Road the only kinetic object from here to any and all horizons put your hands on your hips and feel those pulsing muscles like pistons like atoms like gears. Okay listen up you did good boy you're counting down the miles. It wasn't a clear voice in his head that he could say was male or female or speaking or whispering or smiling or breathing or the inner tongue of his mind but it repeated like his motion repeated and no end to it and okay yall there is no pain you are receding, receding, there is no pain and the same two lines and he pedaled along an infinite road.

Awash with fever chills his bones the stiffness of glass as they raved inside him. Beside him a freight train whistled. There was no one in sight behind him and he saw for a mile back the endless gray highway and the sun shone in spots of glass like a thousand gleaming crowns. No one and still no one. Only blondie but we'll deal with him soon. There's a terrible delight in watching a rival sink without a trace, he thought. Bernard Hinault said that and he watched many of them do it too and there were ten miles remaining and one long climb.

He rode through a stretch of swampland. He rode past still trees and blowing trees and trees bending down to earth and dead trees and trees that razed the sun. He rode beside fields and through them above them on canopied ridges and across knobs and red bluffs and thin isthmuses of wood. An old woman stared bleakly at his sunstruck figure as he swerved past her rutted gravel driveway. At a gray peeling shack two young children sat upon the bank, a boy and a girl, cheering and rising up in spirit as he passed and they were standing, waving, cheering with little clenched fists and eager as they called and fifty rusted shells of cars lurking in their weedy yard behind them.

He turned off the course to the right. He hadn't been on these roads before but it was the way the magnet pulled him and he turned onto it, a half-paved little road with half of two lanes and no road sign, and it would be a shortcut, and he'd catch the bottle man and the only people who'd know would be the people at the turn. They wouldn't see him go through the turn but it's late, it's hot, they don't pay attention. The pacecar wasn't around. Too many wrecks back there. Had to stop for all the wrecks.

His bike felt light. His water bottles were empty. He could throw them out into the ditch, he thought, and make the bike forty-two ounces lighter. He could unstrip his bartape and let it ribbon out into the burning pasture winds and it would be a gram, two grams, that he would be saving. He could toss his shoes aside and drill the clips straight into the soles of his feet, clip into the pedals nakedfooted and rip his skin apart on every pull as his yellow toenails collected all the floating fungi of the current. He spat over his shoulder onto the road. He made fun of the riders who had them but he wanted helium wheels,

a Boreas helmet, titanium pedals, a litany of weightless acces-
sories. He wanted a tuning stand, a good pair of Brikos, a
hundred-dollar jersey. A strand of spit latched onto his sleeve
and hung there, waiting to evaporate slowly into the heat.

It was only a mile till he rejoined a main road. It would be
a right turn, the course would, from here. He turned and rode
a minute and found a place in the ditch by a fence. There were
metal poles on the ground. Fenceposts that hadn't been used.
He stopped and picked one up. He was hot. He spoke out loud.
You are receding. Not many things have been done to me so I
treasure the ones that I find.

He drank the last drops of Powerade from his bottle. He clutched
it in his hand. Did a few practice throws like a football spiral, like
a pass. I haven't forgotten how it felt not to have that water, he
said aloud. He had tried to describe to people the cramps, the
burning, the everything else, but he couldn't think of the right
words. They stared back at him and nodded. They didn't have
any idea. You can't tell anyone how hard it is. You can't convey
the suffering. He sat poised upon the bank with his fence pole.
Arms ajoust above his fallen horse. The man was coming. Chu-
gachuga chug he comes I think I can think I can, wheel out of
true well we'll fix that, fix it good. Sweat dripped from his arms
and helmet. Are your armpits sweating number fifty-three? The
man was fifty-three this time just like Jay was sixty-three the
last time, wasn't that cute. Now that he was a cat 3 the numbers
were two digits. Not that they always were but that was how
it turned out this time, last time. Look here, fifty-three, at my
eyes that are mad at your face no look at me, here, fifty-three,
I know you've got a crush on me.

Feed zone, he yelled.

He yelled it and along the road the sound floated, the two
words feed and zone that the man heard in his crux of exhaust,
and the empty bottle hit him square upon the chin, the pop-top
spinning in for the kill, feeding time, the sharp hole the end that
kissed his bruise awake, and the man saw Jay in his grinning
and that was his story embedded in the sting of its sharp plastic,

observe the pole mister fifty-three, a man become a drone, powerless upon the throne of his machine.

Don't you—the man began, and he stopped in midsentence.

The man swerved to his left and the splotchy air was dotty, skewbald points floating in his panic. Remember me? Jay said.

Don't you fucking dare.

Jay shut his eyes for half a second. Exhaustion pressed upon his muscles like triple gravities drunk or stoned the pole wavering in air in front of him, its weight asphyxiating him as he tried to breathe thirsty in the ditch. You're three hundred dollars you're the corpse between me and my three hundred dollars, you've got two full water bottles, whose did you steal this time? Remember in that movie when the Italian racers skewer that poor kid and he flies up and hits the ground hard ow shit it hurts, which way did he go? Up to the front, up to the back, up to the side, sideways forward, sideways behind him, land on me like a cow from the sky.

The man screeched to a halt inches from the pole. Breathing heavily and deliberately he dismounted from his bike on the right side, facing Jay, shielding his eyes from the sun.

I wanted to wreck you. I wanted to see which way you would land.

Put that pole down, kid.

You crossed the center line. You're disqualified.

Shove it up your ass, kid.

Why didn't you just stay back and let me win.

Jay poked the man's front tire with the sharp end of the pole. He waited for the air to hiss slowly out, the metal rim of the wheel to sink down onto the road.

Why the fuck did you go and do that for? the man yelled.

Look, you're across the center line.

Answer me.

Disqualified.

No air came out of the tire.

Disqualified, Jay yelled, thrusting the pole forward again.

The man watched his tire to see if it would go flat.

Whose water bottle did you steal this time?

The man glanced up with a glint of recognition finally in his eyes. Nodding. Eyes narrowing. Oh, he said. You're that little prick from week before last, aren't you?

Jay stared back at him.

Grow up, kid.

Jay stared him down.

Shit like that happens all the fucking time. The man pulled a cell phone out of his jersey pocket. Dialing up the race people no doubt. Tattletale. I don't think so bitch. With the pole Jay jabbed the phone out of the man's hand and it curled into the ditch without first rising or soaring through any air; it just fell and crashed and the battery fell out and weeds hid it. He heard a crackle as the pole was buoyed up by the man's gloved knuckles, and then a cry of pain.

You little prick.

With a swash the man sliced Jay's rear tire with a knife he hadn't even seen the man draw from his jersey pocket. He grabbed the pole out of Jay's hands and with it pushed him down into the ditch on top of his bike. He hit the ground hard. Jay lay on the dirt and watched the foot-tall weeds that drooped into his eyes as he looked up at the sky, its flowing clouds, its sun.

You'll never win with a bike that heavy anyway, the man said.

As he spoke he mounted his sleek machine.

Hey kid, the man said, what weighs you down more? The lead in your ass or the shit in your brains?

He rode away.

Jay lay still. The wind was knocked out of him. Let me shut my eyes just for a second here oh calllmm yes.

He woke to a spasm in his muscle. Time to get back up on the bike now. He pushed himself up and stretched his aching leg muscles, the sore place on his side where he had hit the ground, stretched the sweaty stench of his jersey and clammy shorts. How long had he been stopped? Five minutes perhaps. He could barely lift his leg up over the bike. It had been the anger alone that had kept him going. What is this. Sixty-eight miles now. Twenty-six average the cyclometer says. He lifted his leg up but nothing was happening; he was a sweating statue upon the road, and his bike collapsed beside him. You have to understand I needed that three hundred dollars, he said aloud as if the man were still standing before him.

You little prick.

The riders came who'd passed him on the hill. Five of them together now. The old guy and the two guys from the Nashville team and the black guy and the other guy. Weren't they just wondering like hell what had happened, why he was down, but the finish line was a mile ahead and who would be the fourth, the third, the second losers. They were all exhausted. So much stronger than them, Jay thought. He watched them as they struggled into the wind and the wheels spun backward it seemed in their torpor, and the faster they went the more backward they were spinning and they were all a great hornet cluster buzzing or a colony of ants or something dry and dead, blazing. Jay reached for his water but it was empty. The five rode past him and thought stay there little boy it's our money; he felt it as they looked at him. Can't convey. He pulled his shorts leg up and watched his spasmodic muscle throbbing down and up and thumping throbs of blood, pressing on his heart. He had leg cramps and stomach cramps. Into the distance he watched the riders tumble, thin and gaunt like gods, trembling toward the finish. He pictured himself beside them, not in the ditch and with no flat tire and he was huffing through sheaths of air, lactate in his legs, in oxygen debt, his bicycle sinking beneath his body into the valley, sinking with the road, bang bang bang along the road cracks.

He practiced his victory sign. He held his arms up open to the airy respiration of the earth, back straight bony arrow at the sun, waved them one above the other, struggling past the other sprinters as they fell behind him and his own hands forward, in front, and lowered them, and raised one tan arm and looked down at his churning shadow. He gnawed at the plastic lid of his empty bottle.

Reaffirmation

Two invitations came in the mail last week for Lara: the ball at the French embassy in Washington and the cotillion in Montgomery. I don't like for her to go to the formals; she is lovely, impressionable, flirtatious, and at such events her dresses frame to perfection every conchoid sketch of her figure. The invitations, which I was swift to catalogue in file thirteen, were embroidered with white Belgian lace, handthreaded in Bruge; had Lara seen their delicate braids, she might have recalled the doilies she herself had bought in that city last summer for our living room, or, as she prefers to designate it, her living room.

Lara, whose sanguine disposition coagulated long ago, wants me out of her life; I can detect her disgust for me vested now in every revulsive breath of air she expels into this humid summer. She worries about her drinking lately, and how can I respond to shit like that? Cognac, fine champagne, Godiva liqueur, so-called gifts purchased by me with her gold card in my attempt to stay one step ahead: I bring them frequently to her.

I'm not going to drink anymore on weeknights, she proclaimed.

I tried to look surprised and hurt. Oh, I said, frowning as I pulled out a bottle of Sheridan's. I bought us this for tonight but I guess I wasn't thinking. Always sensitive, she hates nothing more than causing hurt feelings, and she jumped onto the hook.

Oh Ray, that was so thoughtful of you. She scratched her head. Of course we'll drink it tonight; when I said weekdays I didn't mean Wednesdays too. We always drink on Wednesdays, she said.

There have been oh about three dozen times in July alone when she has turned toward me, mouth half-open in innocent dejection, quivering as if she might speak, but nothing comes. Keep a drink in her hand and nothing ever will. The closest call, I think, was three months ago in Florence when she saw a restaurant where she wanted desperately to eat; we hadn't had a meal all day, but before we could stop we had to exchange money. There was a place next door offering 1700 lire for a dollar, but I insisted that it was a bad rate.

There hasn't been a better one, she said.

I know I saw a place where it was 1760.

I'm starving.

Just hang on.

I dragged us up and down the Arno and around the Duomo and past the train station, back and forth until she was nearly in tears. Do you realize what sixty lire is, Ray? she said. It's three cents maybe. It's nothing.

But we're not exchanging just one dollar, honey, we're exchanging a hundred dollars.

Her face was so pretty when it turned red. So that's three dollars then. I'm rich, Ray, she pointed out. What does it matter?

It's the principle of the thing, honey. They're trying to swindle rich tourists out of their money. It's highway robbery.

She tried to hide any emotion from me but I saw the tears struggling to emerge as we walked by the Uffizi for the third time. Her mouth hung open as it had so many times before and after in her struggle to release her inhibited will, and I laughed to myself. Incidentally, we never relocated her restaurant; instead we ate pastries from a street vendor, Lara sitting next to me munching in disgust on some bland chocolate confection.

We moved into Lara's dead aunt's house in Enterprise last year, about the same time she started taking her medication, actually prescribed to me, not her. Eleven months ago it is now; although she remains sad a lot, she stopped punching holes in the kitchen wall.

I don't feel like we really even live here at all, she said to me. All her friends are back in Montgomery. In Enterprise we know no one, and no one knows us but perhaps a few of the liquor store clerks. I don't want to get to know these people. If I knew them already it would be okay—the people I would know would probably be good people—but how can I devote the energy to it? Already I feel so tired.

In Muscle Shoals, before I met Lara, I knew people, and we went out together to bars, to movies, to high school football games, but it wasn't so much fun really. Sometimes, when you think back on things like that, they seem fun, but they're not really so much fun.

Sean is Lara's half brother, nearly two decades younger than she; he is eleven years old in unbuttoned flannel button-down shirts and baggy pants, and he stays with her when his parents go to Pawley's Island or to the mountains: This happens more than you might think. Go on, you little brat, Lara keeps saying to him, have a beer with me. He is the only person I know whose feelings she isn't afraid to hurt, and that is because making a dent in the little bastard's feelings is impossible.

I'll be damned if I'm gonna turn out anything like you, he always replies.

Once in a while I drive him to the big arcade in Dothan. At the games he is an expert driver, marksman, fighter, but he spends only a few quarters; instead he watches over all the older boys' shoulders, breathing slowly as he lies in waiting like a spy for the few climactic moments when every bit of the player's attention is focused onscreen. He reaches forward, his mind's intent a living claw, creeping: He is a pickpocket.

All that money and not even a habit to feed, I said to him.

This *is* my habit, he responded impatiently, rolling his eyes as if I possessed the intelligence of a speck of dust.

When he's done, he goes to the skee-ball machines—thirty of them are in a row—and as the players toss their balls he stoops between them to snatch their tickets from the slots as they emerge. I wait for someone to notice, I even *want* someone to notice sometimes, but no one does, and he flocks among them without fear, smiling, charmed and shielded. He keeps the tickets in an old Maker's Mark bottle.

Why? I asked him once.

Why are you asking?

I want to know.

No you don't.

Just tell me.

He paused a while. They make me happy, he said, and he smiled as if he had only just then settled on an explanation with which he himself could be satisfied.

It has always seemed to me that the state, mapped, looks like one of the big stone heads on Easter Island: Birmingham is the eye, Phenix City the nose, Lake Eufaula the gaping mouth. Shrimpy salt water murks along through the depths of Mobile Bay like blood through a deltoid reservoir, the carotid artery dripping out of the grinning granite head and throbbing toward its heart. A United States map is on the wall of the spare room where Sean stays, hanging on the bulletin board above the jar of tickets on his desk; I pointed to Alabama the other day and shared my observation about its shape.

What's Enterprise then? he said. Maybe a pimple. A big yellow zit.

He lives in Montgomery and has sworn himself to hold scorn for all smaller places, for any city with fewer than ten Taco Bells and Piggly Wigglys.

Maybe it's a dimple or a scar or a wart or a cancerous mole, he said. Or unshaved beard stubble.

Too precocious for his own good, really. He's fun only when we play sports: football, soccer, Frisbee. He shuts up then and shows some sincerity; he's athletic and nimble; his blond hair shines in the sun.

The only reason I mention him at all is that he started the fight on Friday; it was when he was leaving. We were at the Greyhound station, waiting on a delayed bus that would take

him back to Montgomery. Lara ran her hand through his hair.
When are you coming back down? she said.

He shrugged.

We'll go down to Gulf Shores next time you come.

I hate Gulf Shores.

Then we'll go to Dauphin Island.

I don't know if there are enough bars to get you through the
day on Dauphin Island.

Now Sean, she said and trailed off. She looked hurt.

Sean tilted his head up and yelled at the top of his lungs,
Where's the fucking bus? People all around the lobby turned to
stare.

You hush, Lara said.

Whatever.

Why are you in such a hurry?

I don't know.

What do you say to Daddy when he asks you what you did
down here?

That I sat around all week and watched you drink from sunrise to sunset, sunset to sunrise, and that I managed again somehow to keep you from pouring any bourbon down my throat.
The bus pulled up.

Sean, be nice to me.

For fuck's sake, Lara, he said, it's not anything he doesn't
know. I mean I don't talk about him, at least. He glanced
quickly sideways at me and hugged Lara good-bye and went
outside to load his luggage. I could have killed the little shithead.

Lara and I each drank alone that night: I at the bar and she at
home, sitting on the brick portico, embosomed in heat and
wicker. I came home at midnight and Lara stared blankly into
empty space, refusing to acknowledge me.

What's the matter? I said.

Nobody likes me.

I chuckled. Well, that's news to me.

You know, I realized today I didn't get an invitation to the
cotillion this year. I'm sure they were all sent out long ago.

Aw. You hate those things anyway.

She glanced up. No I don't, Ray.

You always had a bad time, every time you went. I swatted at mosquitoes; they were attacking me already.

Everyone's forgotten about me.

You're delusional.

Sometimes I think that's the way you want it, she said, her mouth curled in a falcical frown, shyly demure and sad.

I'm going to go in and get away from the mosquitoes now, I said.

I went inside and put Muddy Waters on the stereo and poured myself a drink. In the recliner I thumbed through travel brochures stacked in a basket next to me and tried to decide where we should go next. Lara wanted to see Tahiti; maybe we could combine that with a week of skiing in New Zealand, I thought, but I remembered that Lara refuses to ski anywhere but Europe. It's not fun anywhere else, she said to me. Last winter we spent two weeks together at her father's time-shared chalet in Les Deux Alpes. There was a blizzard for two days, and we lay in bed all day both days sipping red wine, eating baguettes with butter and Camembert cheese. It got dark. We made a fire in the fireplace and undressed.

Do you know the names of the clouds? she said to me later, for there were many visible out the picture window in the moonlit night, dancing above the Alps. Cumulus, cirrus, stratus: When combined these names spell complex vapors arming themselves in bodies, cumulocirrus and nimbostratus. Not that we noticed them often. We lay in thought, in song, in drink. There was nothing for me to say to her. I watched the bubbles in my beer.

From a song she continued to play I heard certain lines in an endless chorus. Speakers hide at all points in the walls and ceiling; there may very well be speakers on the floor. All the songs Lara plays are about suicide or murder. Dark brooding pieces of introspection, all of them; one might start to grow suspicious. She has a closet at home she keeps locked and I've never been inside it.

One of her sex games was to handcuff herself to the bedrails. Snowflakes beat against the window like shrapnel, and she shrieked murder me murder me while we went at it; during this moment she and I did not exist and she was flush in her white subterranean pallor, the moisture of her lotion sinking uselessly into her crackling skin, a desperate pixie in the mirror reflecting out at me, fraught with the prettiest chagrin. She hovered, hovered, and we lay in a blanketed stupor. She handcuffed herself to the bedrails where she shrieked murder me murder me while we went at it or at least that's what I imagined she was doing. What she might have done if it weren't for her polo-club upbringing. Squirming and wriggling beneath me hair everywhere wailing but actually she was too sore from two days at the slopes to be able to flex a single muscle. She lay on the bed like a doll motionless and soundless and I had to fill in thoughts and words for her in my mind. Four walls and four closed eyes in the black light, twinkling; a serpentine strap of glowing green was the discarded quilt upon the floor, and in the window the night: two jack pines glowing against the moon. The ceiling fan—was it even on?—rotated and wobbled like the slowest of tilting satellites, and she had her bandanna in hand: It thrust out from her forking wrist like a surgeon's knife, vibrant in the inverted light, and it was silk. Her raspy whisper clawed its way through the breezy black space. Choke me with it. Strangle me. Icy bourbon was in the air, its sweet scent rising from the tumbler; the wall behind her, blood-red above the molding, creaked in the arid heat of winter.

All these moments of our past are one to me: There was before I moved in and there is after I moved in. Say anything to me and I see her face; her name and image have been cliticized, in my mind as necessary adjuncts of life, birth, breath. She's up to her shitchute in money. I can live here forever.

So eventually she came inside, arms unreddened from mosquito bites because the mosquitoes never bother her; she sat down beside me and peered over my shoulder at the brochure I was looking at. I hate it when people look over my shoulder; if I want them to see what I'm reading then I'll show them. She sat down and she sat perched with a rigid back and shoulders as if steel poles had been surgically implanted beneath her skin. I tried not to notice. There was no drink in her hand. She took a few cautious sips of mine. I read about flights to Christchurch in my magazine, and she wandered upstairs.

Eventually I had to go into the bedroom to get a book I had been reading. She sat in the gray shade of the canopy; teeth gritting, nose swollen. Her back with spurning rigidity spoke her scowling mood in silence as her big empty eyes clutched onto one flat band of moonlight collapsing through the shade onto the hardwood floor. It made me nervous to see her like that, her hair unbrushed even this late at night, drinks unmade, messages waiting on the machine. The room was lit in dusky gold. Her cheeks shone in the dust-soaked light, halogenate, her unease illuminated in the hallow glow.

I think I'm going to kill myself if I spend another day with you, she said.

Now, honey. Calm down. You didn't take your medicine this afternoon, did you?

She breathed in an amount of air that seemed as if it should burst her lungs; the glass in her hand was empty, and she slammed it violently against the glazed ceramic coaster on her cedar chest. Shards split beneath her.

It doesn't have anything to do with the medication, Ray, you leech.

Lara, why don't you just get a hold of yourself and *then* we'll talk about what you think is wrong.

She started crying. It's so easy.

Lara, honey. Now, honey.

I put my arm around her shoulder; the conversation was over for the moment, and my shirt and sleeve slowly grew drenched.

I got up and made her a mint julep. Tell me why you think you believe that, I said. Give me more than a load of melodrama.

She was slightly calmer now. She can never stay uncalm for

very long. You're keeping me stuck in these behavioral patterns, she said. You're, you're, I don't know. I don't like it. You're holding me back. She drank the drink.

Tell me why you think that.

You sound like my psychologist, Ray.

For all intents and purposes, I am. I worried after I spoke that I had sounded too smugly sure of myself.

What?

He never would have given you a prescription for that shit. If I weren't here to get it for you then you wouldn't have any. They'd just look in your face and say don't drink so goddamn much.

That's the most ridiculous thing I've ever heard.

Okay, I said obsequiously. You're right.

Anyone with a pulse can get a prescription for it.

I guess.

She shook the ice around in her glass.

He still would have said not to drink so much, I said. She swallowed the mint julep in three quick gulps. Hey, if you're going to get up to get yourself another one, pour me one too, I said. Glaring, she walked to the server.

I've reserved you a room at the Best Western, Ray. I think we should get started on this soon and it'll be easier on both of us.

I'm not sleeping at a motel, Lara.

Ray, I think you are. She handed me my drink.

Lara, I think I'm not.

I see what you're doing to me, Ray.

What am I doing?

She paused. You know what I'm talking about.

Well, why don't you just make sure I do?

Her curls seemed to grow tighter as she argued, as if her follical muscles if such things exist were clenching up and retreating, regressing into her scalp. It made her look more stubborn, more unreasonable. *Bitchier* I guess is the word.

Ray, she said, I think maybe when you reach my age, and

she actually sounded as if she was being sincere, however flawed her logic, you'll agree that my mode of thinking on this is correct. For the best.

This is absurd.

They have room service and a pool.

Lara—

I got you a room on the ground floor because I know that's what you like.

I like the top floor.

No, dear, you've always chosen the ground floor.

It's irrelevant because I'm not going to sleep there.

Ray, you have to sleep somewhere. I hate to think of you just wandering drunk around the county, ending up somewhere being eaten alive by mosquitoes.

What the hell are you talking about? I said. Are you on crack?

She gave me one of those sympathy frowns. As if I were slowly coming to terms with my fate. As if she held the upper hand in this, in life, in anything. I'm talking about where you're going to sleep tonight, sweetie. And I'm very sorry but it's not going to be here. I think you know why. Such a delectable southern drawl, such a rich throaty voice.

Well, I'd been planning on having that last bottle of absinthe tonight but I guess I'll save it for the next girl who comes along.

What?

I said, I guess we—

I heard what you said.

Oh. I waited. Of course I knew what she meant, but this is a very delicate process.

We had two bottles of absinthe.

No, we had three.

You brought back only two.

No, we brought back three.

Two was the duty-free limit, she said.

I began to laugh at her then. At what she had said and at what was going to happen. The nasty shit's illegal anyway, I said. There is no duty-free limit on smuggled goods.

Her eyes had been slowly lighting up as we bickered, and when she was convinced I could actually produce a full bottle of absinthe—which I did, for it was in the dresser beside me, hidden in my underwear drawer—her irises burst into a beady flame of shiny cerulean sparkles that engulfed the once-dull blue. Such expressive eyes: The eyes were what had first caught my attention about her, the emotion borne by her eyes. Of course we had been in a bar at the time, and her eyes had lit up because a drink had just been served to her; it was a triple hurricane, frozen, with a lime slice and a yellow umbrella.

We purchased the absinthe in Barcelona from a bartender who spoke only Catalan. It was the day of the Epiphany, January sixth, and the city was sleeping; closed were the Picasso museum, the Miró museum, the tourist bars. On our quest for a watering hole we were forced to wander out of the city center into the piss-soaked slums where half-breed kids grabbed at passing pants legs, where drugs were dealt unhidden; west of Las Ramblas and east of Montjuïc we stumbled upon the dark and empty dives where Lara discovered her potent narcotic drink.

Que es absenta? she said to the man at the bar.

He might not speak Spanish, I whispered to her.

Well, he'll know what *absenta* is, she whispered back, because it says it right there on the sign.

But he might not know what you want to know about it.

He poured two double shots of it while we argued; he chuckled, and I shuddered at the sight of his three missing front teeth.

In our flowery bedroom Lara now clung to the bottle with fierce intent, reading its incomprehensible print, its numerals and Catalonian words. I studied her facial muscles as they expanded and contracted minutely with each expectant breath; I watched her auburn eyebrows rise and fall. In her top dresser drawer she kept a set of eighteen-carat-gold shot glasses; she lifted them gingerly out into the room, dusting them with the gentle tip of her index finger. The absinthe was mellow but strong, its afterbite greater than it had been in Spain. Lara phoned the Best Western to cancel the room. Colors slowly grew brighter. We went downstairs: The sunstruck navy blue of the sitting room was the blue of every southern mansion, and the lavender of the upholstery was the shade of aristocracy.

I haven't worked a day since I came here, I thought to myself. The absinthe burned my throat.

Lara can drink it more quickly than I can.

In this state of mind we can be happy together: Her thoughts, untinged with their usual distrust of me, their guilt and dishonesty, are weak and singular; she can speak and answer questions but like those of a prodded amoeba her responses show no awareness, awakeness; her treachery is undone.

If only she were conscious to enjoy it with me.

You don't really mean any of what you said earlier, I said to her.

No.

If I weren't here then you wouldn't have anyone to travel with, or anyone to figure out your itineraries for you.

No.

Don't you remember what you said? Cross my heart and hope to die and stick a thousand needles in my eye.

She shut her eyes.

I'm going to stay with you forever, I said. I'll never let you go.

She is in my arms, her blouse draped over the back of the bentwood rocker; I run my finger across her mouth, leaving a wet line of red impression that trails downward toward her uncovered chest, my finger resting at the plexus of all warm flesh. I feel the blood inside her as it pulses; I feel the blood rolling inside myself, and it is what I want.

Your house—what do you mean exactly, *your* house?

She is murmuring drowsily in my arms, her auburn hair red in the chandelier's light as it displays its array of glints and gleams, its exothermic sentience. Every breath a mantra. Stay here, she says to me, states, implores; stay with me, sleep with me, smother me, suffocate me. Her little heart, rising and falling, pounds beneath me; it seems to me that it too glows red in the light. It's good to feel so wanted. In the yard the live oaks are creaking, croaking. The incense is smoking. She purrs in my arms, gently breathing, releasing alcohol and the other gases of her breath into the night's bold humidity; she is unconscious. Suffocate me, she says. Against my skin I feel her naked body shivering.

Sleep on Stones

You gotta point her arms out toward the open road, the house, the barn, the big whatever-it-is that's going to disappear. Her hairs will scrape along the tubered dirt, ripping friction burns into her veiny skin, uprooting the pretty little clovers. Stop cowering. You're not putting a corpse in the ground for chrissake. You gotta lay her down against the soil and dig that hole like you really mean it, give her a little patpatpat a little stroke of the hand, don't go against the veins and don't breathe too hard touch too hard nothing too anything; there's warmth pulsing out of your fingertip, unhindered as it springs from your heart to the sharp edge of your nail, and if she likes it she'll go sproingy sproingy against the dewdrops; she'll shiver in the wind, the cold will recoil out beyond the stars as night falls quiet—shhhhh—shhhhh—in the morning she'll be bigger.

Under the trees it's laughing at you, at me, that's a song, and the vines grow a foot a day that's half an inch per hour that's one-twentieth of an inch per minute I could go on forever but if you arrive right at sunset, wade through the ugliness just around dusk when the orange rays pierce everything and you can see the cells, feel the rhizomes speeding beneath your feet ready to go, the soil is alive with poison, it's bleeding green.

How about the pruned stems. When it grows up to the road and they prune the ends off. Who cries for the pruned ends? When the cars drive over it. When the animals eat the leaves. When you wipe up the mowed guts from the tarmac.

. . .

When I was little I saw the flowers on it. They were purple, they were pretty. I was six years old. Can we plant some of that stuff in our yard? I asked. My mother shrieked. Are you crazy? she said. It would kill us all. At the plant nursery a few weeks later I asked her again; she was buying pyracantha bushes for the backyard. I said, What was that stuff with the purple flowers called?

Kudzu.

Can we plant some of that in our yard?

The man behind the counter overheard us. Where do you live, son? he said. Cause if you live in my neighborhood, I'm movin out.

He laughed, and my mother laughed. Mom, I said, answer my question.

She wrote silently in her checkbook.

When I was nine, about the same time as the silo was out in the lake, I confused kudzu with poison ivy. There was a nightmare where I was stuck in the middle of a never-ending field of it. The rash was going to be terrible; I was crying but no one could hear me. A few weeks later when my cousin and I were in the woods near my aunt's house we found a hillside completely bare except for a network of leafless, tangled strands. We walked straight through it and struggled to keep the stringy limbs from catching on our shoes and tripping us. When we got back to the house we asked my aunt what it was. Kudzu, she said. It loses its leaves in winter. I shivered in horror; it seemed like such a nightmare for us to have been walking through it.

When I told Bonnie about it she laughed at me. We'll see who laughs last.

Bonnie laughed at me a lot. She laughed when I was fat and then she laughed when she thought I was too thin.

You just can't find a happy medium, she said. You have to do everything all extreme like. And then she laughed. My stomach growled. Why don't you just eat? she said.

Cause it feels better this way.

Then why do you come here? she said.

You have to quit eating; that's how you feel it. First it's your stomach and your bowels. You get thinner and you feel your liver, spleen, rib cage and your lungs against your skin. Every little heartbeat kerclump back and forth in tune with your breathing, you can match it up, seven heartbeats for every breath is what to shoot for: ten full breaths per minute at pulse seventy. You have to line it up and once it's there you can't let go, you have to focus, you gotta get where it works even when you quit thinking about it. Where you go to sleep for six hours, wake up to a pulse aligned with the quaking of your lungs, breathe deeply and spit out the asthmacoated dustmites and the mold. You have to keep track or it doesn't work anymore. Breathe faster during a rush of epinephrine. How else are you going to feel good. How else are you going to breathe.

Eating dulls your mind.

Seven heartbeats for every breath. You feel healthy, that's what you feel, and it's like a kudzu vine pulsing ever outward, a foot a day that's half an inch per hour, it's crawling for your throat, constant rate constant time, a shining clockwork machine, cocksure and ready for the world.

They've got a kudzu club that has kudzu festivals every year and they give out the kudzu crown to the kudzu king and kudzu queen. Guys dress up in nothin but kudzu and drink kudzu tea and eat kudzu pie. They got a kudzu haiku contest well I don't really get into that shit.

Ain't it poisonous?

You'd think so.

What else do they do?

I don't know. That's the only part I can recollect.

If you're wondering who was talking just then, and who the person was talking to, it was me talking to myself. Don't react hypocritically; you do it too, as do all God's creatures. Pardon the hokey downhome speech patterns in my little conversation. That's just my imagination getting the best of me.

Poisonous. You'd think so. I want to see a science-fiction movie where kudzu takes over—postapocalyptic, Stone Age, writhing on the ground with a whiteknuckled grip on the goddamn thing take *that,* I'll eradicate you or die trying, the vines grow, men lie dead on the ground, there is an unspoken theme, the vines grow, giant kudzu leaves are looming above them, the music plays, the blood, the kiss, the end. Films have used kudzu before but they never do it right. I can remember when and where it has been done and it's good sometimes but it's never exactly right.

Here are descriptions of books, songs, films, porn flicks, paintings. Their central theme is kudzu. Some of them are not solely about kudzu but merely contain occurrences or overtones of kudzu. I won't tell you their identity although you may recognize a few of them.

1. A pamphlet promotes the proper method to grow kudzu. It is meant as a parody. The author advocates the use of motor oil as a lubricant for the swiftly growing kudzu leaves; she also suggests planting the vines in concrete. Her irreverent tone is misguided and somewhat offensive.

2. A nature documentarist documents the growth and spread of kudzu in the southeast. He wades through a meter-deep sea of it, gesticulating up at the drowning trees. Kudzu is choking them to death. The shape of the kudzu mounds is overtly phallic. The documentary clearly tries to present kudzu within a sexual context.

3. This is an obscure recording of a bluegrass song. Two old men are singing. Is little Margaret in her room / Or is she in the hall? / Little Margaret's in her cold cold coffin / With her face turned toward the wall. There is a fiddle solo and then the singer improvises additional lyrics. Kudzu shoots grow up around little Margaret and suffocate her. They grow into her nose and out her mouth. They part her long yellow hair.

It makes me hungry to talk about this but I can't eat again today; I ate this morning. Eating dulls your mind. You feel more as you get thinner. Muscle tissue as it regrows, bones as they absorb calcium, toenails as they lengthen. My brain is still just one big blob. I can't differentiate yet. Another few pounds. How do you lose weight from your scalp?

You know, when I lived up in Philly they didn't even know what it was.

What what was?

Kudzu.

Whatever.

I'm serious. I told people about it and they just stared back at me.

No shit. I'll be a son of a bitch.

The wind is picking up. I'm still in the car, driving to Bonnie's house, her little country cottage that looks so cute and cozy in the trees, the wood that looks so naked with nothing to cover it up. There's no green anywhere on her house except for the green plastic of the hummingbird feeders. Hummingbird: That was her pet name, that was what she liked, that was what I called her. The feeders were full of the nasty red nectar shit. Hummingbirds don't like kudzu. That's what I've heard. Oh my little hummingbird. Don't say a word.

There are thirteen places I know in the county where the kudzu is bigger than an acre I mean a cubic acre because you can't just use a square acre to measure something like kudzu: Height is majesty. There are thirteen places distinct like separate species separate leaves, they creep alone, they're not connected underground. The plants I'm planting come from all thirteen different sites. What a hybrid this will be.

Samples Road. The vines are tight and stringy, tall, I think the trees are poplars, sunny, the vines are stretched out, muscular, straining themselves, sore, feigning pain and torture. No houses or barns beneath it, I don't think. Not so tangled, raw, throaty, the trees are bones and the bones are tall, the bones are under there somewhere, you never see the bones. The sheet of big gaping green leaves covering the ground is thick and impenetrable, a membrane, and when the wind blows it ripples like a lake beset by storm. There's water under there. There are waves and beasts and depths.

Hughes Loop Road. This is a place that doesn't have any kudzu but it would be so beautiful if kudzu were growing there. I saw it one day on my way home from deer hunting. It was on the left and I slammed on the brakes, backed up, turned down the gravel driveway; against the ribbon of blue mountains on the horizon loomed a ten-foot-high heap of McDonald's signs, red and yellow, the big arches. Hundreds of them, whole signs, half signs, signs broken and in pieces on the ground. Billions and billions served. Some of them were older and said 20 billion, 6 billion, all the billions you can imagine. The arches were too tall to fit in the car. I wanted one but they were immovable. There was a storm coming, and I watched the timid protuberance of cloudlimbs as they stretched their tendons toward me over the backbone of the mountains. The signpile was set back in the trees; I looked around in stealth, wondering if I was being watched. There was no kudzu. Kudzu could bind these all to the ground. Thick kudzu fetters. I can plant them. Soon if I want to. Now or tomorrow or anytime for the rest of my goddamn life.

This is turning into another list. I wasn't finished with the previous list, though; let me continue.

4. There is a grove of dead walnut trees. Kudzu grows unchecked. It droops from the tree branches like formations of solid rock. Two black children stand beneath a tree looking up at the kudzu; one of them is holding an apple. They are praying to the kudzu, although they show no outward signs of it.

5. Men return to earth from a spaceship journey. Due to time distortion they arrive back a century later than they expect; meanwhile, a fluoridelike chemical in the water has made the entire human race sterile. There are some people left but they have reverted to an animal state. Cities are overgrown. There is no culture; only nature. The space travelers walk through the Channel tunnel to England, where kudzu is known as Japanese weed, a fact which goes unmentioned in the book.

6. A sinister man with red hair develops a virus that will wipe out every human on the planet. He buys his plane ticket; he will travel to a lot of different countries. Airport policemen shoot the only man who knows about the plan. Classical music plays, and the glass vials rattle ominously; this is the end soon. There is no literal kudzu but the allusion is obvious. The man's plot will work, the music will play, the vines will grow.

Imagine if you could graft kudzu onto your hair and beard. They would reach the ground in a week.

You wouldn't want that.

Yes I would.

Think about it, dumbass. Hair is dead skin cells. If it were a plant it would be alive; think about how it would hurt to cut it.

It would be an incredible experience.

Take your shoes off; leave them in the car. The best part is soil between your toes; feel it squish and squoosh beneath your muddy feet, it's cold, it's wet. Trowel in hand: This isn't just throwitontheGroundandrun, we're not going to cut any corners. The little saplings are lined up in a cardboard box lid, count them it's eighty-three, they're tangling together and dancing, throwing their stems to the wind. You want to point them toward the lonely gravel road, the house, the barn, the porch, the tractor, the spiderweb clothesline, it's all going to disappear. Bonnie mows her grass every two weeks, that's eighty-three fourteen-foot-long vines, that's 1,162 feet. It's gonna be green, it's gonna be growing forever. Just you try and mow it all down, you lying dime-store whore.

I picked out the digging sites ahead of time; I know her yard like the back of my hand. You have to think about the terrain, all the little curves, is it a hill or a valley or a ditch, is the slope rising falling waxing waning, how thick is the grass? I had them numbered in my mind. I went around the yard counterclockwise, starting on the northwest side by the driveway, opposite the mountain view. The tip of the trowel was sharp. Gonna gouge this blade into the ground like it's never seen, gonna plow it up good hard tight, it's gonna be my baby for a while.

The grass is thick in her yard; she uses fertilizer. There are a lot of dandelions and clovers and wild violets. I threw the flowers through the air with their roots still attached; the dangling dirt added enough weight to launch them all the way to the trees. There were eighty-three vines. What can be said about the act of planting them? What can be said about climactic moments at all? I don't want to undermine this image.

The rain pissed down harder and harder. I can't say it pissed down, though, because piss would have been a lot warmer, and I wouldn't have shivered so much. Sometimes the moon shone through the thick clouds. That's not very important at all; forget I said it. The worms came out and rolled around on top of the dirt; there were hundreds of them; they writhed around in ecstasy as if taking part in an orgy. When I saw them I cut them in half with the trowel. There were two worms side by side and I cut them both in two and I grafted the front of the first one onto the back of the other, but they didn't stick together. Maybe I didn't cut them evenly. They didn't make any noise. I flung them into the trees to get them away from the kudzu.

When I was planting plant number forty I went back to look at plant number one; growth was visible already, and it made me smile.

This is what I see. Six months from now in the dead of winter when it's drizzling and windy and cold, when the sky is darkly gray at noon, I walk up the driveway through the trees into the square clearing. Instead of a yard I see a kudzu-covered plain; instead of a house I see a house-shaped mound of kudzu. Also laid out before me like a frozen pastoral painting are a car-shaped pile of kudzu, a kudzu nest shaped much like a tractor and three tree-shaped kudzu pillars. Bonnie wades out onto her porch, kneedeep, sees me standing in the distance and waves me closer; as I scythe through the jumbled vines my heart lifts at the sight of her isolation. I arrive; we embrace; she is very sorry, she says, for all the bad things she has done. The kudzu is nice, she says; it creates a strong shield against the outside. She won't fight it anymore. Light no longer streams through the windows, she says; the glasspanes are cold black squares set into the wall of each room and they're very nice and cold and she isn't distracted by the view of the mountains anymore. The leaves keep rainwater from beating on the tin roof so loudly.

I listened to my Walkman as I worked. It's not until the roots start to take hold that you need to be able to hear them growing. I listened to the radio but it started to piss me off; it was all a bunch of love songs. There are too many love songs; can't anybody sing about anything else? Murder death disease, adrenaline, your heart beating fast while ants crawl all over your body, impalings, scalpings, teeth being pulled, songs about people drowning. Songs where everyone's scared and they're all down there in the kudzu somewhere crawl around crawl round & find em honey, the vines are grinding them into mortar, they know where to hit you, your muscles are flexing in the night. I feel aware; I don't want it to stop. I'm munching on a kudzu leaf; it's the first thing I've eaten in twelve hours. It speeds you up, there's a definite strength. We all get off on this, don't we.

I put a tape in. The music got slower as the batteries died down. The headphones made my ears ache; they felt like they were bleeding, and I pictured the blood dripping down onto the kudzu. I have red-green color blindness and it all would have blended into one image. People always ask me if red and green look gray; well no, you fucking morons, it doesn't look gray. The blood is the kudzu is red is green but none of it looks gray for God's sake. When the light shines on it there's a little tinge of everything; maybe it's a color you people can't even detect; maybe that's what is whispering to me. The blood drips down rips a gaping hole in the leaves it's roaring, ultraviolet, humming in the buggy, muddled dark. I left the earphones on; I was haunted by the sensation of their foam as it became soaked with blood, but when I felt them with my fingers they were dry.

Here is a song I want to share with you. It is not a love song. I have heard it more times than I can count. It has violins and thick dark guitars and a deep green-black bassline and I was listening to it as I planted the vines and when it plays water flows through it like an underground river through a cave. I feel the warmth of my body as I listen; I feel the oversoul of my mind shackled in darkness in a falling forest; at the hallelujah when the trees laugh two doors float open and through the speakers flood endless weights of kudzu; it grows up toward the sky and down to earth, on and around trees and upward through the miry clay; the land is wild and feral where the kudzu takes root; all stars disappear into the darkness as it drums its way earthward and the tin drums echo against the vulture leaves that stream out of the soil to light the world. The rain is dirty. Seven musical instruments weave out spidered strands of the benighted vine. I shut my eyes, and the song builds, and blinding kudzu creeps across my eyelids.

Her house is quiet. I think about what will happen when she wakes up in the morning, how many days till she notices it; I think about the cold. It's her yard yes but this is about me; I want you to be interested in me. I am rubbing my fingers against my warm cheekbone; it feels extraordinarily good; do you wonder why? I can feel my breathing as if my lungs are a mace being cranked outward; as I become more aware of them I breathe more slowly, and it makes my pulse beat more slowly, and that is good. If it approaches even sixty it feels like my heart is racing wildly; my eyes swirl and I can feel that too; they feel lusty and I shut them, remind them that it is dark truly dark this is not the time to swirl. There's a tickle on the cheek of my ass: I smile and imagine that the kudzu I have planted behind me has grown three feet already and wedged itself beneath me; it's growing still, poking itself into my flesh, it's saying hurry, hurry. When you lie upon a bed of kudzu it feels like levitation, like no surface is beneath you; your weight is an airborne seed's as it germinates in the summery moisture, as it floats across currents of swiftly channeled air. You can sleep on it; it's like a waterbed. When the kudzu takes over we can sleep at all points in space. The ground is rocky now but in three weeks we'll be sleeping everywhere in the yard, hitting the ground nodding off instantly and without knowledge of mass or form or being, passengers on a weightless carpet dreaming, the realms of night exposed in shining color.

The batteries die down further; I take the headphones off. The silence is screaming back at me and my ears burn and there's the barred owl screeching painfully upon the naked tree above me, writhing in agony, wishing to God it had some kudzu to perch upon. There have been many times when I have felt this way; it's good to feel it because it reminds me of those past times; I remember them. When I'm not thinking about something I don't remember it. It's that way with nearly everything, the remembering, the metallic glint upon your tongue as you canter down the tracks of your days; am I making sense? I remember going down the country open alleys and they all looked the same, the roads, and as you're riding down them if you just close your eyes you can feel the asters against your face, carried in the air like they smell like they taste, in the closedwindowed backseat of the car but it all feels the same. Here is a memory: There was a house somewhere off Thompson Bridge Road with a field of flowers and Mama asked the woman what they were and they were okra and she showed us and I stepped in a steaming pile of rooster shit, and the flowers were pretty, and they looked like kudzu flowers but not as nice, and they don't grow as fast, and you can boil or fry their fruit but no one eats the leaves raw cold and brittle. You know what I mean. You can't roll naked in their majesty; you can't crush their leaves with a pestle and snort them so they get to your brain faster. The vines aren't long enough to wrap around yourself, the fields aren't crowded, their cold knots aren't complete.

Do you want to count along with me? Here's number sixty-seven. The trowel penetrates the soil and roly-polys hop out and unroll. I'm not going to slice them with the trowel, I'm not, really I'm not, oh shit I lied sswisshh they're bleeding. I can't see the blood though because I'm color-blind, remember? I nestle the rootsac into the ground gingerly nudging it into place; I'm being very careful as I tuck them in. I've been told I would make a good father. I'm pressing the unearthed soil back in around it, I'm smoothing it out, I'm spitting on it because there's no water. You can scoff at this but the effect is psychosomatic, like talking to a baby. It just needs to hear you speak; it wants to know you care. Spruce up the leaves with your fingers. The point has been plotted. Moving on: Number sixty-eight is right over here by the japonica bush.

I know what you're thinking. Connect the dots. It's a big picture of something. Isn't it. Well, in two weeks you're not gonna be able to tell where the points were. So that would be a big fucking stupid waste of time, now wouldn't it?

It makes a U around her house though. So it's kind of shaped like a silo.

There wasn't any food when I was stuck on the silo. It seemed such a long time not to eat; it seemed like such an injustice. Why isn't somebody finding me and giving me food? That's what you're supposed to do. I'm not some crack baby in the ghetto; I shouldn't be here; my stomach isn't supposed to growl. I couldn't swim any farther; I wasn't a strong swimmer. The water went up and down; I never knew the lakes had tides too. I started to get weak from not eating. This isn't supposed to happen, I thought. It actually felt painful then not to eat. The bones pressed out of my rib cage. My clothes were wet when I climbed up to the top so I took them off; when they dried the wind blew them off into the water. I looked down at my naked chest. Sometimes my nipples were flat against my skin and sometimes they pointed out like angry pimples. I didn't know if they were supposed to do that. Maybe it was because I hadn't eaten. I saw fish swimming around in the water. Algae floated by, and I smelled dead things beneath me. The closest land was an island of treetops in the middle of the lake; it was to my north, and the North Star rose above it after sunset. I stared at the trees because what else was there to stare at. Something was in the branches. It wasn't honeysuckle; it wasn't snakes; it wasn't alive. Brown desiccated strands of dead plant matter were marooned out in the lake in the trees turning and squirming until the roots were too waterlogged to bear. It wasn't moving; it wasn't blowing in the wind. Maybe it was a vine, I thought. Maybe it's that stuff with the flowers. Grow across the gulf of stormy water, reach for my face and with canid slobber lick me straight into your arms. It's not dead it's just bare for the winter. It's not winter though. What month is it? Where am I? My cheeks burned with fever. I stared weakly at the dead brown vines all night; naked atop the metal island phallus I sat shivering, blind in the aquatic wind and wondering if I would drown, and an airy swarm of fireflies floated palely above the distant spit of land.

I'm digging hole number seventy-one. That's the year I was born. As I rip into the dirt it occurs to me that I've come to my part of the century. I'm bound by birth to plant seventy-one. It is the plant whose growth I will feel in my veins, in the bubbles of my blood. We're partners. All these numbers. What year was Bonnie born? What does all this have to do with her? I can't remember the date of her birth. I never really knew her that well. Her face always looked so pretty in that little cafeteria uniform. I always loved it when she said, Lemme fill that up again for you, hon. She went and got the pot and she filled me up, and she filled me up again, and her hair went crooked but I never let on I knew it was a wig. She told me her birthday. I don't remember the year, but she was older than me, and I'm already on plant seventy-two. Seventy-two was the year I said my first word: black. I said it a lot, because there were a lot of black things to name and that was how I named them. Plant number seventy-two will have leaves with a tint of black. There are so many numbers. As I dig I try to figure out all the con-nections, all the meanings, all the things that are going to come together because I'm doing this.

You might think something would have happened by the time someone finally rescued me but nothing had happened. Mama was cooking pork chops and flour biscuits. The baby was cry-ing. I got whipped with a hickory switch. There, that one's for not having any brains, and that one's for keeping me worried so long, and that one's for just being so goddamn dumb, goddammit, you're so fucking stupid sometimes. Get me that box of Kleenex, she said, laying the switch down on the porch. The bark of hickories is rough and scaly. The branches tend to be thick and heavy, painful when they strike you, unlike those of a kudzu vine, which can grow larger than a blue whale but still fall softly and gently against your skin.

She said I was never the same after that but I couldn't say because there's not much I remember from before it. I remember everything that happened afterward, all the dreams where I sat atop the silo. The water was a giant whirlpool sucking itself away and below me in all directions stretched a deep plantless canyon. I surveyed the horizon slowly. The silo was a hundred feet high as my toes dangled over the edge and it was slippery, my heart stopped, I fell into the waterless pit; my bones crashed upon the rocks that lay atop a thousand kudzu roots.

7. A family lives in a house in a mountain holler overtaken with gargantuan mounds of kudzu. The little girl wears red ribbons in her hair. The mother dies, and the father buries her in the yard. Kudzu grows up through her grave and curls around the headstone. Rats live out in the kudzu and make a lot of noise at night. The father leans the girl against the porch railing and sodomizes her; as she suffers through it she glances up with teary eyes at the soaring shoots of kudzu that have loomed above her every day of her life.

8. A slender teenage boy is kept prisoner by a motorcycle gang in a cabin in the forest. Lashmarks scar his torso. He says he's hungry; this is in Spanish with English subtitles. He hasn't eaten in four days. Two of the men bring some kudzu branches in from outside; they untie the boy's left hand and he munches on them savagely, salivating. The men watch in excitement.

9. Two lesbians are having sex in the woods. Their clothes are hanging on the branch of a kudzu-covered tree. The redhead rips a long, vigorous strand of kudzu out of

the ground. She folds it up against itself several times and uses it as a dildo to screw the brunette.

10. A man is stuck out in the wilderness. Rain is falling. He squats down between two trees to take a shit. He has no toilet paper, so he wipes his ass with freshly plucked kudzu leaves.

I never finished the list of places. Let's see. Trigonia. A bend in the road. You see a field of damp, dark green that reaches down into a deep trough in the landscape. One dead tree remains and its one dead branch, rotten, knobby and black and reaching eastward, stabbing at the hillside. It's going to crawl all the way to the lake and it will creep across the water's surface to the silo islands; it's going to crawl inside them and eat the hoarded grain. Sometimes if the wind stops you can hear the plants climbing up the hill. Close your eyes it's a beautiful sound aaahhhhh listen there's nothing else. The leaves are leering at you mooning grins that see nothing and there's a chimney sticking up, a television antenna. The house is down there somewhere, groaning in the dirt, crumbling and constricted. Vines thrash through the bricks like slimy vipers, coiling around each other in the dark; they're filling up the empty rooms. The dust will go away.

You know two of my uncles worked in Oak Ridge making the bomb. They helped make it work, the kudzu. If there had been a ground war with Japan there might never have been a chance to bring the kudzu over here at all.

Downtown. A hundred years from now—crash—that's the sound of a thousand bricks crumbling into oblivion all at once. The kudzu atop them will droop but it won't fall all the way. It can stand on its own. Strong beautiful fronds dangling up dangling down, suspended in air, hanging from nothing, hanging from streetlights that have fallen, from the covered walkways that have long since collapsed. Dark and vivid green. Strong pointy leaves. Shining in the sun.

I would keep telling you about this but somebody needs my

attention out there in the yard, somebody's growing toward the structures of the night, somebody's gonna gnaw right into the surface of your skin, blow right through you, soar on toward the light. It's midnight but yes there is brightness. I can feel the neurons pulsing in my skull. That is enough. I would keep telling you about this but a hundred little vines are free to fly. Blood you see is pressing against my fingernails, and dirt, and the churning water membranes of the flora. They'll grow on their own but I like to feel useful. This land will all be underwater someday soon. One last four-leaf clover will be eaten by aphids and it will all be wiped away. Not real water of course but it's easy to picture it that way, deep green like the distant foamy sea, broiling in stormy growth, waving in the wind like pirate sails and whitecapped when the starling-herd shits on the leaves.

Scintilla

The waves are talking. Kneel down they're horsemen in the sand, little white triangles plowing across the distance. Their crests, their troughs, their cries. Anthony took me straight to Tybee from the bus station. We'll go straight out to the beach lookin for honey, he says. Honey's everywhere on a Sunday. Oh but you're not into that. He laughs.

Marsh grass waves in the wind.

We'll work on our tans then, he says. Smile up at the sun gods.

This is the first time in three years I've seen him. Show me a big smile man. He's coy around me as always, even I who am the progenitor of his flight, his existence at all in the visible world. When I look at him he looks away.

My eyes catch the sun and I sneeze. Three times in a row. This is because my eyes are blue, he says. His hazel-browns bring no such eruptions. If they were blue, oh boy, I might have broken the silence long ago, tackled him and been the hero before he hardened into his age, but no, it still exists to be had.

He's happy to see me but shy, subdued. I don't think he has many friends here. I try to explain to him why I came, why now and not before. About David and the—

Stop it, he breaks in.

Pardon?

Just try to remember I don't want to hear about any of that disgusting shit.

Adamant but without intended malice. He speaks in a flat

cockstrut of a voice that wavers every dozen words or so. As if he believes everything he says is right but wants you to think it's funny that he thinks so. I begin again. David was the one who—

No, I mean it, he interrupts. Just shut the fuck up.

Something is hanging out of the pocket of my backpack in the sand beside me. Flapping in the wind. It's the letter I got from Amanda the day I left. I reread it:

> Dear Ryan,
> How are you? I am writing all by myself. The Knoxville zoo does not have a white tiger. I want to see a white tiger. The Tampa zoo has a white tiger there the Oklahoma City zoo has one too. Do you think we could go to the Tampa zoo when you come home from school. It is 679 miles to there. I looked on a map at school. Also Disney world is there and Busch Gardens and Universal Studio. It has some rides I want to ride. I don't want to go upsidedown but if you ride the upsidedown ones I'll wait for you while you ride them. I hope you come home soon. The hamsters are in your room now.
> Love, Amanda.

I look up at the birds above me. An egret trots down the beach. Yellow in the light. How come you never see egrets in the sky? They've got wings, they fly don't they, they're birds.

Anthony says something about the circles under my eyes. Says I look like a junkie.

I'm just tired out from the bus, I say.

The bus. The fucking bus. You're really slumming it up lately.

What's that supposed to mean?

I'd never stoop to taking a Greyhound.

That's silly.

No matter how much you paid me.

That's because you're a snob.

There's something to be said for snobbery. You used to know

something about it yourself. Still can't believe you sold that MX-6.

Only way I would have had money to move.

What happened to that clunker you told me you bought last year? Why didn't you just drive that piece of shit down here?

His voice wavers like a prepubescent boy's. Full of himself: He's riding a wave, speech decibels rising, pissing me off. He bitches about cars every chance he gets.

It broke down, I say.

Well, he says, go figure. That oughta teach you a damn lesson. His car is a Cobra with tinted windows. Mine is a gray flaking shell of an '81 Datsun dumped cold at a corner on Rivington.

Everything gray. Got rivved up all gray dirty, sooty, black. It's dark when no home is your city. Anthony is talking again but I ignore it; his words are not much louder than the rush of incessant waves, than the honking seagulls or the scouring wind. The same wind down here as back home but it's warmer here, not so bad, you don't feel it. He's talking about the car. Wants to know how much it cost me. Four hundred bucks, I tell him, that's what I paid, four hundred and a few services he won't want to know about. Now the estimate to fix it is eight hundred, master cylinders and loose transmission mounts and brake pads. Eight hundred: a month's rent in my ghetto apartment, one month of alive in the Vault. I can't afford it. The car leaves a square unsnowed upon the road, hawks its oil and air into the sewers.

We eat lunch at Fannie's on the beach, gouda cheese pizza and six-dollar frozen drinks. When we go back outside the tide is fully out. With towels from the car we walk to the beach. I lie in the sand and wonder whether to be sorry I made the trip down here. The weather feels good. Everybody back north always says it's so nice down here. Savannah. Isn't there a language where that is a phrase, sa va something something, perhaps Portuguese, sa va na na na, or maybe it's just a song I've heard.

· · ·

It's been thirty-six hours since I slept. The heavy, oliveskinned woman next to me on the bus snored from Newark to Rocky Mount. I could tell from the moment she stepped on the bus she'd sit next to me.

I'm from Bethlehem, she said to me when she boarded.

Bethlehem, Pennsylvania? I asked, but no, the accent was foreign, the desert steam and scansion of the Middle East, raspy and sweating.

No, she said, Bethlehem the birthplace of our Lord Jesus Christ. Slow and self-righteous, a faint glaze of awe in her eyes. The bus moved slowly through the snow. Thirty miles an hour all through New Jersey. Tiny little state; how the hell can it take this long. Bethlehem woman's soda from McDonald's rested loosely between her legs, sweating through the wax paper of the cup. She fell asleep. I watched the drink edge closer to the dropoff, vibrating with the bus and with her breathing, here it comes here it comes. Crash: It was on the floor, rolling around. The lid was on; it didn't spill immediately. I nudged her, nudged her again, and she finally roused.

Huh?

Your Coke. I pointed to the floor.

Oh no, she said. Oh no.

Well, just pick it up.

She moaned and put her face in her hands. Oh no. Beneath the pulmonary mass of black hair her head shook back and forth, rocking like a baby, forward and back.

Ma'am, just pick it up so it won't spill on anything else.

She raised up, hands still covering her face, barely audible whines peeping from between her fingers. So clumsy, she moaned. So clumsy.

Ma'am?

Her face was buried and invisible and I heard a stifled sob. So clumsy.

My seat alone stayed illuminated. I donned my headphones and read Amanda's letter for the first time. Everyone else had gone to sleep. Am I keeping you people awake? I wondered. I can't sleep sitting up. I wished I'd remembered to buy Nytol. A few beers and two Nytols and then I can sleep on a bus. I stared out the window at Baltimore, Washington, Richmond.

Sunset on the beach. The temperature is dropping, and my bare chest shivers in the wind. I go to the car to get warmer clothes, and Anthony follows me. With towel and drink in hand he approaches the parking lot and the phone, handsome in his bathing suit. Soft olive skin. Don't look at him too close. It makes him nervous, and he yells about it sometimes, but he won't yell at me in public because he hates for people to hear him.

Gotta call home, I tell him. Meet you back on the beach.

I tell my parents I've arrived in Savannah safely. They act like I never told them I was coming in the first place. Is there an ulterior motive for this, I wonder, or can you really forget so easily, or did you never listen in the first place?

Ryan, Mom says, you waste so much good money going to all these places.

Don't list the places, I'm thinking, but I know she will. Her litany begins.

Just last month you were in Boston, and there was the time you flew out to San Francisco, and the time you drove to Chicago with that man you live with.

I don't live with him anymore.

Whatever, she says, continuing. And all those places up in Canada. The waterfall. What's it called? I close my eyes and shake my head and listen. I can feel Amanda's distress building up. Shut up Mom just talk about it some other time.

And Mexico last New Year's and someplace else I'd never even heard of and—

How come I never get to go anywhere? Amanda asks quietly, speaking aloud, not whining but straight and matter-of-fact.

You hush.

Ryan gets to go all these places and you won't even take me to Pigeon Forge.

That's not true.

But I never go anywhere.

You go to school every day.

That's not what I mean.

You get to go to West Town Mall.

That's different, she says.

You're being ungrateful.

What is it you want me to be grateful for? Amanda snaps back, trying hard to have leverage in the argument. Probably hasn't been out of the house for a week except to go to school.

I remember what it felt like. The tiny six-bedroom rancher. Not so bad on school days but on a weekend what do you do. Pace back and forth along the hall. Go play with the other kids in the neighborhood, Mom always said. Didn't know it was such a stab in the back. I couldn't explain it to her. I want to tell Amanda this. How it gets better.

Well, when Ryan was your age, Mom says, he never got to go anywhere either.

I listen to their bickering. The television schedule, which one of them washed the dishes last night, who was supposed to buy the buttermilk at Winn-Dixie. I rest the phone on my shoulder and watch the ocean waves lapping and the water all of it ten degrees too cold to swim.

Amanda, you get off the phone and go brush your teeth.

I just brushed them.

Well, that didn't take long enough. You go brush them again.

How would you know whether it was long enough?

I interrupt her: Mom, I say, this call's costing a dollar a minute.

Well, I think whether or not Amanda gets her teeth clean is a little bit more important than that.

Ryan, when are you gonna come home? Amanda asks me.

I don't know, I begin. Maybe in—

I told you to brush your teeth, Mom yells. Spitting every word out like a curse.

Swarms of seagulls hang in the air above me, festering in single spots, sand falling from their dirty feathers. The sunset's mirror forms above the ocean. I lay the phone upon the metal surface of the booth and stoop down to the sandy road, soon kneeling, bringing my eyes low to see if at earth level the horizon will touch a higher line of sky.

The voices still are loud enough to hear.

I told you I already bought the damn green beans for crying out loud.

But they're not the right brand. I can't use Del Monte beans. They don't taste right.

These are Luck's.

Well, I can't use those either.

I pick the phone back up. I'd better get going, I say.

We shuffle awkwardly toward a good-bye.

On the beach again Anthony asks me about the conversation. What did you talk about? he asks. I tell him about Amanda, how she's depressed.

How old is she now?

Thirteen.

Got knocked up yet?

Don't talk about her like that, you piece of shit. He laughs aloud, louder than he needs to. It's an hour until he has to be at work; we drive back to his house over the tall bridges and the thin tidal islands.

Eight o'clock. Anthony drops me off at his house before he goes to work, but I leave again after a few minutes. In the hot night air I take Habersham to Oglethorpe, walk past the cemetery, turn north toward the nightlife. The music is loud on Congress Street. I go inside the Velvet Elvis for a beer, a single pint of Bud. After a few minutes the guys next to me get up to leave. They think the girl behind the bar is sexy, they've been flirting with her. Let's see what they've left me. They're out the door and I lean left to look. Jackpot. Between two wrinkled dollar bills is a dimebag of coke. This is her present for being sexy. I put it in my pocket. Maybe they meant it for me anyway. Didn't they notice I was sexy too.

The waitress comes to collect her tip, skeptical as she approaches, eyeing it, is that just two fucking dollars? Count em yourself, lady. One two. Fucking bastards, she's thinking.

Looks like those fellows shortchanged you a little there, I say.

Damn right they did.

They been in here long?

Just all fuckin night, that's all. Just tryin to get down my pants all fuckin night. Two dollars for all that shit.

If you'd like, ma'am, I'll go beat em all up for you.

She grins.

Just give me another quick shot first for strength.

She laughs. Gap between her teeth. You're cute, she says.

I try.

I move down the street to Savannah Blues. I go to the downstairs bar, play tabletop Ms. Pac-Man. The room's pretty full. Soft folk music playing. There's a woman swinging her arms back and forth, mouthing the words of the music. The way you move is right in time. The way you move is right in time. She's sneaking glances at me, she sees me looking back at her, she smiles as if beckoning me to dance. I put another quarter in the game.

They play the whole album. She's mouthing the asks and the secrets and damn if it's not every single word she knows, dancing oh so slow, when the songs end she goes into slo-mo, sitting the gracefullest down in her chair of all the drunks around.

My mother's words echo in my mind. When Ryan was your age he didn't get to go anywhere either. Half true. I want to tell Amanda how it gets better. How everything she says I remember saying myself, everything she does I remember doing. The same favorite color, pink, the same number, seven.

Every little misconception, too many to name. And I do. Like twins born ten years apart. But my parents were in their forties. Hers are nearly sixty.

I save Anthony a line for when he gets home but he won't do it. Sneers at it. I'm not the fucking moron you think I am, he says.

Okay. More for me.

We don't talk to each other. Not that there's nothing to say but it just doesn't feel right to say it. I've known him since I was twelve. Even on the phone we don't really talk. I can't remember whether we used to talk more when we were younger. It's not even a comfortable silence. We just stare at each other.

I can't believe you walked home alone at this time of night, he says. Such a faggy little voice he's got. Cmon figure it out, Anthony. Get your head out of your ass.

This neighborhood's fine, I tell him.

So you can just waltz in from the murder capital of the world and figure the whole city out in one night.

Honestly. It couldn't be any safer.

Oh yeah? he challenges me. Well, all but three of my female friends have been raped. Raising his voice as if he's bragging. Just let me come and pick you up in my car next time.

I didn't know your phone number.

I gave it to you earlier, he sighed. Don't tell me you've already forgotten.

We drift out to the back porch. It's hot and muggy, the neighbors are drinking on their porches too. We talk about boats. Anthony went all the way to Daufuskie Island last week. He tells me about the new supplies he bought earlier this spring. Thousands of dollars' worth. It's where all his money goes. How else can two months' salary last a lifetime? he says. Assuming there's no one else to spend it on.

He has a new sail for his catamaran. What was wrong with the old one? I ask.

It had that big pink stripe down the middle.

Pink was my favorite color when I was a kid, I say.

That's because you were a little pansy.

I know.

He drifts back into his memories about boating. Reminiscing about the water still keeps him in a good mood. The only thing. Remember that summer we went out on the lake every damn day? he says. Caught so many fish I'm surprised we didn't sink the entire boat.

Yeah.

Went through the lock at Fort Loudoun Dam and you got all claustrophobic on me. Hyperventilating and all that shit.

Thought Lifestar was gonna have to fly right down into that big concrete pit and get you out.

Blades would've been too wide.

Then it's a good thing you snapped the fuck out of it.

Spanish moss blows around in the trees. You're always hearing about the Spanish moss. You wanna tell somebody what it's like to sit on the porch here, you just say hot, muggy, quiet and the moss blows around in the trees. But it doesn't even blow around that often. Air's too still. You just think it's blowing. Cause that's what it oughta do, you think, that's the way the world should work. It's hanging everywhere. There's some shouting in the distance, maybe from over in Crawford Square. Maybe from the cemetery. You can't really tell.

I spend three days like this. He works seven at night to three in the morning, we sit up till five or six, we sleep till two. While he's at work I walk around past all the old houses, the live oaks and the mansions. I wonder what this architectural style is called. Whether it has a name. Every day the sky is bright blue. Not a cloud in it. My grandmother used to call the sky heaven. It's cloudy in heaven. Heaven's looking a little gray.

Three days there. On the third night I tell him I'm leaving pretty soon.

But you just got here, he says.

Well, what's the point in my staying? I ask. We hardly talk to each other. You won't even, even, I begin, and I pause.

Won't even what?

Never mind. I didn't mean it that way anyway.

Won't even what? Sleep with you?

That's not what I was going to say.

Nine hundred miles down here to see me and you stay three days.

You don't seem to give a shit whether or not I stay.

Nine hundred miles. First time you've come here since I moved away from home.

Well, you might as well not have moved away for all the good it's done you.

You nagged me for years to move away.

Whatever. I pause. You want me to stay longer?

I hear there's a lot of cock to be had down in Jacksonville. Why don't you just hop on the next bus that's going south.

You're twenty-six, Anthony. You've never even been on a date. Why do you really think we always connected so well?

Why don't you just hop on the next bus that's going south?

Listen to me for once for Christ's sake.

Or north. I don't care.

The next morning the bar calls, asks him if he can work the day and night shift both. He'll get overtime pay. As he showers and dresses I lie awake silent on the floor and I smell the cologne, the aftershave, the omelet in the kitchen. I know he's being quiet to try not to wake me, thinking he'll duck out the door and when he gets home tonight I'll be gone gone gone. He leaves a window open in the kitchen. The breezy air seeps in and at nine in the morning the room already is hot, humid, sunny.

I don't have any money. I look around the house. Anthony has anticipated this. He has hidden all his cash away. I'm going to have to call home.

I stand by the phone for a minute to think about how I'm going to ask it. Talk about other things first, work it into the conversation how expensive everything is up there in the city, how fast the money goes. But there's nothing to talk about, nothing to work it in with, because we just talked three days ago. Ask about the weather. Say how it's still real nice down here. Ask about the cats.

I speak my name into the recording for the collect call. I hear my mother's voice accept the charges.

Hi, Mom.

Amanda ran away, she tells me.

What?

The night you called. She left a note.

I breathe into the silence.

I can read you the note.

Does it say where she's going?

No.

My mother tells me about the people they've talked to, the people at school, the things the police have said. Trying not to cry in front of me. I don't know why she wastes the energy to hide it. She talks and talks and I can process barely half of what she's saying. How they had call-waiting installed immediately in case she calls. How she took the tent with her. Finally she starts crying.

She's probably just camping out in the woods somewhere, I say, trying to reassure her.

There aren't any woods anymore, she sobs. It's all suburbs now.

There's woods if you go far enough. You just told me she took the tent. You know how she likes to camp.

That's not what the psychiatrist thinks.

What psychiatrist?

The one I took her to when you first moved away. Back when she wouldn't do anything I told her to do. He said it was because you were gone. He said that's what did it. That's what he said.

Whatever.

That's what he said, Ryan. I'm just repeating what he said. He's got a doctor's degree so I think he's qualified to talk about this.

I guess you think she's off trying to find me or something.

She sighs loudly. I swear to God, Ryan. You don't listen to anything I say.

What?

Listen to me.

I'm listening.

You've spent all your money, she says. Haven't you?

Mom, that's not what's important right now.

That's why you called, isn't it?

Mom.

Answer me.

Things are expensive.

No one told you to leave New York.

You know how I get when the weather's bad, Mom.

No one told you to go to New York in the first place, it was your decision and I don't want to hear you blaming anybody for it but yourself. Her voice breaks up as she speaks. It was your decision and it was Amanda's decision what she did and I just hope you both can live with the consequences.

Well, you can't really call it a decision when there's no other choice.

What the hell is that supposed to mean, Ryan?

I don't know.

That's right. You don't know. She pauses to swallow. You and her both. Always saying things you don't know what they mean.

I should come home.

I don't see what good it would do.

Well, there's not much I can do about the situation from here.

No, there certainly isn't.

I shower and get dressed, step out into the daylight. It's still a shock to my body to leave the house and encounter warm sunshine on the street. I toss my coat back indoors, relock the door and walk toward town.

Standing at a coffee-shop counter I'm pouring sugar in my cup. A big black man stands next to me. He picks up the paper, and it falls open to a two-page ad. He points at a picture, says to me, God-DAMN, that's uncanny, un-cann-NEE.

Huh?

That looks just like you, that shot right there, would ya lookit that now?

The photograph is of a two-year-old girl, red hair, baby face, baby skin, finger near the bridging of her nose.

That's crazy, the man says. You must feel just like you're lookin in a mirror.

I move out onto the street. I know the round sun shines, yellow splat the little drops come, I know it's the sunrays pushing up at my armhairs that buoy my muscles while I'm standing, it's why I'm standing, why I'm walking around at all, why I got the little paper map, the Historic Savannah map, it has Accommodations Dining Shopping Tours ATMs Real Estate Mortgage, plopped on the ground in the paths of the vitamin sun; the streets are crowded with women in straw hats and the hats have ribbons.

The sun makes me feel so good for a few minutes. What I'm thinking during those minutes is how in a few it'll go away, in a few minutes, and I'll think back, think how those were a pretty good few minutes, sorry for myself how they go away, and what I'm also thinking is how the sun is an elevator of moods and if it would just stay around, if I would stay in such a place, if this were where I was. How there are men in the Arctic their entire lives and they never know of this at all is that better?

Falling off the sidewalk. Beep beep.

Those few minutes. You can't erase it in your memory but it just sits there, you don't quite remember what they were, it might as well be gone, you forget in the cold to look.

I can see the Talmadge Bridge in the sky before me. Biggest tallest structure in the city. I don't go up there no, not up on top of that thing the looming creature of the skyline God it's high. Not so high compared to other bridges but high here, wide, tall, great. Amanda loves that shit. Every time she went to Dad's office building she said mama, mama, can we go to the top floor? I wanna look out. That was the fourteenth floor was the top. Wanna be high. She'd be crying for the bridge, walking along it if she could get leaning into the empty. Stand there with her hair blowing, her dolly, her Coke. Eyes get so blank. Wondering how tall is the killing point, whether this jump here can do it, not because she wants it or the sweet crisp taste for danger is ablaze but *come on DOWN* coo the restless whitecap fins in churning water and you can't help but be curious, that's why it scares me is because of the can't help but be curious. Why does it kill you. Why don't you sink and rise like diving from a board, does it hit you like dirt, wavy wavy seagulls on the beams, the steel water a single one great thing alone, blue in its concrete reflection.

Maybe that's where she ran to. Always liked bridges. The water beneath the Buck Karnes bridge or the water beneath the Charles Cates bridge or the water beneath the Bonnyman bridge. I was never brave like that.

A bus takes me to Victory Street, Highway 80, where I can follow the road until it ramps itself straight into the ocean. It's hot. I take my shirt off, tie it around my waist. Thumb pointed at the shore where I'll glisten baby in the brown sugar sun in my toes, ridges that fall in armies on the sand, where I'll watch the sailboats. I'm gonna hitch out to the beach, I'm gonna find me a beach boy. Little-kid eyes, blond hair, only the hints of muscles. I want him yellow, to wear yellow, swim yellow-trunked, be yellow in the fountain of the sun.

Someone takes me as far as Skidaway Island. Says he's sorry he can't take me farther. Has to get his shrimp boat out in the water before the tide's too low. So I start walking.

After half a mile I come to a billboard: Taste and see that the Lord is good. A church's name under it. This is a place to stop. I'm standing by the road with my bag on the ground and my back hurting, waving these cars down. They say thirty years ago you could always get a ride easy, anywhere in the country, people weren't so afraid. Last year I couldn't even hitch a ride on the road I lived on. Folks stopped for Amanda though.

She was seven, the time I'm thinking of. One year before I moved away. She wanted to go to the beach. Not enough money. I'll make some money myself, she said, stomped out of the house into the garage. She found a trowel, went down to the ditch under the tulip poplars and dug and dug, picked the worms up, held them in front of her eyes, said five cents each, put them in a Styrofoam cup. The long ones were ten cents. On a cardboard sheet she wrote Worms for Sale with a black permanent marker. Jumping up and down as the cars passed. She yelled so loud. A woman stopped to take a picture. My Lord, sweetie, who you think's gonna buy them worms?

Fishermen, she said.

Law law. Ain't nobody fish this time of year.

The lady gave her fifty cents. Probably could have spared a twenty. Amanda stayed out in the ditch till dark. Nobody bought worms but she sure got money, almost ten dollars at the end of the day. Mom yelled at her when she finally went inside. Amanda Leigh you've torn up half my yard.

There wasn't much traffic on that road. There's not much traffic on this road.

I want to yell at these people driving by. I'll dig up some worms. Quarter apiece; the cost of living's higher now. Give you the whole cup free for a ride to Tybee Island. Worms for sale, worms for sale. I'm standing there winding my fingers along my breastbone. Worms for sale big fat juicy ones little dirty ones long nightcrawlers squirming same as all the rest. I'm snaking my sweaty fingers along my chest. Left ones that is. Right hand pointed at the road. Thirsty, nobody stopping. What do they think I am, a robber, a pimp, a killer. Caesar-clipped locks warm in this sunlight. There's a billboard: Dixie Boy, a silhouette kid in the cotton, slyly awake. The right face grinning, the right chin. One of the drivers will see me, or one of the crustyfaced passengers, and like what he sees, affixing my face to the kid's muscular frame.

I wonder for a minute if on that day seven years ago she took her ten dollars inside the house and said mama, mama, is this enough to go to the beach, but no, even back then she knew how it is.

An airplane lurches through the sky. Small as a distant loon. The electric wires are drooping crooked and I move my eye to keep the jet behind them. Three clicks left and one click down. The smokestreak gets wider behind it; the wire can't hide it anymore. I look down. A car passes, driven by a thirtysomething man. Is he blond. Sandy a little maybe. Wife and kids in there but he's eyeing me, sly and nervous and haha I caught you. He looks away nervous, at his wife furtively to see if she's noticed. He speeds down the road. I've had no chance to finger my tanned nipple smile back at him, be complicit, give him a little nibble to keep him going, keep him dreaming through his life-long ruse, dreaming through the daddy-are-we-there-yets.

· · ·

Another man drives me to the beach. He's staying in the Days Inn on Tybee Island. It's hot today, he says. You know what that means.

I'm getting a headache. His voice bothers me. No, I say. What does it mean?

Means the chicks are in skimpy little bathing suits. He whistles. You lookin for a girl down here? he says. I don't see a ring on your finger.

My head throbs when he hits bumps on the road. No, I say, actually I'm looking for a guy. Someone much like yourself.

He stays quiet for the rest of the ride.

At the shore I find an abandoned beach chair to sit in. Watch the seagulls. You can give yourself nausea just from rocking back and forth in a chair. If you've eaten or not or drunk or whatever you want. I don't know why you'd want to but you can do it; it happens to me, not on purpose but you rock and rock and it's not what you're really thinking about, the rocking, it's not like you're jabbing a knife into your fingernails, or banging your head back against a brick wall, but there's one spot on your head where you can bang it bang it with no pain, you don't know when to quit. Stop and think about why your head hurts. There's hammering up in there, the round part is hitting the square part, the bruises come from the sounds hit from the side, the ears, the only way in is your ears. What are the bugs, the little buggers eating in there, what meat do they chew, what cold tit do they suck on.

I wedge past a young couple on my way to the toilet in the public restrooms. They're shoulder to shoulder, arms linked, talking so I can't hear. Both of them eye me as if I don't belong there. I shut the stall door, sit down, they're right outside, feet shuffle closer and they're inches from the door, kissing, slurpy slurp slurp. This is making me nervous. Go away I'm trying to take a shit. Now their lips are apart and they're arguing, Yes you did. No you didn't. Now they're kissing again.

I'm three minutes in the stall.

When I open the door they're staring at me, they're waiting.

The man's watching me jealously, as if he's afraid I might look at his cunty girlfriend a second too long. He's got a crew cut, red face; looks like an army guy, or a marine, a cunty little man himself.

I walk to the end of the fishing pier. Don't throw fish heads in the water say the signs. If everybody did it they'd fill up the whole ocean. From the end of the pier I strain my eyes to look for the lighthouse. I can't see it.

Amanda would want to go up the lighthouse if she were here. The high things. But it costs four dollars so I forgo the experience.

The bottom half's black the top half's white and walking up those stairs in there she'd count them and wonder which stair is where it switches from dark to light, whether it looks any different, which stair is halfway up to the big round window. Up through the white part to the top thinking get the momentum and I'll soar all the way to Talahi. Yes she would have remembered that name, she remembers road signs, billboards, mile marker numbers, all of them flashing signs in her mind, so Talahi Island yes is the island to the magnet north like a big transparent label floating above it, that's the direction, you can go so far this way. She'd tuck the blue dolly down her shirt, over the railing arms birdwinged, soar over to the big sky word name.

Yellow in the sun fountain. The fisherman at the pier's end is twenty years old. His face is perfect. Flaxen yellow hair straggles down toward the water, straight yellow locks clipped at the neck. Mouth yellow like a sickle, big lips, puckered all up so young. To the palmlined southwest glistens the sun, ducks under the pier's roof, illuminates our bodies and our skin. I wonder how thick is the boy's country accent. I watch as he casts the line. This pigment is pulsing out into the air. Gold. Nicotine. Sulfur. I want to talk to him, touch the skin that shines gilded in the citrine glow, but I'd sooner jump off the pier and drown, twenty feet into the water, down into the wet pit of fish heads.

Back on the beach the people are thinning out, going away.

This is a weekday, a Tuesday I think or a Wednesday. I dig a moat around myself in the hard wet sand. I have some postcards in my bag. Amanda asks me to send her postcards from the places I visit but I always forget in the end. It's hard to find stamps when you're traveling, hard to find a mailbox or a pen. Now I have those three things but she's not at home. No address. What do you say to someone you've never talked to.

Dear Amanda,

In my dream last night a nuclear winter had come. Your braces were still on your teeth and they were hurting a lot and all the orthodontists were dead. Bad sores formed in your mouth. You cried. I got on my bike because there was no gas left for cars and I rode toward Maryville to try to find someone who could help you. As I rode dust fell from the sky and red bony things and lightning flashed and wind blew dirt up off the ground. Around a curve was a dead body on the road chewed off at the waist. It made me wreck my bike. I lay on the road looking up at the dust and the patterns it formed in the sky. Eventually a boy came walking down the road, and he bashed my head in, a baseball bat his bludgeon of choice. As I bled into death I said, Take my teeth, my teeth are good, give her my teeth. Just cut my whole jaw out and give it to her. Don't leave me here until you take the teeth. Don't go. She's in pain. Why didn't I think of that before.

These words I write in the sand with a palm stick. One of the little bark rods from the trunks of palmettos. I write it on the wet part of the beach. It takes some time but there's nothing else to do.

You had to get braces because you sucked your thumb. It made your teeth come in crooked. When you were six years old I tried to get you to quit doing it. We were alone in the house—I had to baby-sit you in the summer—and when you put your thumb in your mouth I said stop it, Amanda, stop it. Why do you suck your thumb, Amanda? Quit it. You cried. I tried to remove your thumb physically from your mouth. You ran into your room. I followed you and unlocked the door with a Phillips-head screwdriver. Why do you suck your thumb, Amanda? Why is it so hard for you to quit? Why do you want your teeth to get so crooked?

You're so mean, you said to me, spitting out the words between your little sobs.

Well, just suck on it all you want then, I said, but I stepped back ashamed. You cried, slipped your thumb back in, watched your tyrant brother duck quickly out of the room.

Seven years have passed. I wonder if you still remember that day and a thousand others like it and if you don't, if it's gone, does the aura of my evil remain somewhere in your head, you can't like me that much, it can't be that bad for you that I'm gone. I think about the things I'm missing by not being home. Your skin hardening. Your face erupting in zits. I want you to know that I hated myself at that moment, and that I cried more than you did, and the horror that was dead above us at that moment in the air.

The waves erase the words. I stare at the retreating ocean foam and its saltine shaft of bubbles; my mouth opens at the sand words gone drifting out to sea, my letter, a minute scared, a single second dead. The sounds distract me here. Can't think about anything very long. Music churning through my lungs. My hair blows adrift in the quantum fluid of the blues and the wind drinks up the Spanish moss thirsty, the wind is weightless straws that vacuum out their lice.

I could have worked another week. I could have stayed on for one more paycheck and that would have fixed the car. It goes a long way back. Did a lot of shit in that car. The riv rav riven car dead in the gray snow blabber up there up the shore a ways. One more week. But if you get stoned enough it just presses down too hard, all the windows up above you from the street, the strip of sky you can see like a long squinting eyehole in the fabric of space. The buildings blink together and it's night. I could have worked another week but I cashed my check, got drunk, waited a while, just be patient and wait long enough. I woke up and there I sat moving, on Greyhound 756, strungout and zagging along the shallow eastern seaboard. I was sloshed, ripped, the name of the shore sounded big and important, seaboard like a big electric defense gray grid, like that game Battleship I used to play with Amanda. So there I was. Look out the left window, go far enough and it's the rootless not routeless eastern seaboard, bleeping its hollow coordinates to nuclear sailors out on the water, who see windows as pinprick lighthouses at check from their weapons, me as a speck of sand, busing along night to night, New York, et cetera, et cetera, et cetera, here. Seven cities sloping off the shelf.

Quotes hang on the wall at Fannie's, the restaurant on the beach, and there's one from Mark Twain that says travel is fatal to bigotry and narrowmindedness, but the one everyone likes and is talking about is below it, it's about smoking, it says cigarettes are the greatest lover. Find me someone else I want forty-five times a day and I'll quit.

I don't have a pen. I can't copy it down. I'm paraphrasing. I can't smoke, never could. I pour my drink into a plastic cup, carry it across the glassy parking lot to the boardwalk where my feet rub against the wood and sand; I go to the edge of the water sit and away dash the crabs.

Find me someone who wants me, myself, forty-five times a day, or forty-five people who want me, or the forty-five radians of yellow sunlight that will shine on my hair and bring one of them to me knelt before my widening eyes, hairs of skin ablaze, and I'll want him enough for the both of us.

Evening now. The sun sets and I sit on the beach eight at night, windy, chilly at night here the sand's cold against the toes like wet dirt toes of worms, at night anyway, a toe is the whole worm, what it is is a toe. An old man passes by. You sure do rub those toes in the sand like you mean it, boy, he says. So many people just talk to you here. Everybody just talks to you. None now but when they come here they gonna do it, everybody gotta talk, good for you, makes your bones grow. Talk with the words that love you. I never knew how to do it. But walk down the streets of any city you'll see that's what they're doing is talking, the words if you stretch them will wrap the earth thrice like a ribbon, even at night if you listen close sometimes it's what they're doing. If you watch a while you see the way to do it. It's how the air is built, light so the waves don't sink below your ear, clear like nothing there, why else would air be built that way. Ping: It blips straight out to the straight white line of night. So I sing a little, my voice nervous because it's the only sound on my frigid slab of sand, unsteady. Out toward my sweetest friends. The little white triangles shining in the moon: the bodies I can talk to, and I'm moving,

on the road again,

on the road to get just can't wait.

III

Gegenschein

The stars winked out. At night the moonlight shone upon the surface of the springwater. It was a harvest moon and the autumn blackness carried scents of wheat and corn through blacksand skies. As his campfire smoldered Thomas captured lightning bugs, imprisoning them in an empty apple butter jar with two airholes as he had done in childhood twenty years earlier. Thirteen in the jar. They flapped their wings faster than his eyes could detect. With two wings they were fast but if he tore off one wing then the other wing didn't flap very fast anymore. Then they slowed down. He wondered if they had nerve endings on their wings. Splat against the hard dirt ground and then the wings didn't flap at all. Their storming yellow lights illuminated the inner surface of his tent like oil-lit lamps in ancient taverns. Thunder struck. As Thomas smeared the bugs onto the black tent fabric a damp and moldy darkness gave way to the pale green glint of his organic lanterns. His frosty breath hovered in the unseasonably cold air. He wondered why he couldn't see the bugs' breath too. As they died he bent his ear slowly closer to their shining light but heard no sound. Why don't they hum like lamps when they glow? he wondered. You can hear a lamp or a flashlight or even a candle when it's burning. He listened for noises, his ear pressed up against their naked phosphorescence. Water spilled through Potato Creek at the bottom of the mountain. In silence the dying fireflies dangled from the tentwall by the strings of their sticky yellow viscera.

Thomas didn't know who owned the land. No one was around.

The hills were calm and tranquil as he sat on the hillside watching cloudstrands stain the sunsets. This was the third week. He bought groceries with money from his student loans. He whittled with his pocketknife; he wasn't very good but he was getting better. He learned the proper way to whet the blade.

His camp was on a red hilltop clearing in the copper basin in Polk County. It was near Stansbury Mountain where the basin reclamation project was going well and there weren't many red patches left. McGeetown had trees now, and Dogtown had trees, and there were trees in McHarg. At the overlook by the old mine only small red splotches remained among the pine saplings. Thomas had headed south on Highway 68 from Tellico Plains. When he saw the sign for Ducktown: A Quacking Good Place he got off the highway. The weather was cool for September. He drove around on gravel roads, gazing out at the pale panoramas.

Chhrrooooke, said the tree frogs.

On certain nights the moon was gray. Once it was apricot, the color of Crayola-shaded skin. On some nights it was red, black, gone, a vacant spot of nothing in the starscape, shining through the fading nylon gloom.

That night he had another nightmare about the school: the hellish horde of people and the signals they emitted, and their energy. He was drowning in a flood of pheromones. Forced physical proximity with so many people. It was a terrible restlessness. The darkest prison cage and it was driving him out of his mind. He didn't read anymore. Couldn't think couldn't rest and at night there were so many rooms full of voices. Dead sounds fell through the rotting drywall of the dorm like salted slugs. There were so many people perched on so little land and how could you even think at all with so many minds snipping and snapping, how could any of them think, how could they breathe? He couldn't relax. At every instant he felt the urgent need for company and everywhere else in the building people were talking and he was alone in his room and there needed to be other people. He sat in his metal deskchair, phone in hand, calling everyone he knew. When no one answered he paced anxiously from wall to wall, wondering where they were and what they were all doing, why they hadn't called him. He brooded alone as the gregarious animal tentacles in rooms around him bit at him like fire ants, and he itched incessantly, flea-ridden.

You know you don't remember anything but the last couple of dreams you have before you wake up. One out of a thousand maybe. For every dream a thousand disappear beneath the thick clay membrane of your brain. The scary ones and the bloody ones. You think you remember nightmares but the ones you don't remember are the nightmares. Thomas replayed this theory in his head as he lay awake from his dream at four in the morning, when he couldn't go back to sleep for half an hour. He shivered in the damp fall air. You don't remember them but that doesn't mean they don't affect you. When everything gets all fucked up it's the ones you don't remember that are doing it to you. They melt you into a tarblackened puddle of blood. You'll be locked in the darkest asylum.

His back ached when he woke up at sunrise. It was seven A.M. He stretched and shivered in the dewy air; with a groan he pulled himself out of his sleeping bag. The campsite was on top of a bare hill, isolated, and he was expecting to step out onto an empty clay clearing when he unzipped the tent. He didn't notice the steady sounds of breathing as he fumbled for his thermos. When he opened the zipper an old man was standing three feet in front of him: It was a wiry, wrinkled body, stonelike, and it stretched up into the pale morning sky. A yellowtoothed grin crossed the man's face. Thomas screamed in panic, and the man laughed, and their sounds bounced against the distant haze of hills.

Law law, son, the man said, shaking his head.

You scared the living shit out of me, Thomas said, his heart racing.

Well.

Thomas watched the man's jaw twist back and forth as he chewed tobacco. He was sixty-five or maybe seventy years old;

his skin was thick and red. He had the thickest eyebrows Thomas thought he had ever seen. His nose was turned up in a permanent scowl of disgust, and his round Teutonic cheekbones gave stares as piercing as a second pair of eyes. Thomas introduced himself and found out that the man's name was Cole Ogle. When Thomas asked him how he had gotten up to the hilltop he said he didn't remember. He didn't think he had spent the night there but he didn't remember being anywhere else when he went to bed. He didn't know what had happened at all. He didn't think he had driven but he didn't remember walking.

You must remember something, Thomas said.

How come you ask so many questions? Ogle snapped back at him.

I thought you were lost.

Shit, Ogle sneered.

I was just trying to help.

What are you doin here?

I'm on vacation, Thomas said.

You ain't from Ducktown, are you?

No, sir.

You know why they call it Ducktown?

No, Thomas said.

Guess why.

Thomas thought for a minute. Were there a lot of ducks in the area? he asked.

No, they ain't no ducks.

There must be ducks somewhere.

Nope. They ain't no ducks.

Why do they call it Ducktown then?

Ducktown, Ogle began, and he paused. Law law law.

Well?

Well what?

Why do they call it Ducktown?

Why do they call what Ducktown?

Ducktown. Why do they call Ducktown Ducktown?

Ogle spat through pursed lips. Cause of the outlaws, he said.

What?

Cause of the outlaws.

I heard you, Thomas said. I meant what do you mean?

Cause they was always a gunfight goin on back then. When you come through on the train and stopped at the station the conductor he'd yell for everbody to duck.

Oh.

Cause of the gunfightin. So the folks on the train wouldn't get shot at by all the outlaws.

When was that?

Not too long ago.

In this century, you mean?

Ogle shrugged.

Thomas got up out of the tent and put on a pair of pants. He changed into a clean T-shirt as he tried to figure out what to do about Ogle. He wondered if the man belonged in a nursing home or had Alzheimer's disease. He walked around the perimeter of the hilltop, looking down into the trees for signs of other people. He wondered if Ogle was going to rob him. The woods were quiet. He looked at Ogle as the old man stood in place staring back at him.

My folks didn't want me to grow up and be a copper miner, Ogle said. Figured if they was to name me Coal then at least I'd mine coal instead of copper.

So it's spelled like the mineral?

Huh? he shouted.

Is it spelled like the stuff you mine out of the ground?

Huh?

Never mind, Thomas said. He dug around in his rucksack for a clean shirt to put on. Ogle stood upon the same spot of red clay where he had been standing since before Thomas had opened the tent. Thomas was getting anxious about Ogle's presence. He tried to keep a conversation going to keep from feeling awkward.

So you didn't mine copper? he asked.

I mined copper, Ogle said.

Thomas stared nervously out at the hills.

They named my little brother Silver and he mined copper too, Ogle said.

Do you own this land or something?

Huh?

I thought it was Forest Service land.

It ain't Forest Service land.

Is it your land?

Ogle thought for a minute. I don't rightly remember, he said. It might be and then again it might not be.

Do you own land?

Mmmm. Fair to middlin.

Huh?

Fair to middlin, Ogle repeated a little more loudly.

What I asked you was if you own land.

Where?

Here. Anywhere.

I don't know, Ogle said. It don't look right no more cause they went and planted the damn trees.

You don't remember if it's your land?

Nothin looks the same no more. All these damn trees gets in the way and you can't tell nothin about it no more.

There were a few minutes of silence. Thomas organized his belongings in the tent, glancing back over his shoulder at Ogle once in a while; the wiry old man was sitting down upon a rock smoking a cigarette. The age lines on his face looked as if they had been formed by sixty years of twisting his mouth back in glowering anger. His ears and nose were bright red. Thomas tidied up the camp and wandered down the hill to the spring to fill his collapsible water container. He was gone for four or five minutes, and when he returned to the hilltop Ogle was gone. Thomas quickly surveyed his scattered heap of possessions, and everything seemed to be there. He shrugged and prepared breakfast for himself. He spent the morning and part of the afternoon hiking a new trail he had found the day before, and he didn't return to his tent until two-thirty.

. . .

To the south and east Coal Ogle trudged slowly through the woods. Thomas had already forgotten about him. Ogle stumbled through the thickly budding forest and mumbled to himself. It didn't feel right. The only sense of direction he had was that the town was somewhere in front of him. He maneuvered slowly and clumsily through the trees and although there was no trail he felt the pull of the town tug at him like a compass magnet. He couldn't find anything in the woods anymore but he could find the town. It was the only thing that was the same and it wasn't even the same really. He swayed back and forth between the thirsty pines. The red dirt felt hard beneath his feet. He thought he was probably somewhere near the old mine. The place where the train used to be. The little path down to the tavern. The spot where they had buried old Cobb Cobbler when he had collapsed from sunstroke. The spot where they drank. The spot where they played cards. The spot where they fought.

With eyes glazed over he stared in confusion at the evergreens surrounding him, sticking up out of the ground like a thousand jousters' poles. He wondered where the empty spaces had gone. The copper hills had been moonlit for so many years, barren red like Martian mountain valleys. The shine was light on mud from surface mining. Nothing looked right anymore with the trees all grown. The hills were mossy, mazelike. As Ogle made his way past a billion pinetree clones it was dark blackcharred and owly among the trunks. He thought back to the time of the ravenridden open copper basin. Everything was lit up. The cabins, the thin spread of dusty soil upon the ground; the broken redlit windows of the bar.

Chhrrrooke. Chhrrrooke.

Some nights now he couldn't even see the stars. Under full moons without moonlight he failed to find the oak cabin or where the still had been. They had called it moonshine because the moon shone down on rocky dirt because the land was a fledgling desert. He stumbled through the evergreen jungle without course or bearing. Squirrels twittered in the trees.

. . .

Ogle was standing in a gravel ditch beside the road when Thomas approached him in the truck on his way to the town to buy groceries at four in the afternoon. Thomas squinted his eyes and slammed his brakes when he realized he was seeing the same man who had appeared at his tent that morning. He leaned over and opened the passenger door. You want a ride? he said.

Where to?

Ducktown.

What?

Town.

What town?

Ducktown.

Ogle stood still without responding, glaring up at the sky.

You want a ride?

Ogle looked back with empty eyes, silent. Look up at the sun, he said finally.

Thomas glanced upward toward the light and then quickly averted his eyes from the blinding yellow glare.

No, I mean really look at it, Ogle said as he stared straight into the sun.

You're gonna hurt your eyes, Thomas said.

After a minute Ogle turned his head downward. His pupils were so small Thomas could barely see them; his eyes had become two pale cataractic circles. He opened his mouth to speak ten seconds before any words came out. If you look at the sun long enough, he said quietly to Thomas, as if he were telling a secret, you see a man in the sun too.

A man in the sun?

It smiles at you a little more than the one in the moon, Ogle said, grinning. It ain't as pissed off all the damn time.

Ogle looked back up at the sun. Thomas realized he wasn't even sure which way Ogle had been walking. A salamander slithered across the gravel road in front of the truck, and it disappeared into the ditch as Thomas waited for a response from Ogle. He shifted uncomfortably in his seat.

Hey, mister, Thomas said.

What?

You want a ride to the town or not?

The town?

Ducktown.

Ducktown?

Yeah, Ducktown.

You know why they call it Ducktown? Ogle asked, scratching his agespotted scalp with one bony finger.

You told me already, Thomas said.

Ogle looked back in confusion, turning down his mouth in a slightly forlorn frown. Yeah, he said. I guess I did.

Get in and I'll give you a ride down to the town, Thomas said, and Ogle silently obeyed. Thomas drove them downhill around the dusty curves. He listened to the radio without speaking; Ogle stared out the window. It was only a three-minute drive to the highway, and he pulled into the parking lot of the grocery store when he arrived in town. Thomas heard Ogle's stomach growling.

Is the grocery store where you were going? Thomas said.

Ogle acted as if he hadn't heard anything.

When they arrived Ogle climbed out of the truckcab without speaking and walked hurriedly into the store, brushing against two exiting shoppers. Thomas followed him back to the bakery.

Hey, Ogle shouted loudly as he leaned against the glass counter, pounding his fist against it until a young employee came out through the door that led to the back.

May I help you, sir? the clerk said.

Gimme some of them nigger tits.

The clerk stared back at him. I beg your pardon, sir?

I want some of them nigger tits, Ogle shouted in his thick mountain accent.

What?

Nigger tits.

Two black shoppers turned to stare. Thomas moved away in an attempt to disassociate himself from the situation.

Them cream things with the chocolate on em, Ogle barked. You used to always had a whole tray full.

Could you maybe point to what you're talking about, sir?

If I'd saw where the fuckin things are I'd of told you. Why don't you go back there in that back room you got back there. I bet you they's some nigger tits in that back room.

I'm sorry, sir, we don't carry anything by that name.

Ogle cursed under his breath and walked away. He lifted a chocolate cream doughnut out of a self-serve bin and stuffed it into his mouth whole, smearing its filling on his rough gray moustache. He pushed a row of cans onto the floor on aisle five, and as he passed the checkout aisle he lit a cigarette. When the cashier complained about it he blew smoke in her face and stomped out of the store. From the deli Thomas looked down the center aisle toward the window and watched Ogle's receding figure trudge across the road and into the distance.

Thomas bought marshmallows and bread and peanut butter and beer. He had the money to get more, but he couldn't think of anything else he wanted. Peanut butter was the only food he had eaten for four days. As he walked out to the parking lot with one brown bag he thought about getting something to eat at a restaurant, but he hadn't showered or shaved in a week; his clothes smelled bad, and all he really wanted to eat was peanut butter.

When he left the store he decided to drive up to the Copper Basin museum. The sign by the highway had caught his attention a dozen times, but he had never turned off the road to see it. Its driveway's pavement was narrow and broken. He parked next to the chain-link fence at the top by the overlook and went inside.

Good afternoon, said the woman at the counter.

Hey.

Admission is four dollars, she said.

Thomas stared back at her. The museum was only three or four rooms. There weren't any windows. He looked around the corner at the exhibits: There were black-and-white photographs on the wall, information sheets, a life-sized model of a miner. A hallway had been painted black to look like a mineshaft.

I don't think I'll go in, he said.

Are you sure? she asked. Thomas saw a tinge of disappointment in her eyes. He looked down at the guestbook; the last visitor was from two days earlier.

Yeah, Thomas said, I'm sure.

We've got an informational video that runs for twelve minutes, she said. You can watch it in that room over there.

No, thank you, ma'am, he said, turning around to leave.

That's a long way to drive not to even see it.

How do you know how far I drove?

You've got Knox County plates, she said. I saw you drive up.

He shrugged. I think I've made up my mind, he said, and he walked outside and closed the door behind him. Even though he had been indoors for less than a minute, the sunlight hurt his eyes when he stepped out. He walked to the overlook and gazed out through the fence at the hills and knobs stretching out in front of him. There was a large blue-green pond that he thought was probably an old rock quarry. Only small red scars remained upon the land. He tried to picture what it would have looked like when all the trees were gone. No trees as far as the eye could see. He wondered whether the people who had been born in the basin after the trees were gone got upset when the reclamation project started. He tried to picture the dry red land. There were photographs in the museum, he thought. If he had stayed he could have watched the video.

When Thomas was back in the truck he barreled quickly down the hill. He drove past empty structures of cracked, decaying concrete, and he wondered what their purpose had been. He supposed they would have been identified inside the museum. When he reached the highway he went left and traveled several miles to his turnoff. The weather was good, and he rolled the window down. Full-bodied white clouds rested upon the hilltops. Deer grazed in a field on the left. As Thomas rounded the curves he wondered which of the houses and trailers he saw would still be standing in a hundred years. Which derelict wood heaps would decay into dirt without varnish or color, and whether the trees would reclaim every bare space. His thoughts did not coalesce into phrases in his mind; he saw them instead in pictured sequence as if they were panels of animation. It was muddled. He saw his father twenty years in the past, shortly before his death, the old scratchy voice telling him the story of how all land east of the Mississippi was once a single forest whose treetops from above blended into a boundless sheet of green. Squirrels scurried from the Gulf of Mexico to the Chesapeake Bay without ever touching the ground. No wind penetrated the thousand-mile shield. Rotting autumn harvests of withered leaves coated the sunless earth.

He had always remembered the image. Squirrels five hundred years dead dashing along on continental odysseys. He felt sorry for the ones he saw in yards and open meadows, darting in the chaos of their schizoid patterns, wondering where to go. The squirrels must not have liked the copper basin. He wondered if there had even been squirrels there at all when the mines were open. He could have asked Ogle, he thought.

They were everywhere now. There had been a lot of squirrels on campus, big bloated ones, fat from the offerings of passing students. Whenever he dreamt about the school there were squirrels. Mad rodents frothed rabidly in his dreams. Darting lividly down electric wires, looking sadly down at all the brown grass, all the gravelly pavement. All the big strange empty land. So they panic across fields as if trapped in a hallucination, a beastly apocalypse feeding off their lingering forest instinct. So the sky at night is a violent incarnation of deathly purple, stained by their echoed roar of rage that dyes the light.

He parked the truck and walked up through the woods, speaking to himself as he climbed up to the campsite. The drone of his broiling voice arced from hill to distant hill. Whaannnh, whannnh, whannnh whaannnh. He ran his fingers through his dirty hair as distant thunder shook the clouds.

Thomas read his book for two hours when he got back up to the hilltop. He drank three of his cans of beer and ate a peanut butter sandwich, and by sunset he was already drowsy. He leaned back against the ground twenty feet away from his tent, and without meaning to go to sleep he closed his eyes and drifted out of consciousness.

A disembodied voice spoke muddled thoughts in his dream. Red clay and the crunch of roots pressing through it. The sound of the speech ran through the bowels of a dozen young softwood conglomerations. An imagination that was forever questing. He remembered thoughts and commands. The red clay is very hard very thick you can't be buried in it. Unplunged earth. Wrench breath and eyes out of their prison lifeline and alone you'll bleed in ether, softly floating, as minutes scowl in time.

Chrrrrroke. Chrrrrroke.

The sounds spilled out of his ears. Have to pay attention. There are no pavement lines. He remembered a prayer they had taught him in church. I see the moon and the moon sees me. God bless the moon and God bless me. In his eyes the moonlight, and the things that danced in it, and the glowing moonlit dome of treecloaked land. In both cold ears the shining tree frog trumpets of the night. They basked in blighted blackness.

A shadow separated him from the moon when he awoke. It loomed above him. He saw the lit end of a cigarette as it floated back and forth in the darkness.

I followed you up here, he heard Ogle's voice say.

Thomas screamed. Jesus fucking Christ. What the hell.

You snore real loud, Ogle said. If you was an Indian they'd of sliced you with a knife for bein so loud. The animals would of heard it.

Goddammit, Thomas said.

You would of scared away the meat.

Thomas fumbled for his flashlight and turned it on, shining it into Ogle's face. What are you doing here? he demanded.

I followed you up here, Ogle said again, grinning into the narrow beam of light.

Where the hell do you live?

Not far from here.

Why don't you just go there?

I'm on my way, Ogle said. I'm just takin my time.

Thomas looked at his watch; it was eleven. The moon was near the horizon; he wasn't sure whether it was rising or setting. Still confused from sleep, he sat down upon the ground outside the tent next to the dead fire and wondered what to do.

Hey, Ogle said. What was it I told you earlier that I'd told you before?

When?

I don't know when it was, Ogle said. It was sometime. I don't know.

You mean about Ducktown?

What about Ducktown?

How they named it that because of the gunfighters.

Yeah, that was it, Ogle said. There was somethin I wanted to ask you about that.

What did you want to ask me?

I don't remember.

Thomas rolled his eyes. Maybe it'll come back to you, he said sarcastically.

Ogle stared at him for a minute. Wait, he said, I remember. I wanted to ask you where I was when I said it.

You were right here at the clearing.

I was?

Yeah.

Ogle thought about it for a minute. Well then, when was it?

This morning. When I got out of the tent and you were standing there. When you scared the shit out of me just like you scared me tonight.

Oh.

Did you ever remember how it was that you got up here this morning?

Ogle looked up at the sky for a few moments. No, he said finally. But I know how I got up here just now. You know how?

How?

I followed you.

Thomas sat on the ground and rubbed his eyes. He picked

up a knobby stick lying next to him and used it to sketch lines and patterns onto the loose dirt. Several minutes passed.

Why don't you start a fire? Thomas said.

I don't like fires.

Thomas sighed through his nose in irritation and impatience. He was sorry he had stopped to offer Ogle a ride earlier. Well, this isn't your campsite, he said. Since you're following me around you could at least start me a damn fire, don't you think?

Ogle stood still.

Or do you even know how to start a fire?

Used to be you could start a fire out of dirt around here.

How the hell can you start a fire out of dirt?

It used to be the clay was harder than a skull, he said. I always wanted to get buried in dirt that was as thick as the bones in your head. He paused, cleared his throat and lowered his voice. I don't know that you could even find dirt like that anymore, he said. It's all under the trees now. That's why I like it so good up here. This clearing is the hardest spot left. It's cause the moon can still shine down on it. The moon shinin presses it down real good.

What does that have to do with starting a fire? Thomas asked.

The moon presses it down good, Ogle said. I just told you that.

Thomas got a beer out of his cooler; he stood up and paced around the clearing as he drank it. He kicked at a few tufts of grass growing up out of cracks in the hard dirt. He looked at his watch; he was nervous, and he wanted Ogle to leave.

It was the clearest night since he had arrived. Stars dotted the glowing sphere of the cosmos like pulsing points of acupuncture. He saw the Milky Way. The air smelled crisp and leafy as he ambled through the darkness. Near the southern horizon he saw a tangled counterglow of asteroids; he stared at it, and Ogle walked up and saw him staring, and the old man poked him hard on the fleshy part of his upper arm, knocking him out of his reverie.

Hey, Thomas said, what the hell?

Tell me what's that you're lookin at.

It's the fucking sky. What do you think?

I mean that glowing stuff. Right there where you been starin at that other light spot up there. It's like they's two moons in the sky.

That's gegenschein, Thomas said. He smiled slightly, knowing that Ogle wouldn't recognize the word. He could have said counterglow instead but he didn't want to.

Gay gun shine, Ogle sneered. Now what in the tarnation is that?

It's when a cluster of meteors in space reflects the light of the sun.

But it's nighttime now. They ain't no sun.

The earth doesn't block the rays of sunlight that hit the meteors though.

Where the hell did you learn about shit like that?

In my astronomy class at UT.

Ogle thought about it for a minute. Well, I ain't never heard the likes of that bullshit, he said. Sounds like a bunch of that smart-people shit.

What do you mean?

You go to UT?

Yeah.

You're one of those book people, ain't you?

What do you mean?

One of them book people, Ogle barked. The ones that reads the books.

Thomas got some sticks from his woodpile and tossed them down on the ground where his fire had burned last night and every night that week. He gathered some dry pine needles and nestled them beneath the sticks and lit them with his lighter. When the fire was going, they both sat down; Thomas had already finished his beer, and he opened another one.

Hey, Ogle said. Let me have one of them.

Thomas passed him one of the warm ones, and they drank in silence for a few minutes. Owls hooted in the distance.

Look, Thomas finally said, you just can't stay here at this campsite with me. I came here to be alone. I don't mean to be rude but if you're gonna stay here then I'm gonna pack up and leave.

I don't plan on stayin, Ogle said.

Well, when do you plan on leaving?

Won't be too long now.

Could you be a little more specific?

Say, Ogle said, tell me about that truck of yours.

What about it?

It looks different.

Different from what? Thomas asked.

Different from other trucks.

Thomas nodded his head and shrugged his shoulders, unsure what to say.

Is it a fifty-six or a fifty-seven? Ogle asked.

It's a ninety-four.

They didn't make trucks in ninety-four, Ogle said, grunting out barely intelligible words. First trucks was maybe in the twenties and even then they wasn't really what you could call trucks.

Thomas stared back at him.

For all your fuckin gun shine gay shit you ain't really all that smart.

Thomas shrugged, turning his cheekbones up in a cynical expression of confusion.

It's like when the mines was goin. The men that ran it. They had book sense but they didn't have no common sense.

Then why do you suppose they were running it and you were just a miner?

Cause I wanted to be a miner.

Why the hell would you have wanted to be a miner?

Cause I just did. That's just what I wanted.

Thomas finished his beer and opened another one and drank it too before Ogle had finished his. He watched Ogle watch him drink, and he waited for the old man to tell him he drank too much, but he didn't. Without standing up he stomped the cans flat with his shoe and threw them onto his growing pile. Hey, he said to Ogle, it's late.

Yeah.

I really don't mean to be rude but I want to be alone.

Ogle looked up at him and narrowed his eyes, and Thomas thought he heard him emit a low growl, sustained for several moments until it finally died. It could have been an animal in the woods but Thomas thought it was Ogle. Cinders lifted up through the air between them as they stared at each other. Ogle fumbled around in his back pocket as Thomas rolled his eyes impatiently. Get the hell out of here, he repeated silently to himself. I've had enough of you. Go the hell away.

Does it work like all the other ones? Ogle said.

What?

Do you have to do somethin special when you start it?

Start what? Thomas said in irritation. He had opened the bag of marshmallows, and he was roasting two on a stick without looking up at Ogle.

The truck.

No, it starts like any other car, he replied. Thomas went along impatiently with whatever Ogle said. Anything to get him to leave, he thought.

I didn't see where there was a choke.

A choke?

Yeah.

Why the hell would it have a choke? Jesus Christ.

So they ain't no choke?

No, they ain't no choke, Thomas said, mocking him.

Okay then, Ogle said. I guess I'll get out of your hair now.

He turned toward the trail. Thomas reached for another can of beer and breathed a sigh of relief. Thank you, God, he thought. The cans were all gone, so he lifted a bottle out of the cooler and felt in his pocket for the bottle opener on his key-chain. It wasn't in his pocket. He glanced around his scattered belongings and in the silence heard Ogle laughing faintly in the distance as he descended down off the hilltop.

Fuck, Thomas yelled.

He chased after the slow-moving figure in the distance. Ogle heard the commotion and turned around, standing still. Thomas got as close as five feet away from him before he saw the black revolver in Ogle's hand, half-hidden by his jacket. Its surface shone in the moonlight.

Give me the keys back, Thomas said.

Shit, Ogle grunted in response.

I'll go straight down to the sheriff's office and report it. I know your name already.

You gonna get down there before I do?

No.

Well, I ain't givin you the keys back, Ogle said.

He pointed the gun at Thomas and marched him back to the tent, instructing him to climb into the tent and keep it zipped up until Ogle was down below the treeline in the woods. Thomas walked toward the tent, cursing himself.

You see what I mean? Ogle said. You're just like those guys that ran the mines.

Just shut the fuck up.

I remember them bein exactly the same as you.

You don't remember shit.

I remember it just fine, Ogle said.

No you don't.

The hell I don't. I remember it. All the big red empty hills. All my brothers, they mined too. If they was still livin, you could ask them and they'd remember it just like I remember it.

You don't even remember whether you had brothers or not.

Yeah, I do, Ogle said, his voice rising. I remember all of it.

No you don't. I bet I remember more about the fucking copper mines than you do.

The mines was all shut down by the time you was born, you little shit.

That doesn't matter. Just from what I've seen around here I bet I know more about the mines than you do.

Ogle grabbed him by the neck. It was all before you were born, you little shit, he growled. You don't remember none of it.

Thomas smiled. I do remember it though, he said. Everything you've told me I already knew about.

I ain't told you shit.

Yeah you have. You just don't remember what you've told me.

Get the hell into the tent, you little shit.

You sure you remember where the truck is?

Shut up.

Thomas drank late into the night. He had bought beer he thought would last a week but had consumed half of it by three in the morning. Drunk as the stars swirled above him he laughed about the truck and laughed and continued to laugh and it was half past three, and his mouth was dry, and there was a full moon. He didn't really need the truck anymore anyway, he thought to himself. He could walk down and report it and file the claim but he didn't think he would do it tomorrow or the next day. Maybe on Friday if that was what day it would be after that. It wasn't urgent enough to bother with right away.

He could walk down into the town when he needed to. It wasn't more than four or five miles. At the store he would glance at strangers nervously, trying not to make eye contact. He would feel their piercing stares against his neck and back and head as they speared the bony shield of his skull. He would go shopping only once every two weeks. It was very quiet down in the trees, he noticed. With a Miller bottle in hand he wandered between the pines.

Nothing was really urgent. It was easy to forget about other people when there was no human presence for miles in any direction. The pheromones needed much more proximity. He felt no need for a partner anymore, and it was relaxing to be alone and to be glad to be alone. He was happy that no one was around who knew him, who knew how long it had been since he had broken up with his last girlfriend. He was glad there was no one anymore who could deduce how long it had been since he had last had sex. He wasn't embarrassed about it anymore; it wasn't important. Animals rustled across the blanket of dead pine needles, and when the raccoons came into the clearing he fed them Lorna Doone cookies. The moon shone through the wispy clouds, injecting its deathly rays into the thin chasms between the pines, and they fell upon him as he mumbled to himself, crawling through the woods' haunted copper conduits.

This is where I live now. To the wormy soil he spoke aloud: I've loved you since the day we met. It seemed to whisper back to him. He saw the trees growing; he saw their roots spread out to hide the copper. He barely remembered the faces he had known back home. Sometimes he felt reflected in his consciousness the shrill hive of minds that he had hated, black, putrid and glowing in their mania, but it was very faint, and it went away if he ignored it. They glowed and then they didn't glow. To the soil he spoke aloud: Something good is happening.

The key turned, and Ogle started the truck. Trees muffled the sound and it didn't carry through the trees and no one heard it but himself. The evergreens were closing in and it would all be one big forest again. Squirrels jumping on trees from the Ocoee to the Nantahala National Forest and that's seven miles apart and if it's not red you might as well be anywhere else. Ogle thought of all the places he could go. Harbuck, Burger Town, Wehutty. He had courted a girl from Wehutty once. That was a long time ago. He tried to remember her face but could not. He tried to remember her name, and how many years it had been.

The truck sped down the hillside. There were a lot of places he could go. Wolf Creek, Grassy Creek, Ogreeta. He tried to remember why those names had floated into the forefront of his mind. The land around him was dark and brooding but in the lunar illumination he saw clearly the woods in frozen closeness; he turned the headlights off and navigated by the moon's sullen gloss of chalky, ashen light. It shone upon his creviced face as he drove up toward the state line. There were a lot of mountains. In the absence of his headlights there weren't going to be any more signs or yellow pavement lines. The mountains were going to get thicker and stronger. He left the copper basin. The stars were stark and rising and the road was going to climb three thousand feet into the sky. He careened through the curves with no foreknowledge of his destination, breathing heavily in the euphoria of his mind's oblivion and remembering his life like a collection of his most recent dreams, and the full moon shone off the truck's black hood as he drove through the newly forested wilderness.

What I Remember About the Cold War

Hector died today. I spat out into the yard from the back porch and called Hector, Hector, heckyheckyhecky as I smoked my last cigarette. Stay outside the whole damn day, it's fine with me, I said to him, but I went to take a piss and there was the little bastard right in front of me, dead and stiff, facedown in his kitty litter. It was funny the way his tail stuck up. I laughed. Hey, Raina, I yelled down the hallway. Looks like Hector finally bit the dust. Now we can get a dog.

I didn't have anything against the cat. If I antagonize Raina, though, while she's already weepy and blubbery about it, maybe she'll leave me and I won't have to deal with kicking her out of the house.

I walk home from work every day the back way, through the trees. Beer bottles gleam. They get filled with dirt after a while. I wonder who fills them with dirt. Down the littered trail I follow the red centipedes as they crawl; I crawl behind them, grimy, a pupal lump; my motion decays. The towers loom through the trees. The land on which I walk is for sale. They'll build more towers, and more fuckups will come. I mentioned this to Bruce on Monday, that the land is for sale. Disjunctive thinking, Bruce said. He is a philosophy student. Disjunctive thinking. If it's not one thing then it's the other, the opposite. For something to change then its opposite must change.

So if I kick you in the balls, I said, what else changes? What

else is going to happen while you fall to the ground and squirm?
What is the opposite of your balls?

It takes me twenty-three minutes to walk to my apartment
from work, unless a train is blocking the road, in which case it
can take up to thirty. I count my strides, but the total varies from
day to day, and I have not bothered to calculate an average. In
my apartment building there are forty-two steps up to my door.
It never changes, because there is no opposite of number.

When the Locust and I were still living together, I was surrounded by numbers. She printed them out on long strips of
paper, font size thirty-six, and hung them on the walls. We had
the square root of two hanging on the bathroom door; I faced
it while I sat on the shitter. She printed it out to a hundred
digits. You can memorize it while you take a shit, she said.
We had π in the kitchen and we had e above and below the
television screen, seventy-five digits each, and I think she knew
all the digits of all of them. I took a book into the bathroom.
Why are you taking a book? she said. Just memorize the square
root of two.

I don't really want to, I said.

She told me she wanted the thirty-third line of the Fibonacci
sequence tattooed around her waist.

It'll stretch out if you ever get pregnant, I said.

I'll never get pregnant.

But what if you just get fat?

Verity buys coke from me every Tuesday. Just a little bit at a
time. I don't think she ever actually snorts the shit herself; she
just wants me to think she's addicted. Bruce told me that her
eyes lit up when she heard I dumped the Locust. So she wants
me, I guess. Sometimes I call her Rarity, and she laughs. Sometimes I call her Clarity. Sometimes I call her Variety. She thinks
I'm flirting with her. Whatever, hon. I just think you've got a
dumb name.

The toilet's stopped up again, Colin says to me.

So use the plunger.

There ain't no fuckin plunger, man.

So piss in the damn sink.

You should do something about that, he says when he gets out of the bathroom. Everybody's always over here. Raina's friends sprawl across my couches like sloths. She associates with drunks and druggies because the idea of a man irreparably addicted to a substance seems to turn her on more than anything in the world. Think I even heard her say it once. The more substances the better. They sit on the couches and watch *South Park* and take bong hits. They suck the energy out of the walls. I should do something about the toilet, should I, Colin? I think not. I think it will remain stopped up indefinitely. In fact, if it makes you stop coming here, I'll start digging holes out in the yard to take a shit.

I tell them about the revolution. They smile and grin and hawk up a laugh, as if I'm joking, as if I'm making them complicit in a fiction. I tell them some of the basics. Montana, Idaho, and Wyoming will use the electric downtime to secede. They'll bomb all the major news networks, and they'll bomb most of Los Angeles, Silicon Valley, and Seattle. Hunger pangs grow in my stomach as I think about all the changes that are going to happen. Sleeping will be more difficult. Watch for the predators. This is a continent that needs predatory fauna. I can't wait. I see a lot of predator bait when I walk around the city.

My room is full of lamps. Forty or fifty of them: They hang on the walls and they sit upon the floor, and they burn.

I don't spend a lot of time in my room. My walls are black and purple, and I hang lamps from them. I don't have any of the usual stuff. I don't have a chest of drawers or a closet; all my clothes are in a heap beneath the window. I have hardwood floors.

I've had this place for nine months. When I'm inside it, I feel like I'm gestating. It's like a womb: a womb with lamps.

There's no hope this time, said Daddy on the phone. She won't walk again.

You'll have to move to a new place.

We can't afford it, you know. There's still the lawsuit. To think that that bitch will sue an invalid.

You're on the fifth floor and there's no elevator.

We'll have to work something out, he said.

There's nothing you can work out.

I wish you'd come home sometime.

Don't nag me. I already told you that I will. Don't nag me.

It would make your mother very happy to see you, you know. She doesn't have many pleasures left in her life.

Shut up, Daddy, shut up, I repeated to myself. If you make me cry again I'm going to hang up the phone.

Let's stop the music for a while, says Mona, ferret-eyed Mona. Let's just listen to the air. Crickets chirp. Wind blows.

Mona just doesn't get it.

Bruce is ranting again. Russia in 1991, he says. Yanayev and Yeltsin. They pulled it off. No one even knows that they pulled it off. They could be the same person for all we know and all they tell us and all we want to hear. The strategy was immaculate. Who in the western world even remembers the bastard's name, no? They went under and lost the war and now they're just another struggling emerging democracy and we won, right? No one sees.

Sees what? says Mona.

The computers. They don't rely on numbers. Everyone thinks that they're fucked but they've got their land and you can't be fucked if you've got that much land, and they know their land. It's not computerized. In seven years they've set themselves up perfectly for the millennium, and no one even thinks about them anymore.

Shut your fuckin trap, man, says Colin.

Bruce leans back and shakes his head and puffs the bowl. I'm just saying they're gonna be ready, he says. I give it two hundred years and then they emerge from the dark age and start technology over, and this time they'll do it their own way. A million deaths is a statistic. Know that you are warned.

Bruce is the only one who understands.

I remember Yanayev. I saw that shit on the news way back whenever it happened. I was at the beach, on an island; it was a family vacation. There's been a coup, they were saying, a bloodless coup. It sounded like "bludlisskoo." They talked about the bombs. It was a long time ago. They talked about Yanayev and what he could do with the bombs. It was the only time I remember being scared of the bombs. Well, shit I don't want the world to end, I was thinking, because I hadn't even gotten laid yet. I was seventeen years old.

I'm not worried about Y2K. I want something to happen. Nothing ever happens.

If nothing happens when it hits, I'll be disappointed. I want something to happen. On every street corner I see restless strugglers. Dye yourselves black and dye your colors as you stand, seventeen, cattle upon the bland American grazery, churning for godheads. They smoke a lot of Camels. They're all going to explode.

I had custody of Hunter over the weekend. He's five years old. Kids are hypochondriacs. You can really scare the shit out of a little kid. They'll trust you like you're God. The kid actually believes what I say. Ohmygodinheaven Hunter you didn't spit your toothpaste back out? You swallowed it? You'll *die*. Don't worry; you're not gonna keel over right here on the bathroom floor. You'll live a few months. Do you think it was less than a gram? You'll live if it was less than a gram, maybe. We'll just have to wait and see.

If it weren't for Y2K, I'd pay more attention to him, but as it is, he's just a burden. I'm forced to write him off as a loss. He'll be too young to be self-sufficient. His mother is too stupid to be self-sufficient. They'll probably both die.

All their new words have infiltrated our minds, Bruce says. They're giving us new words and we don't even know what they mean and we say them more more more and when they take away mechanics, electricity, medicine, we'll be stuck with their words. Their words will be coming out of our mouths. They're buggering us with evil words, he says.

Like what?

Quonade, he says.

What the hell is a quonade?

How the hell should I know?

You're the one who knows the word.

I don't know the word. *They* know the word.

Who knows the word?

The man.

What man?

There is no what man. It's just the man.

I've never heard that word before, I said. Quonade.

That's the way it works. You don't notice it on your own. But you'll sure as hell see it now. It's everywhere.

What's a quonade?

It's whatever they want you to want it to be.

Bruce went home to go to bed, and Colin showed up. I gave him a beer. He sat in the recliner and rubbed the space between his left thumb and index finger with his right thumb. His mouth showed no emotion, but his nose ring gleamed and dominated his face. There was no need for an expression: The silver ring shaped itself into a huge grinning sneer.

This kid the other night, he was saying. This kid told me he wasn't gonna wear a condom. I said the hell you're not and he said, Look here, I make the rules. You play the game or I don't even unzip my pants.

We don't wanna hear about this, Mona said.

Shut up, I said to her.

Shut up, she said with derision, mocking me.

I asked him why, said Colin, continuing his story. You know, like what the fuck, you know? The kid looks at me he says, he's like, I've never been tested for anything before. I might be squirting poison up your ass, or I might not. It was a wicked little smile he gave. It turned him on; it made him stiff as metal to think he might be killing me. My dream, the kid tells me, is to have a loaded pistol and to shoot the guy in the head when I come. I said to him, That's an interesting dream. His eyes narrowed and he grinned and he said, I know. He was a beautiful kid.

I looked into Colin's eyes. So did you do it?

Mona shrieked. You're horrible, she said to Colin. You're horrible and I want you to get out of my house. And you, she said to me, are horrible for wanting to know whether or not he did it. Don't you dare say another fucking word about it, she said to Colin. I don't want to know whether or not you did it. No. Never mind. Of course you did it. I know you and I know what you are. Tell me, Colin, how does it feel to know the closest you'll ever get to any pussy was when you plopped out of your mother's green slimy snatch?

He smiled at Mona.

Tell me, Colin, she said, can you tread water using nothing but the loose lips of your own asshole?

I ignored her and watched Colin and said again, So did you do it?

He blinked his eyes twice and glanced aside. Never mind it, he said. I don't really want to talk about it with you anyway.

I like my gun. You can get used to just about anything but a Glock is very good. That's what I want in my hand when Y2K hits, when the skyscrapers are chopped down like trees. I walk down the street and laugh at the heads that will explode. A man walks out of the Rendezvous and stumbles upon the stair, glances around in embarrassment, turns left, puts his right hand down his pants and scratches his ass. I see ingrained civility; I see folds of fat. Metamorphosis is coming, and you sir will be assimilated into a mound of dirt. I love it. Every day it comes closer: The last bulldozer will pave the final acre of asphalt, and we'll hear the last traffic report on the radio from the eye-in-the-sky helicopter watchmen, and my game will begin.

The most dangerous game. My test. I love it. I can't wait.

Clara, I don't think you'll survive the revolution. Don't expect me to help you. Don't expect to look me in the eyes with a last-ditch damsel-in-distress plea and see sympathy. I won't be here anyway. I'll be on my way out. I'll be roading it toward the forests. I'm going to collide with our country.

At Clara's place after work. She always has to rate the sex after we screw. She uses a scale of one to one hundred, one hundred being the highest. Why do you always do this? I said. Are you my teacher? Is today report-card day?

I saw an article about it in my magazine, she said.

So what do I score today then, Clara?

Today I'd give you a seventy-eight, she said.

The sky got dark outside. Gray like the gray in a dream, black like the black at night, color in your eyes. Thrashdoom tenants in gold lamé pants, silver shoes, lipstick running out of their eyes like mascara. Time to freeze the new round of hamster heads, she said. Her hamsters have babies and then they eat the babies and the babies are heads with paws, bleeding and squeaking, sawed-off strokebodies, scooting toward mother.

There was no room in the freezer; the vodka was already in the freezer.

Clara set the pipe on the table and stomped across the room to lower the shade. See right the fuck in, she sneered. The room became dark. Don't you get it, Clara? I don't *care*. I don't care.

I saw my body that night in full futurity, wrinkled careening, hungrily reeling through the years. Tight hoary skin. I saw a torn ear and I saw widely the scars. In the mirror my face grew gaunt, and I was conscious, and I removed my red shirt.

In the mirror. Glass in a three-by-five wooden rectangle. I am a head.

I weigh one hundred and fifty-four pounds. I stand one hundred eighty centimeters tall. Crawlupinmylapandrepent he says to me whoa. Do you know why you're seeing me? he says. This is what I'm telling you. Don't go to school don't save money don't pay social security taxes don't opt for 401k and don't quit smoking. Charge credit cards up to the limit. Have your fun while you can, little boy, because soon we'll be going to war.

You'll probably die. It's probably about a one-in-five chance that you won't die.

Humans are the prisoners of their landscapes. In the cities, the people will be killing each other, and also in a lot of the countryside. Florida, for instance. Think of the Seminoles. Romania, Carpathia: Think of the Huns. The land can calm you or the land can piss you off. I've been trying to think of the calm places. Greenland; the Easter Islands; Oregon. Think about the history and who was indigenous. I'm going to drive out to Oregon or northern California sometime in 1999 and take up residence. The land will be too lush for fighting, and I can farm and it will be good there; I'll be away from the death. Think of the Seminoles; think of Mongol hordes; think of the Huns.

I sat at the desk with my diary. Quit being so fucking antisocial, she said, sneering by the cold weight of her hair—her hand on my shoulder, tugging, goddammit come back to bed, hookdick—but I said all along I'd write a sentence today, one miserable little sentence if that's all forever, and here it is.

When the city showed up. Knock knock knock. Come in, said Bruce. I was sitting on the couch weighing bags of dank. They walked through the door and though not one of them smiled I could feel each aura glow as its person looked around the room. My heart pounded out of my chest, and I stared at Bruce in his chair. He was calm. He looked up at an officer, and I saw a glint of recognition in his eyes.

I saw a glint of recognition from the officer in response.

Ah. I see then.

I had suspected no one. I looked at him and glanced down at the floor and glanced back at him, and my heart pounded, and I tossed the weed back and forth inside the bag with my fingers. It wasn't just the weed. There was more shit there than just the weed.

I asked him, Why'd you do it?

He shrugged.

I asked him, How much money do you make a year?

He paused for a moment and then said, Sixty grand.

I asked him, Do you really believe any of that shit you say you believe? Y2K. Crash and burn, baby, when it hits.

No.

None of it?

He stared into my eyes. Hell no, he said. I think you're crazy as a fucking loon and I'll be glad to see you locked up.

I had never noticed all those little pockets of fat on his face.

You were pretty careless, he said to me.

I shrugged. No reason not to be.

I remember the smell of new paint in the cell. It was a peaceful mauve paint with a blue wallpaper border, like something you might see in your grandmother's house. It reminded me of autumn, of the fall of the leaves, of the first frost. It's all the synthetic smells that I smell every day that I'll miss. You can't record smell, after all. We'll forget what paint smells like.

I'm laughing so hard at all of this, I can barely breathe.

The judge put me on probation. When I saw the little globules of sweat streaming down his wrinkled head, I knew he'd let me go. He was a wimp. I saw his ugly face, and I saw his wart. I looked around. What the hell is anybody doing here? What the hell are you doing? People shuffled uncomfortably in their seats, squirming in the heat of their revenge. They couldn't look at me. They acted like it was the end of my life or something. He deserves more. What must he be thinking. What was I thinking? you wonder. I was watching the cameraman as he zoomed in toward my face, inching slowly forward, the red light blinking on and off and on and off and on, the room's blueness reflected in the convex glass. The lawyer said don't be surprised about the cameraman; they always have one these days. I was watching the cameraman and thinking that I was glad I had shaved that morning; I was thinking, Hey: now everyone can see the beautiful angles in my face.

Everything is stockpiled. There is a small cave in the woods out in the country. There are a lot of dead trees in the woods. The path hasn't been cleared in a while. I have a small cave. Everything is stockpiled. I'm rubbing my hands together and the minds are going to crash and I can't wait. Leave the life nothing. No one left.

The Locust came to see me once. She brought me some numbers to memorize. I threw them away. The only number I think about now is the countdown. Four hundred seventy-four. Four hundred seventy-three. It's not a big number anymore. It makes me happy.

There will be only a few of us, I hope. It will be a beautiful complicity. We'll see each other: the survivors, looking into our vast surviving eyes.

Deseret

salt is taking back the land
  is taking back the land
  krrsshkrrsssh
  (on the radio the empty noises) krsh krsh
  salt is taking back the land.
  krsh.

out in the gray grainy salt flats the things that happened. We had the cabin you know. I mean fucking hell it was five miles off the highway in the salt flats. Did I say they were gray? Well, they were gray.

Not even a driveway. Five miles off the main road and you just jerked the wheel out into the desert and zoomed south toward the lake. The water is so salty you just float on top. Big water big desert. Bonneville is not far away, you know. The races and shit.

He tied the chain around my neck and padlocked it and hooked it to the ceiling. It was a thick chain about 130 millimeters. I had about eight feet of radius from the hook.

When he went at it it was a soft lash gentle against my back. He said it left red marks. Not really what you would call welts but you had to give them a day to go away, you know. Let me out once a day to go out and get in the lake and the salt sink in oooohh oooohh the salt is changing it all.

There was a hook on the outside of the house. Every morning at nine and the sun was bright he dragged me out hooked me up onto one of the dogleash lines where you can move thirty feet from the house out to the pole. Why was there a flagpole? For flags I think. The people who had the house before were Mormons and I guess they flew the Mormon flag maybe. Matt sat in his lawn chair by the lake naked in the sun, red, and wrote in his journal. The land is very flat, you know. Gray cracked earth for miles and then the gray cracked mountains. The lake recedes a bit each day. Someday a dry basin. The air force will take back the land; nobody sees them.

He goes out only once a week now for food and water. Drives to the big truck stop at the interstate. Comes back and collapses in the bed and won't move for the rest of the day. More than a month now since he's been anywhere else.

It's getting serious. Some days he won't get up at all anymore. White skin like bad prosthetic movie makeup. The stringy thinning hair. What do you do. Pimples on his face. Watery eyes, running nose. Nuclear waste coming out of his ears, the cascading waxy filth. I sit in the dark real still in the dark and watch him. He doesn't sleep at night. I didn't know until the other day that he never really sleeps.

Never been to a doctor in his life but he knew the day he first started to die. I'm dying, he said.

Oh, are you now?

Yeah. I've got maybe three months to go.

It took me a while before I realized I should believe him. Never been to a doctor in his life but he knows. He stopped getting out of bed as much. He moved the fridge to my side of the room so I could get to it without being unchained.

Mumbling at night. Kneel down ohmygodohmygod scratch me make me bleed.

The day when I first came down he said to make him a crackpipe. A test, he said. You've got whatever's in this room. The house was empty. Stone walls and a bed and a refrigerator. Shirtless and sitting on the floor.

I got a beer can out of the trash and poured out the last dregs and bent it in half. In the crease I poked two little holes with a fork. Give me a cigarette, I said. He lit one for me and as it burned

I let the ash fall into the crease. I poked another hole at the back of the can. There's your carb, I said. Put the rocks over the ash.

You're hired, he said.

It was an ad I had answered. On the Internet. Forbidden zone dot something dot org. The contract is for me to stay for eighteen months. No permanent injuries or scarification, he promised. The house was just one big stone room and I had one side. A bed and a toilet and in the corner a showerhead with a drain in the floor. There was nothing on the walls. His torso was muscular and his head was shaven. Okay, I said.

You're sure this is what you want?

I shrugged. Yeah.

It gets hot in the daytime, he said. And it gets cold at night.

Why are you out here? I said. Where do you get your money?

What the fuck do you think?

I don't know, I said.

It was a meth lab in the basement. He screamed the answer at me over and over as he lashed me and on the floor I felt his boot upon my neck pushing me down against a book he had placed on the ground before me. He tossed down a straw. Do this line, you piece of shit, he said. Fucking meth lab and don't ask me about it again.

I snorted.

Get used to it, he said. That's the way it's gonna be.

What a crazy fucker, I thought.

It was good.

There are twenty regular customers maybe twenty-five; they buy in bulk. Up from Salt Lake City and a few from Provo and one old man from up in Pocatello. When Matt brews up something new a bunch of them come at once. Fucking test parties, you know. He makes it so strong, laces it with no one knows what. Lets me join in sometimes but the chain stays on you know. Crystal when you're tied to the wall when it ohmygod ripples and veinbursting the whitest eyes are blind. When you're tied to the wall roaring struggling. Makes me hard as a fucking rock.

Screaming you know. Can't control. Down boy, he says. I'm barking and crowing. They're loving it.

One time Matt told me to stand against the wall and then he threw eggs at me as hard as he could. Vivid pain. He was careful and meticulous as he scrubbed the yolk off afterward. It goes back and forth you know. Violent then reverent. He licked some of it off and got salmonella poisoning; he vomited for two days straight. The puke rotted in little red piles out on the salt flat. That was back when he was still cooking up the yellow roses. He had trouble etching the roses onto the pills. The one guy with the spider tattoo made fun of him for it.

At first I was embarrassed when people came over to buy the shit. Standing there naked you know. The chain. Then they'd come again and I didn't give a shit anymore. Just a bunch of speedheads and in what other capacity do they know me anyway. This is my role.

I watched them snort their shit. The chain wouldn't go over to that side of the room. Go ahead and whip me before you get yourself stuck in a K-hole and can't move for three hours.

Matt liked it sometimes too. Once he was watching me as I finished a cigarette. Put it out on my forehead, he said when I reached for the ashtray.

No.

Shove the burning ash into my skin, you bastard.

No.

I exhort you.

He liked it too. It was kind of cute coming from someone who looked so tough, who wanted to be so tough. He had an anvil tattooed on his left arm and a skull and crossbones on his back and two vipers on his ass and a cattle brand on his thigh. Shaved head. He wanted to get the grim reaper tattooed on his scalp but he was afraid it would hurt too much. He had me draw the image on with permanent marker one time. Kind of cute then that his rough voice would get soft when I asked him about his journal. It wasn't a diary, he said. Just stuff he wrote down sometimes. He sat still but swirlingheaded lit-up in the mass of blasting air, the vast mass of air; he flipped off the light and with two sharp splintered fingernails tampered with the skin of his chest. The sticky wildfire. He thought of it and looked at the shining face: the fiery scrubby shine: straight through to his thoughts. Shards exploding outward. He sat still but lit-up mazes sedimenting in the rocklayers of his skin and as he read the words bugs flew disconnectedly, dreamlike as they devolved into darkness. He sat swirlingheaded, eyes racing around the anonymous hordes of bugs. As the bugs flashed on and off in the back porchlight there were flashes and Matt sniffled and read a few words.

Despite.

He pronounced it DESSpit, as if it were *desperate* without the *per* in the middle. DeSPITE, I said, jiggling nervously the stick in my clammy hands, you know what they say about the size of your hands, and he stared at me dogeyed and slightly lippuckered and curling his tongue as if he were wagging it, as if he were salivating at the sight of a bone.

Feed the anonymous hordes, he read.

Shards exploding outward. Nail nothing. Tamper with the shards. A considerable bleakness. These were things he had written. Despite a considerable bleakness the anonymous hordes. Some sort of bad poem with sloppy scansion, half-finished already. I wasn't paying attention. When someone reads aloud to me I don't listen to the words. It's not that I don't want to.

He was playing with his left nipple, rubbing it with the back of his thumbnail, hardening it into a red lump. He had a hairless arching chest. He was sitting still consuming the silent unbearable force. You're looking very britpop tonight, he said, and I smiled. The music probably made him think of it. These songs that he listens to over and over. Stuck in the house with no other music. Do you realize how many days in a row. Shutting my eyes and actually praying at the sounding of the sounds they sing are sounds shut open. The powerchords sounding out like killing machines bbbaBEAT-bbaBEAT, you know. The muddy voice:

Like all the boys in all the cities
I take the poison, take the pity.

Out in the yard at night although it wasn't a yard only salt flats. He was rubbing his nose. I saw the circles deep and reddened. He was playing with his left nipple. The blank stare he gave me perceived no gleaming body before him. How did I end up out here is what I wonder sometimes. I don't really remember you know.

The next day he wouldn't get out of bed at all. Just lay there breathing and sweating. The toilet's not working, I said. You gotta get up and throw me the plunger. The chain won't reach that far.

Piss in the kitty litter.

I have to take a shit.

So take a shit in the kitty litter.

Get up, you bastard.

Do you want me to have to hurt you? he said, and he chuckled. Dumb question. Anyhow I'm not moving.

Get the fuck up.

He sighed. I looked at the lines in his face. He looked old. Thirty-three. Tired as if never not to be tired again. Do you know how much, he began, and he trailed off. Look, I'll tell you where the key is.

No.

It's over in the—

NO.

It's—

I covered my ears. Shut up, I said. Shut up. He cocked his eyes and shifted slightly in the bed, raising his head to see me above the bedframe. He smiled and was silent; he fell back to sleep.

I wondered what he was going to say when he trailed off. Do you know how much what. Do you know how much pain I'm in. Do you know how much I hate this.

He bolted awake at midnight, shivering and focusing his eyes as if jolting out of death. He saw that I was awake. Does your family know you're here? he said. He had never asked before.

No. How would they?

Do you think they're upset that you haven't talked to them?

I shrugged.

Did it break somebody's heart?

I don't know. Maybe.

He went back to sleep.

He still never lets me go down into the lab. I wouldn't know how to do anything down there because he never told me how. I have no idea what is involved. Long dark rows of bubbling vials I imagine lining wooden casings, a single red bulb hanging by a frayed wire from the ceiling, buzzing as it sways. I don't know.

He says he's going to let Lee take it over when he dies. Lee is the man with the long fingernails, whose hands quiver when he speaks.

He woke me up in the middle of the night last night. Wake up wake up. Kneeling by my side.

whawhat

Wake up, he said.

You're out of bed.

Yeah. He sat down on the concrete floor.

What's the matter? I said, and he didn't answer. Are you bringing in enough money? I asked. Nobody's been over here to buy shit lately.

I haven't had anything to sell lately.

Well, how the hell do people know it if there's not even a phone here?

They know.

He drank from a bottle of black rum. The door was open and the cold desert air streamed into the house. I wrapped up beneath the blanket; a few minutes passed. He was breathing loudly. He stroked my face and forehead.

Even now, he said.

What?

He paused. It was hard for him to get the words out, it seemed.

Even now. How long have you been here? Months and months. Not even now.

What? What not even now?

I don't love you.

I wouldn't expect you to, I said.

That's not what I want you to say.

What do you want me to say?

I don't know.

I wouldn't expect you to.

Not even after all this time. I thought I could bring you out here you know and maybe it wouldn't be so bad then. I think it wouldn't be so bad if there were something where I could just have some reason not to be so passive about the whole thing.

You're not necessarily dying.

Shut up.

You gave me what I wanted.

I'll give you some money. There's not much but you could take it and go back down to the city.

I'm not going back down to the city.

You should go back.

You gave me what I wanted.

He sat on his bed and scribbled in his journal. I sat on the floor and watched him from across the room. He wrote for three or four hours. Every ten minutes or so he glanced up and stared at me, intently into my eyes. I tried to look like I didn't notice it. My eyes were starting to water.

I hadn't talked to anyone else in nine months. I hadn't done much talking before that either. It's not what I do. I tried to think what would happen when I had to leave; I pictured myself trekking out through the desert toward the mountains, walking miles and miles across the basin looking toward the peaks as they hovered in the unreachable distance, never seeming to get any closer. I pictured myself on the interstate hitching north but that doesn't really go anywhere and I'm not going south. I haven't thought much about it, I guess.

You want a line? he said.

No, thanks.

Bump?

No.

Nothing?

No.

He cut some for himself. What are you going to call the book you write about me? he said.

I'm not going to write a book about you.

What else would you write a book about? he said.

I'm not going to write a book.

Well, what *are* you going to do? he said. After you leave here. Where will you go? he said. I just stared back at him. He sneezed a few times and rubbed his nose and coughed and flung his arm behind him to scratch his back. I don't think he has any concept of it all.

He told me if I ever get around to writing a book about him to begin please with an epigraph from Genet, from *Our Lady of the Flowers*, ten words he always loved. Lying in the bed palefaced he whispered it, suppressing his hacking cough as I saw the hint of a smile again. Lying in his bed by the window facing the open waste. Hard to say just what I'm losing. The cool breeze blew in gently from the window as he mouthed the words slowly through the mute white room above the ticking cuckoo clock and whispered but I knew them already:

I have made myself a soul to fit my dwelling.

Emaciated and speaking to me. Heartburn belches coiling through his throat. Naked under the covers and mouth drawn down in pain. In a sort of prison you know but that wasn't what he wanted. Shouldn't it have been me not him who liked the quote.

I haven't been outside in a week now. I want to lie down on the parched soil at noon and coat my naked back with salt-specks. I want to scorch my pale pink skin until it is red, wrinkled and old. The hawks if there are hawks will circle in the air and for short split seconds block the sun. Salt will seep into every wound.

They say the ground is so salty here that when you're on it you don't sink to the bottom of the earth; you just float right on top.

Matt asked me please to begin with the epigraph because he

was reveling for once in its naked lucidity. The dead cells fell from his fingertips as they dangled over the edge of the bed. Rainy mold coughing coughing in the air. Back in the days before he came to this place, down in Salt Lake City, the blue skies and the puffy white clouds. He liked it, he said. He listened to the grinding violence of his music. He ground his heels into the rough concrete; spikecollared he walked the streets armed&ready a weapon in every muscle and faced angrily the omniphobic human grains of energy circling all around him, the antagonizing cuticles and skins, slobbercoated, fists out toward the city.

Stop Breakin Down

At Tin Mill Canal the left headlight burned out. Darker now: eight eyes blinking at the nailing darkness. The sewage treatment plant and its sooty gray sewagetreated smoke rising openly into pinkblack air went grayer. Near the end now nothing to worry about—did you do that, Vince?—you saboteur you sly bastard you it'll take more than that. We approached the bridge looming tall before us and soaring. Upon the western skyline Venus and a crescent perched above the towers. Line of sight. The radius clutching nightgloom all the darktime; close to the end now, and Tobey tossed his empty beer bottle into the backseat, thrusting it against Phoebe's forehead. Clunk. She punched him in the shoulder, and the action of his reflex swerved the wheel in a sharp skid to the right. Watch it, he said. I'm the driver. You're the passenger.

We approached the bridge. Don't see you in the rearview, you slow shits. Win. The engine sputtered. Always. He reached beneath his seat for another beer and opened it against the dashboard. Drunk and darting across space. Eight eyes roaming across the gray industrial postdusk dark. Displacement. A moment, I think.

Tobey laughed. Full circle, he was thinking. Isn't that what they call it?

Last call at Sudsucker's was at two. The seven of us had sat in the back by the Atari, two in chairs and five squeezed together on the couch, which we had occupied since dinnertime. The tab was over a hundred dollars. Vince poured out the contents of the final pitcher.

These your songs on the jukebox, man?

Yeah.

Vince and Tobey were playing Maze Craze. My eyes ached from the flashing colors. The bright monochromatic screens. Red and blue dots racing along corridors to the right-hand side of the screen.

Won again, Tobey said.

Get your kicks now, man.

That's nineteen for me.

Just wait till we're on the road.

Phoebe rolled her eyes.

Can't wait, Tobey said.

You're not serious about this race, Adam said. The bartender came to wipe off the coffee table, and they all lifted up their drinks. Adam watched the next maze appear on the screen. He didn't want them to see that he was worried. Around the beltway. What are they talking about? They're all drunk. How the hell did this get started? he was wondering. You're not serious, he said to them.

Is that a question or a statement of your opinion? Tobey asked.

Adam glared at him.

I'm looking at the video game but I can feel you glaring at me. Answer the fucking question.

You answer my question.

So it was a question.

Jesus help me.

No.

No you're not serious? he asked. The others had stopped their conversation to listen.

No, no you're wrong that I'm not serious. We're serious. You'll be in the car so you'll be serious too. We're all serious. We'll all be serious. We'll all be serious together.

I'm not riding with you then, he said. Fuck it.

The buses don't run this late, Adam. You can't afford a cab

all the way back to Hamilton. You can't even afford the beer you just drank. Can you.

I don't think you should do this.

Whatever.

Shut up Adam, Ben said. Everyone nodded in agreement.

In the cold air on Fort Avenue we stood by the cars and smoked. Here are the rules, Vince said. We go down Ritchie Highway to Exit Three and the race starts there. The on-ramp. That's where it starts.

So it ends at the Exit Three off-ramp, Ben said.

No, Vince said. It ends at the end of the Key Bridge. Go around the inner loop and whoever crosses the end of the bridge first wins.

The people in that car pay the others back for tonight's tab, Tobey said.

That's not fair, Vince said. There's four in your car.

I guess that will be added incentive for you to win.

I should just hitch a ride home, Adam was saying to Phoebe, shaking his head in disgust.

Then do it, she said.

Whose side are you on here?

I'm not on anyone's side, she said, gently nudging his shoulder. I just think it will be fun. You shouldn't be so uptight.

How fast does that baby go? Tobey asked.

Hundred twenty and it don't even rattle. Hundred forty you might start to feel a little shake.

Phoebe rolled her eyes.

Shit, Tobey said.

Shit's ass.

Quit your braggin and let's see it.

How many miles is it to go around? Ben asked.

I don't know; the numbers don't correspond with the exit signs.

It's gotta be fifty at the least.

At the very least.

We'll do it in half an hour tops, Tobey said.

I'm with Vince then, Ben said. I wanna do it in twenty minutes.

Tobey drove a turbocharged Cougar. Eighty-nine model year but a ninety-four engine. Black body and a red hood. Surprised they let you across the state line with that ugly hunk of metal, Vince had said when Tobey first moved to Baltimore. Surprised they don't levy a special redneck tax on your ass. He followed Vince's Camaro down Ritchie Highway. No traffic. Vince was running the red lights, and Tobey had to run them too to keep up. He glanced around for cops.

Past the fast-food restaurants and gas stations. Mile-wide strips of pavement. Down the hill to the exit onto the beltway. Neon idiot lights.

Sprawl.

At the on-ramp Vince screeched his tires as he turned right and accelerated quickly down the ramp. Tobey stayed on his bumper. As they pulled out into the lane we could see Ben in the backseat of Vince's car flipping us off. He signaled something to us, pointing toward the hood and bumper of Tobey's car. What's the bastard trying to say? Tobey said.

Hell if I know.

Vince sped up to a hundred and went into the left lane. Tobey followed. Vince sped up and slowed down, slamming on his brakes and speeding up and switching to the middle lane and darting around cars. He turned his left turn signal on. He turned his right turn signal on. He turned his rear wipers on.

What a dumbass.

We're gonna win.

When we passed the Harbor Tunnel Thruway the road had more traffic. Tractor trailers. Vince pulled into the Washington Boulevard exit lane to pass a pickup truck and managed to steer back onto the road barely in time. Adam gasped when the Camaro jolted back into the main lane.

Pass them, I said.

No don't, Adam said.

Just let him drive, Phoebe said. Even more traffic came onto the road after we crossed under I-95. Tobey gripped the wheel.

Pass all these fuckers. Steadily smoothly. What they must be thinking. Twice as fast as them at least. Turn their heads. Excitement in their lives. Scared. If they're scared then they'll get out of the way. We felt the car pulling to the left, toward the concrete barrier. Out the side window no look out the front window. Reflection in the night.

Control. Feel it in the air. Stay out of our way.

Phoebe packed the sherlock as we passed Arbutus. Tobey was still following behind the Camaro. Pass them I said but he was waiting for something to happen. They'll get stuck behind someone, he was thinking. They'll have to brake. Gotta do it when they can't respond.

You got a light? Tobey asked when it got to him.

Use the cigarette lighter, Phoebe said.

You can't light a sherlock with the fucking cigarette lighter, he said.

The beltway wall had been completed. Infinite sienna squares. Meant to look like something. Adobe maybe. As I lit the pipe the passing wallsquares began to dominate all the peripheries. Count them one two six ten no it's far too fast. They're getting away, Phoebe said.

They're not getting away.

Just let him drive, Adam said sarcastically. She glared at him. Just let him drive, he said again.

We bounced along the broken pavement. Sure do see a lot of Maryland license plates in this damn state, Tobey said. The bowl was cashed, and I put it in the glove box. We bounced along the ridging pavement and the CD player skipped on the bumps. Tobey and I clicked bottles together in a toast, beer sloshing out upon our hands and arms. Rebel yell. We passed Frederick Road. We passed Edmondson Avenue. We passed Baltimore National Pike. Phoebe was wrestling with Adam in the backseat, trying to cheer him up, and she snapped his seat belt undone and pinned his arms and neck in a twisted half nelson. He didn't fight back. She pushed him playfully back into his seat, and he refastened his seat belt. We passed I-70. We passed Security Boulevard. Through the cracked window the cool fall air sucked against the glass with a shrill sinister hiss, and every passing car whined lowly in fading Doppler hyberbolas of stunted sound.

Whose idea was this? Adam said. It was Vince's, wasn't it?

Phoebe rolled her eyes.

I don't remember, Tobey said. The dashboard's loose brown plastic rattled loudly.

It was Vince's, Adam said, wasn't it?

Vince wouldn't have been smart enough to think of it, Phoebe said. She rolled her eyes. What the hell is he doing, anyway? she said. The Camaro was in the far left lane, halfway into the left shoulder, the yellow line centered beneath them. Dumbass is gonna get a flat tire.

Blowout at this speed, God could you imagine?

The Camaro moved back onto the road. Tobey stayed in the middle lane. There's a car up there in the shoulder, he said.

Cop.

No.

Could be.

No, man. This is it.

Huh?

They'll think it's a cop. This is it. Soon now. He counted: Three. Two. One.

The rear of the Camaro swerved twenty degrees to the right as Vince slammed his brakes. Screech. Eighty sixty fifty. We watched them try to right themselves from the side window and then the back windshield as Tobey downshifted to fourth gear and floored the gas. Redline. To the floor. At eighty-five hundred RPMs he shifted back up into fifth gear. He shot past the motionless blobs of metal, one hand on the wheel and one hand on the stick, head pressed back against the seat and eyes staring straight ahead as if he were playing an arcade game.

Damn.

We gained more ground.

Damn, is that them way back there?

Don't slow down, man.

Adam shut his eyes and made the sign of the cross.

What the hell are you doing? Phoebe said. You're not religious. He didn't answer.

Damn.

Good job.

The car on the shoulder was a rusting engineless truck. A dead black hulk. You lost it for a shadow. This is fast. In the Cougar we sped north along the bulging eight-lane ribbon. If we get pulled over I'm fucked, Tobey was thinking. The red in his eyes. The worried red. Don't know what Adam's worried about. I'm the one going down. Is this Thursday? Chugachuga-chuga rumble hurdling above the speakers.

Scratchy stringy voices on air: Take me down little Susie take me down. I know you think you're the queen of the underground. He maintained his speed.

Eyes shut no eyes open. We were all getting tired. Tobey was feeling the disturbances in his stomach and the insidious night exhaustion. As he belched sorethroated and loudly the air and inner lining of his stomach churned heavily and slow, the enzymes coating wet pink fleshwalls with thick gray mercury—we heard this—fastening themselves to the gas and slime like murky algal muscles. You'll have to take the wheel if I puke, he said.

You better not.

Tobey didn't answer.

I can't see them at all now, Phoebe said. The road was emptier. We passed the Northwest Expressway. We passed Reisterstown Road.

You know, Phoebe said, you never notice the curves. It's a circle but you never see it curving.

But you feel it curving.

We passed Park Heights Avenue. We passed wooded subdivisions and houses sticking up above the wall. Swooosh around the curves. See there are curves. He belched again. We passed Greenspring Avenue. We passed JFX. Above the hum of the engine rose the sounds of old metal rattling and metal against metal in grating metallic friction. Above the hum of the engine rose the whirs and the hammering thuds and thunds of thunder, the whines of rubbed-raw body fronds. The rhythm. Stronger now. Later. Heated motion, and the dull cracked shoulder, the yellow reflections reflecting back in yellow. The wall standing dark hushed hale as rubbertracks pithed the thin magnetic chords of open road.

Why don't you drop me off on York, Adam said. I'll walk to Walter's apartment.

If you wanna just jump out of the car then do it but I'm not stopping.

Come on, Tobey, he said. They're nowhere in sight.

But they will be if I stop to let you off.

Come on, Tobey.

No one spoke as we drove past 83 north, Charles Street, York Road, Dulaney Valley Road. Providence Road. Tobey maintained his speed. He was wondering if something had happened to Vince's car. He was drumming his tongue against his teeth. He was listening to the pains in his lower left quadrant wondering if his spleen was swollen from drinking again before he had fully recovered from mono. He was wondering whether or not he'd get pulled over for reckless driving. Over a hundred and you can spend the night in jail. He could feel the tension in his shoulders forcing his shoulder blades up and outward. He could feel his neck. He could feel his eyes glazing over, and he scrunched them tight and opened them again to snap himself into alertness. Dirt and birdshit on the windshield. Eight eyes staring at gray-white blobs of hardened shit and slime.

We never have conversations anymore, I said.

Yes we do.

No we don't.

He tried to think of something to say. You got anything goin on right now?

Ain't been laid in forever, I said. Back in opwaga again. In the backseat Phoebe rolled her eyes.

What's opwaga? Tobey said.

You know.

No.

Organization of people who aren't getting any.

We went down the hill. We curved around past the Cromwell Bridge exit. Do they call it Cromwell Bridge because of Oliver Cromwell? Adam asked. There's a conversation, he was thinking. Now I'm helping out and we're having conversations, he was thinking.

No, they call it that because there was a bridge there named Cromwell Bridge.

Tobey sped on around the curves. Cops are here with radar sometimes, he was thinking. He kept his sight focused on the shoulders, watching for stopped cars. His tires were skidding on the turns, and he was always conscious of the loose slippery feel of the wheel. The car was getting old. He thought about the rattling and looked in his rearview mirror and wondered why they weren't catching up.

Are we gonna run out of gas?

Shrug.

Tobey squirmed around in his seat. Coffeemarks stained his jeans legs from knee to waist. Brown streaks of bile and booze and brown and remainders of coffeemarks that stained his jeans; he hacked loudly the trailing smoker's cough that drumbanged our ears. His eye met the eye of a snowflake splinter in the glass of the windshield, locked, front and away and sandy stringy hair brushing against his collarbrushing shoulders. Two weeks' beard growth falling from his face; bird-blue eyes; chapped lips whose sheaths of dead skin vibrated against each other at the sound of oncoming car horns. How long for you now? I asked him.

Three months.

Quitter.

Huh?

Like it says on the sign at Crackpot. Right by the back counter where you ask them for cases from the fridge. He swerved back and forth within the middle lane as he massaged his hands against the wheel. Rehab is for quitters.

Tobey stared out the window. We passed Perring Parkway. South and north.

Isn't it?

Three months.

Surprised they don't care that you're drinking.

They do.

Mmm.

The speakers hummed. Click croak creak. Swiftly around the circle. What is the word? Tobey was thinking. Circumscription. Circumnavigation. Stringy sandy hair dangling in his face blocking his view: He tossed it back to the side. Whatever. He was tired. In the mirror he saw the redness of his eyes. Where the hell are they? In the mirror he saw what seemed to be a box-shaped shadow at the far bend of the road behind him; as we rounded a bend it disappeared.

How's Angeline doing? I asked him.

Angela.

Well?

I don't know.

The violence of his scoliotic shrug carried spite and scorn. Tension vectors untangled like a snapping coiled skein. Oh that's right, she left.

How's your mom doing?

She's all right.

Coming down this weekend.

He nodded. Curling up his nose. Coiling up his nostrils.

I could see it. Just want a bump, man, he was thinking. Single fuckin bump. With spittle swishing in his throat he tapped his wart finger on the wheel. White Marsh. Belair Road. How far now? All I wanted. He kept time with the rhythm of the music, sliding his middle finger up and down the plastic, imagining the murky tablature. Where are they? We're winning. Die in the attempt if. In lockjawed teethgritted clarity he saw the bloody bodies crashing into shivery baybrine, the barricades of the bridge soaring clunk into the water. Concrete will sink. Dyou do you know this?

Change the song, Phoebe said from the back. Put it on the radio.

Tobey looked to the right. Do it you die.

I don't like this tape either, I said.

It's the Stones.

But I don't like it.

What are you trying to tell me?

I'm telling you that I don't like it.

That's fine. But I'm not going to change it.

Every time I'm walking down the street. Some grandmomma start breakin down on me. Stop breakin down.

The road was nearly empty. We had the left lane to ourselves. We shot past the walls and trees and I-95 and cars streaked backward in strong and straight trajectories into the rearview. Tobey kept the speed between a hundred and a hundred five. Still no sign of them. He looked at his hair in the mirror and adjusted a curl and tossed beer solemnly down his dry throbbing throat.

Past I-95 through Dundalk. Everyone was sleepy. Tobey rewound the tape back to the beginning of the song again. It was the fourth time through the song. He could feel Adam's agitation. The nerves running down his spine. Tobey listened to the words and waited again for the moment. The twelve or thirteen notes in perfect succession. Seven seconds of melody. The only part of the song he wanted to hear. Otherwise he wouldn't have repeated it. Wait for the melody to come: fingerdrum on the wheel as the melody drills down into fingerbone. The nerves in his spine. Plucked like guitar strings. Here it comes again. He gripped the wheel for a curve to the right. Here it comes here it comes here it comes.

The tollbooth, Adam said.

Goddammit you made me miss it again, goddammit, you piece of shit.

The tollbooth at the bridge.

Goddammit I listened through that whole song to hear those few seconds you piece of shit and you picked that moment to talk.

We're going to have to stop at the tollbooth at the bridge.

Tobey hung his mouth open.

I guess no one thought of that, Adam said. They all stared forward. Tobey shook his head in disgust with curled nose and gritting teeth speeding on toward the bay and in the rearview mirror peripherally he saw Adam's smug smile. The curt smile of Adam in the backseat.

You knew about the tollbooth all along, Tobey said, didn't you? Huh?

You knew it was there.

We all knew it was there.

You remembered it was there.

Whatever.

They're going to catch up, Tobey said.

Adam shrugged.

We'll just speed through it, Tobey said. How would you like that? How does that make you feel? Sitting back there in your preppy turtleneck sweater rolling your eyes at me thinking, you can't drive, you're going to wreck, you're going to kill me. Worrying. Thinking the tollbooth, the tollbooth, when we get there it'll all be okay. Your little trump card. The chips you were hiding under the table.

Whatthefuckever.

Silence. Driving on. No lights outside. No one talked and we passed some boring shit out on the road and Tobey tapped his finger on the wheel and we didn't see them behind us and the tollbooth and what are we going to do about it and we looked for cops and nothing happened for a while and it was boring. There were about eight or nine minutes which probably didn't actually happen which probably in a very literal sense did not exist. Driving on. Silence.

I looked out at all the houses. I couldn't see them but I knew they were behind the wall behind the trees behind the shopping centers. Somebody dose me. I see you ha ha I see what you're up to. Why do you want me here? Give me the reasons. In your red eyes next to me the reasons where are they.

I need to piss, Tobey said.

Piss into a bottle and throw it out the window.

I can't do that while I'm driving.

Oh well, I said.

You know what they should have for cars? he said.

What?

Some kind of tube that comes up that you could piss into and it would just be a hole straight down to the road. It could just pull up from the floor and you piss into it and just let it snap back down into the floor when you're done.

That's disgusting, Phoebe said.

You'd never have to stop. You could just keep driving forever.

You'd have to get gas, I said.

But you'd never have to stop except for gas.

I guess.

I should design it, he said. I'll patent it. I'll make millions. Thousands maybe.

Whatever.

We were coming up to the tollbooth. One mile. Well, Tobey said, we'll do what we can while we can. He pushed the gas to the floor. Pedal to the metal, Adam. The car shook. To the left. To the right. He was stretching out the tension in his neck. He was thinking about sex. How it had been three months. How Phoebe always ignored him. He was thinking about sex. He was thinking about jerking off. He was thinking about how the white lines on the road looked short but someone had told him they were six feet long on the interstates. He was wondering whether anyone could know what he was thinking. He doesn't know I can see his thoughts but something makes him nervous.

The one woman at the Grind. Eyeing me and I could see the connection as she latched on drooling for me to signal. Long smooth raven hair big brown eyes looked like a Paris model.

What are we going to do? I had said. Now that you've hooked onto my mind. We've got this power now the two of us as one. What are we going to do?

Her mouth hung open for a second before she turned and rushed out onto the street. She didn't understand I thought it was just a mistake I'd made but she understood. It scared her. They don't want me to know.

I can see these things. It's why I'm not scared in the car.

Nothing will happen. Alone on a mountain at the age of eighty-seven heart failure painless plink into nothing. Until then nothing. Nothing will happen until then.

Where do you think they are? I said. Vince and them.

He didn't answer.

Are you listening to me? I said.

What?

You don't listen to me.

Well, what did you say?

You're not listening to me.

He'd been trying to hide it for so long but I found beneath his disguise the cold words the deadly hemlock raw concoction see glowglowing in our lofting little airboxpocket speeding toward the bay: gloat smirk many many layers but beneath it all of course the old riff. Can't do a damn thing without you tagging along. Staring. Hate it when you look at me, he was thinking. Your one beastly eyebrow, connected to itself. You think you know me. You think you're clever.

I think old Sudsucker whatever his name might have been saw the lonely purple aura. Above my head as I ordered the drinks. So he laughed.

I think this is very fast; it's a high bridge. The cold air hangs in frigid pockets waiting frail and bald hanging in heterogeneous suspension. I think it's almost three. Waiting outside in the spaces between thrusting airpockets looms the salt and the stench of the bay: I think I can smell it twisting off my nostrils. I think they'll catch up now. I think this is silly. I think I'm going to do something drastic. We're going to go swimming, I think.

Shit, he said, there's a line.

He screeched to a halt. There were five cars in front of us, and it took almost a minute for us to get to the front. Headlights approached slowly behind us. The car in front of us had to wait for a receipt. Tobey put his head down against the wheel as Vince pulled up behind us. I saw their smug smiles through the side mirror.

Goddammit, Tobey said.

We paid the toll and took off. The car sputtered forward. Behind us Vince didn't even stop at the tollbooth; he tossed the change at the attendant and followed us, never leaving our bumper.

Goddamn fucking piece of shit, Tobey said as he shifted from second to third. Fucking goddamn piece of shit.

In the mirror the roundness of my eyes and the circle in my skullplate swirling round again in circles. I like it when it looks this way. The whites of my eyes coated by a shiny film of liquid and look at all the white things: the whitecaps in the water and the lines on the road and Adam's knuckles wet with spit from where he has bitten them raw and the stars and the moon and the headlights behind us closer closer. Tobey revved it up to the line and shifted to fourth. You can't do it, man.

Goddamn fucking piece of shit, he repeated all the way across the bridge.

Without the left headlight their car did not shine in the light as they pulled out to speed around us. They jolted into fifth. Adam was smiling and I felt his smile drilling into the back of my neck the vindictive little sonofabitch cocksucker. The wind from miles away hungry you'll be in it.

Goddamn fucking piece of shit.

Glowing the cold words smirking beneath the layered riffs of his mind. Trying to hide it for so long. Lofting pocket of box of air of bay speeding toward the sea. He saw me staring. Hate it when you look at me, he was thinking. I sent a thought and he ignored me. Thinking only about the chase. About Vince. They're all thinking about Vince. Phoebe is thinking about Vince.

Goddamn piece of shit bitchass goddamn lump of a car.

You want to win, don't you?

I grabbed the wheel with my left hand. They were passing us. I pushed the wheel left and Tobey panicked and grabbed my hand pushing it away looking into my eyes all googly-goggly. For a second I couldn't tell anymore what he was thinking. Or maybe he wasn't thinking anything. Vince swerved all the way over to keep us from smashing into them.

All the way to the left edge of the bridge.

Tobey stabilized us and shot us forward toward the end. All the drums on the radio blasting. All the eyes staring straight ahead at eight straight paths of apparition. All the gulls of the bay winding down through the air whining at us all googly-eyed glimmering hotwired shitting into the water in glee.

Fifth gear.

We zoomed over the bridge joints as their headlights wavered in the mirror and the tooting horn zoomed in angry cosine waves through the outer sphere of air.

What the fuck, man.

I shrugged.

What the fuck.

They were winning.

What?

They would have won.

He stared at me.

I thought you didn't want them to win.

He stared at me.

They knew about the tollbooth. Like you said. It was their strategy, I said. This was our strategy. We won.

Jesus Christ, man, it was just a game.

You wanted to win.

I didn't wanna fuckin die, bitch.

You were trying to win, I said. Adam was watching us intently. Phoebe was rolling her eyes.

It was just something to do after the bar so we could keep drinking. Something to do so we wouldn't have to go home.

You wanted to win.

Vince is gonna kick your ass. As soon as we stop the car he's gonna come lunging out his door toward the car and I'm just gonna point toward you and shake my head and watch it all happen. He slowed down.

You wanted to win, I said.

He drove on around the circle. Back to Exit Two. Ritchie Highway. The gas stations the strip malls the sprawl. Vince is gonna kick your ass, he said. I looked into his eyes. There was a moment of doubt but then I knew it. Of course I'm right cause if I weren't then he wouldn't be saying this. I saw the cold and glowing words smirking from the cracks in his skull. I sent a thought:

I knew it would be okay. I knew nothing would happen.

But he wasn't listening. Just watching the lines of the road whizzing by and silence in his mind not listening to me or anything but the lines. Eighty-seven. The mountain. Nothing will happen. Listen to me as I make it not happen.